"The great writers of a
offered again to reader
good to see once more Lord Dunsany's masterpieces in new
dress and available."

—Grand Master Andre Norton

"Lord Dunsany is one of the Founding Fathers. To let his
work fall by the wayside is to lose contact with the roots of
our genre. I'm delighted that another generation of young
readers and writers will have the pleasure of discovering
these wonderful stories."

—Lynn Flewelling, author of *Traitor's Moon*

" 'Beyond the Fields We Know . . .' Lord Dunsany coined
the phrase in *The King of Elfland's Daughter*, and he showed us
all the way. Writers, like me, who read him in our youth, have
been trying ever since to be the ones to take you there. I urge
you not to miss the chance to ride the original vehicle. Like a
pavane played on original instruments, it is slow and stately,
at times unfamiliar, and always unquestionably authentic."

—Ellen Kushner, World Fantasy Award
winning author of *Thomas the Rhymer*

"Lord Dunsany made me a fantasy writer. *The King of Elfland's Daughter* and *The Charwoman's Shadow* led me into realms
whose beautiful and mysterious geography I've been travelling ever since. Read these knowing they are dangerous in
the best possible sense. But read them."

—Delia Sherman

"The ending of *The Charwoman's Shadow* is the finest piece of
pure magic I know in the whole of literature, and now that
I can personally identify with the first sentence I find it almost unbearably moving."

—*New York Times* bestselling author Arthur C. Clarke

Over the course of more than twenty years, Del Rey has built its reputation as a publisher of trailblazing science fiction and fantasy works that have withstood the test of time to become acknowledged classics of their genres. *Fahrenheit 451, Ringworld, Dragonflight, Childhood's End, Lord Foul's Bane, The Sword of Shannara, The Mists of Avalon*—all breakthrough works of their respective eras—continue to enthrall each new generation of readers that discovers them. And Del Rey remains dedicated to keeping these, and all the mainstays it has introduced over the years, prominent in the pantheon of speculative fiction.

But even the occasional masterpiece can slip through the cracks and become buried treasure, until, after years of unfair neglect, its immense value is rediscovered—by happy accident or through the efforts of a lone champion able to recognize a mislaid gem—and restored it to its rightful glory. Now, for an extraordinary selection of books, Del Rey is that champion. And it is with great pride that I introduce Del Rey Impact: a new imprint for a gathering of vintage works long overdue for rediscovery—and eminently worthy of the honor.

From high-tech science to epic fantasy, the classic titles bearing the Del Rey Impact imprimatur will appeal to speculative fiction readers of every taste. *The King of Elfland's Daughter, The Man Who Fell to Earth*, and *The Drawing of the Dark*—to name just a few—are works that touched and transformed readers in their time, and paved the way for many a bestseller that would follow in their trendsetting footsteps. All of us at Del Rey are thrilled to be returning these long-unsung masterworks to the spotlight, in splendid new trade paperback editions. We hope that Del Rey Impact will reacquaint many readers with the old favorites they remember and introduce many more readers to new wonders they never dreamed existed.

—Shelly Shapiro
Editorial Director
Del Rey Books

THE CHARWOMAN'S SHADOW

Lord Dunsany

Introduction by
Peter S. Beagle

THE BALLANTINE PUBLISHING GROUP • NEW YORK

A Del Rey® Book
Published by The Ballantine Publishing Group

Copyright © 1926 by Edward Plunkett
Renewal copyright © 1954 by Lord Dunsany
Introduction copyright © 1999 by Peter S. Beagle

All rights reserved under International and Pan-American Copyright Conventions. Published in the United States by The Ballantine Publishing Group, a division of Random House, Inc., New York, and simultaneously in Canada by Random House of Canada Limited, Toronto.

Del Rey is a registered trademark and the Del Rey colophon is a trademark of Random House, Inc.

www.randomhouse.com/delrey/

Library of Congress Catalogue Card Number: 99-90313

ISBN 0-345-43192-8

Cover design and collage by David Stevenson
Cover Photos: hands © Laura Benedict/Image Bank;
figure on fire © Kamil Vojnar/Photonica

Manufactured in the United States of America

First Ballantine Books Edition: February 1973
First Ballantine Books Trade Paperback Edition: August 1999

10   9   8   7   6   5   4   3   2   1

Contents

CONTENTS

"The Charwoman's Shadow"

I thought I had the old Lin Carter edition of this book at home when I agreed to write a foreword for the new one, but one of my grown children has it, which should tell you something. I read *The Charwoman's Shadow* aloud to them when they were young, as well as *Don Rodriguez* and *The King of Elfland's Daughter*. The latter was the one I started with; and I was two chapters into it at most when I stopped and said—not really to my audience—"My God, I stole from this man!"

I don't mean that I plagiarized plots or characters, or even language from Lord Dunsany. What I stole—or what he graciously gave me—was an *attitude* towards language: an understanding that the right name for a character can imply an entire culture, a history, a music, a world; that a single word chosen properly can persuade a reader that he shares a folklore he can't possibly know; and, as well, that the greatest fantasy is always grounded in some observed reality, no matter how small and private. As Dunsany himself wrote—and it can't be repeated too often, in this age of fantasy-by-the-numbers—*"Bricks without straw are more easily made than imagination without memories."*

So the medieval Spain of this book is, of course, a Spain that never existed; but it is a real Spain within these pages, because Dunsany had sojourned often there, and had the proper light and sounds and smells and tastes—and shadows, too—to lend his imagination the proper colors of the magical Spain he wanted. In the same way, he can have the great, wise, cruel magician of *The Charwoman's Shadow* teach his young apprentice Don Ramon Alonzo Matthew-Mark-Luke-John of the Tower and Rocky Forest nothing more occult than reading—and in Dunsany's hands what comes out is purest magic:

> And then, with sonorous voice . . . the magician
> began to expose the secrets of reading; one by
> one he stripped mysteries, laying them bare to
> his pupil; and all the while he taught in that
> grand manner, that he had from the elder masters
> whose lore had been handed down. He taught the
> use of consonants, the reason of vowels, the way
> of the downstrokes and the up; the time for cap-
> ital letters, commas and colons; and why the
> "j" is dotted, with many another mystery. That
> first lesson in the gloomy room were well worthy
> of faithful description, so that every detail
> of the mystery might be minutely handed down;
> but the thought comes to me that my reader is
> necessarily versed in this mystery, and for
> that reason alone I say no more on this magni-
> ficent theme. . . .

Because Dunsany knew that real magic isn't a matter of spells and summonings, pentacles and incantations, and terrible bargains with diabolical forces. Seen as real magicians—such as Lord Dunsany—see, everything in existence is potentially magical, and forever mysterious; and within something as universal, and universally disregarded, as a human shadow there resides true power, more of the eternally elusive, the wondrous *hidden*, than in the changing of lead, or anything else, into gold. To open this book is, like Don Ramon Alonzo, to begin learning the true nature of enchantment from a master.

—Peter S. Beagle

CHAPTER I

The Lord of the Tower Finds a Career for His Son

Picture a summer evening sombre and sweet over Spain, the glittering sheen of leaves fading to soberer colours, the sky in the west all soft, and mysterious as low music, and in the east like a frown. Picture the Golden Age past its wonderful zenith, and westering now towards its setting.

In such a time of day and time of year, and in such a time of history, a young man was travelling on foot on a Spanish road, from a village wellnigh unknown, towards the gloom and grandeur of mountains. And as he travelled a wind rising up with the fall of day flapped his cloak hugely about him.

The strength of the wind grew, until little strange cries were in it; the slope steepened, the daylight waned; and the man and his cloak and the evening so merged into one darkness that even in imagination I can but dimly see him now.

Let us therefore turn to such questions as who he was, and how he came to be faring at such an hour towards a region so rocky and lonely as that which loomed before him, while the latest stragglers amongst other men were nearing their houses amongst the sheltered fields.

His name was Ramon Alonzo Matthew-Mark-Luke-John of the Tower and Rocky Forest. And his father had lately called to him as he played at ball with his sister, beating it back and forth to each other over a deep yew hedge; and the ball had a row of feathers fixed all round it to make it fly gently and fairly; and the yew hedge ended at a white balustrade, and beyond that lay the wild rocks and the frown of the forest: his father called to him and he entered the house out of the mellow evening, praying his sister to wait; but he talked with his father till all the light was gone, and they played at ball no more.

And in such a manner as this spoke the Lord of the Tower and Rocky Forest to his son when they were seated before the logs in the room where the boar-spears hung. "Whether to hunt the boar or the stag be sweeter I know not; methinks the boar, but only the blessed Saints know which is truly the sweeter: and yet there are other considerations besides these, and the world were happier were it not so, yet it is ever thus." And the boy nodded his head, for he knew what it was of which his father would speak, that it was of lucre, which hath much to do with worldly affairs: the good fathers had warned him of it. And indeed of this very thing his father told.

"For however vile or dross-like," he said, "gold be in itself, and I do not ask you to doubt the ill repute you have learned of it in the school on the high hill, yet is it necessary in curious ways to many things that are good, as certain foulnesses nourish the roots of the vine. For Emanuel and Mark are of such a kind that they will have their regular payment year in year out for such work as they do with the horses, nor is Peter any better in the garden, and it is indeed the same in the dairy. And then there was the teaching that you received from the good fathers on their high hill, much of this dross went also there though the work itself was a blessed one. And now it is necessary to put yet more of this gold in a box, and to have it ready against some day when a dowry will be needed for your sister, for she is already past fifteen. And, the rocky structure of our soil being unsuited to husbandry, gold is not easily wrung from it, and there is little of a worldly nature to be won from the forest; and to me it seems that as sin increases on Earth the need for gold grows greater.

"For myself, if the getting of gold be an art, as some have said, I am past the time for learning a new art; and, if it be a sin, my sins are over. Yet you my son may haply gather this great necessity for us, or this evil, whatever it be; and, if it be a sin, what is one more sin to youth? Not much, I fear."

The youth crossed himself.

"And follow not the way of the sword," continued his father, in no whit diverted from his discourse, "for the lawyers ever defeat it with their pens, as hath been said of old; but follow the Art, and you shall deal in a matter at whose mention lawyers pale."

"The Black Art!" exclaimed Ramon Alonzo.

"There is but one art," said his father; "and it shall all the more advantage you to follow it in that there hath been of late but little magic in Spain, and even in this forest there are not, but on rarest evenings, such mysteries nor such menace as I myself can remember; and no dragon hath been seen since my grandfather's days."

"The Black Art!" said Ramon Alonzo. "But how shall I tell of this to Father Joseph?"

And his father rubbed his chin awhile before he spoke again.

" 'Twere hard indeed," he said, "to tell so good a man. Yet are we in sore need of gold, and God forbid in His mercy that one of us should ever follow a trade."

"Amen," said his son.

And the fervour with which the boy had said Amen heartened his father to hope he would do his bidding, and cheered him on the way with his discourse, which he continued as follows.

"There is dwelling in the mountains, a day's walk beyond Aragona (whose spires we see), a magician known to my father. For once my father hunting a stag in his youth went far into the mountains, as goodly a stag as ever rejoiced a hunter, though once I killed one as good but never better. I killed mine in the year of the great snowfall, the year before you were born; it had come down from the mountains. But my father hunted his up from the valley where it had been feeding all night at the edges of gardens; it went home to the mountains, and in dense woods on the slope my father killed it at evening. And then the most curious man he had ever known came down the rocks, walking gently, wearing a black silk cloak, to where he was skinning the stag with tired hounds sitting round him, and asked my father if he studied magic. And my father said that hunting the stag and the boar were the only studies he knew. And well indeed he studied them, and he taught me, but not all he knew for no man could learn so much. And then he told the magician something of how to hunt boars; and the magician was pleased, for men shunned him much, and seldom spoke from their hearts of the things they loved, before his portentous cloak and his strange wise eye. And my father warmed to the tales as he told of the thing he had studied; and the stars came twinkling out above the magician, and the gloom was enormous in the ominous wood, and still my father told of the ways of boars, for there was never fear in my father.

And the magician asked my father if there was any favour he would have of him, and my father said, 'Yes,' for he had ever wondered at the art of writing, and he asked the magician if he would write for him. And this the magician did, withdrawing a cork from a horn that hung from his girdle and that was filled with ink, and taking a goose-quill and writing there in the wood upon a little scroll that he took from a satchel. And they parted in the wood, and my father remembered that day all his years, as much for what he had seen the magician do as for the splendid horns he had won that day. And when the writing came to be read it was seen that it was a letter of friendship or welcome to my father or to whomever he should send with that scroll to the house in the wood.

"Now my father cared only to hunt the boar and the stag and had no need of magic, and I have had nothing to do with parchments nor writings. But I can find the scroll at this moment among the tusks of boars that my father laid by, and you shall have the scroll and go to the wood and say to that magician, 'I am the grandson of him that taught you of the taking of boars nigh eighty years agone.' "

"But will he yet live?" asked Ramon.

"He were no magician else," replied his father.

And the boy sat silent then, regretting the thoughtlessness that his hasty words had revealed.

"With the mystery of writing, which you will doubtless study there, I have myself some acquaintance, having sufficiently studied the matter, some while since, to be able to practise it should the occasion ever arise: but of all mysteries that he hath the skill to teach you the one to study most diligently is that one which concerns the making of gold. Yes, yes," he said, silencing with a wave or two of his hand some hasty youthful objection that he saw on the boy's lips, "I wot well the sin that is inherent in gold, yet methinks there

5

is some primal curse upon it, put there by Satan before it was laid in earth, which may not cling to the gold that philosophers make."

And youth and haste again urged another question. "But can the philosophers make gold?" blurted out Ramon Alonzo.

"Ill-informed lad," said his father, "have you heard of no philosophers during the last ten centuries seeking for gold with their stone?"

"Yes," answered Ramon Alonzo, "but I heard of none that found it."

And his father shook his head with tolerant smiles and answered nothing at once, not hastening to reprove the lad's ill-founded opinion, for the wisdom of age expects these light conclusions from youth. And then he instructed his son in simple words, telling him that the value of gold lies not in any especial power in the metal, but purely in its rarity; and explaining so that a child could have understood, that had these most learned of men who gave their lives to alchemy acquainted the vulgar with the fruits of their study, as soon as their art had taught them the way of transmuting base metal, they would have undone in one garrulous moment the advantage that they had earned by nights of toil, working in lonely towers while all the world had rest. And more simple arguments he added, sufficient to correct the hasty error of youth, but too obvious and trite to offer to the attention of my reader. Having then explained that the philosopher's stone must have been often found and put to the use for which it was intended, he recommended the study of it once more to his son. And the young man weighed the advantages of gold with all that he had learned in its disfavour, and there and then decided to follow that study. Gladly then the Lord of the Tower and Rocky Forest went to this rummage-room where strange things lay and none interfered with the spider. And in that dim place where one scarce could have hoped to find anything, amongst heaps of old fishing nets that had become solid with dust, where worn-out boar-spears lay on the floor, and rusted bandilleros that had once pricked famous bulls, blunt knives and broken tent-pegs, and things too old for one to be able to name them at all, unless one washed them and brought them out in the light, groping amongst all these the Lord of the Tower found a pale heap of boars' tusks, and the scroll amongst them, as he had told his son: then he left the place to the spider. And returning with the scroll to his son he brought also a coffer out of another room, a small stout box of oak and massive silver, well guarded by a great lock, all lined within with satin. And he took a great key and carefully unlocked it, and showed it to Ramon Alonzo as he gave him the scroll of the magician; he held the coffer open with the light blue satin showing and said never a word; the young man knew it for the coffer of his sister's dowry and saw that it was empty. And by the time his father had closed the box again, and carefully locked it and placed the key in safety, the boy's young thoughts had roamed away to beyond Aragona to the man with the black silk cloak and his house in the wood, where base metals would have to suffer wonderful changes before good thick pieces of dross should chink deep on that satin lining. And where young thoughts have roamed there soon follow lads or maidens.

And then they talked of the way beyond Aragona, and the path that led to the wood. And the father leaned in his chair in comfort at ease, for it wearied him to speak of things that are hard to understand, and especially the getting of money; and he had thought of this matter for days before he had spoken of it, and it had never seemed sure to him that the money would come at all, but now all seemed clear and he rested. And leaning back in his chair he told the way to his son, which was easy as far as the wood, and after that he could ask the way of such men as he met; and if he met none he was likely near to the house, for men avoided it much. Awhile they talked of things of little moment, small matters pleasant to both, till the father remembered that more than this was seemly, and reminded his son of all such things as he himself knew that concerned the decorum and gravity of the study of magic. Indeed he knew little of this ancient study, but had once seen a conjuror produce a rabbit alive from under an empty sombrero, years ago outside a village in which he had sought to purchase a cow, and it was this that he meant when he spoke of the slight acquaintance he had himself had with magic; for the rest he spoke of the hoar traditions of magic, which were as antique then as now, for then as now they went back past the first gates of history, and ran far on the wide plains of legend and into the dimness of time.

"To such traditions," he said, "a grave decorum were fitting."

And the young man nodded his head, his face full of a fitting decorum. And the father remembered his own youth and wondered.

They parted then, the Lord of the Tower and Rocky Forest going to find his lady, the young man still in his chair before the fire, pondering his journey and his future calling. These thoughts were too swift to follow: pursuing instead the slow steps of his father we find him come to a room in which, already, discernible shadows were cast by a want of gold. With its ancient sentinel chairs that seemed posted there to check lounging, and its treasures of tapestries hung to hide ruined panels or wherever the draughts blew most from untended rat-holes, that threatened room would scarce convey to our minds, could we see it across the centuries, any hint of impending need. And yet those shadows were there, moving softly as in slow dances with the solemn folds of the tapestry, or rising to welcome draughts in their secret manner, or lurking by the huge carved feet of the chairs; and always knowing with shadow-knowledge and whispering with shadow-talk, and hinting and prophesying and fearing, that a need was nearing the Tower to trouble its years. And here the Lord of the Tower found his lady, whose hair was whitening above a face unperturbed by the passing of time or anything that time brings; if great passions had shaken her mind or wandering imaginations often troubled it, they had passed across that plump and placid face with no more traces than the storms and the ships leave on the yellow sand of a sunny cove.

And he said to her: "I have spoken with Ramon Alonzo and have arranged everything with him. He is to leave us soon to work with a learned man that lives beyond Aragona, and will win for us the gold that we require and, afterwards, some more for himself."

More than this he did not say upon that matter, for it was not his way, nor was it then the custom in Spain to speak of business to ladies.

And the lady rejoiced at this, for she had long tried to make her husband see that need that was sending its shadows to creep through the Tower, telling every nook of its coming; but the boars had to be hunted, and the hounds had to be fed, and a hundred things demanded his attention, so that she feared he might never have leisure to give his mind to this matter. But now it was all settled.

"Will Ramon Alonzo start soon?" she said.

"Not for some days," said he. "There is no haste."

But Ramon Alonzo's swifter thoughts had outpaced all this. He was speaking now with his sister, telling her that he was to start next morning for that old house in the mountains of which they had often heard tales, and bidding her tend his great boar-hound. They were in the garden though the gloaming was fading away, the garden that met the lawn on which they had lately played, a little lower down the slope where the Tower stood, and shut from the untamed earth and the rocks that were there before man by the same balustrade of marble that guarded the lawn. The hawk-moths appeared out of the darkening air from their deep homes in the forest and hovered by heavy blossoms; it was in the midst of the days that are poised between Spring and Summer. Here Ramon and Mirandola said farewell in the little paths along which they often had played in years that appeared remote to them, under Spanish shrubs that were tall fountains of flowers. And whatever the lady of the Tower guessed, neither her lord nor Ramon Alonzo had any knowledge that there was a glittering flash in the eyes of the slender girl that might laugh away demands for any dowry, and be deadlier and sweeter than gold, and might mock the men that sought it and bring their plans to derision, and overturn their illusion and fill their dreams with its ashes. Ramon Alonzo was troubled by no such fancy as this as he spoke earnestly of his boar-hound, and as they spoke of his needs of combing and feeding and dryness they walked back to the Tower; and the gloaming was not yet gone, but it was midnight in Mirandola's hair.

And so it was that on the following day, at evening, beyond Aragona, a young man was to be seen by such eyes as could peer so far, in his cloak on a rocky road with his back to the sheltered fields, bound for the mountain upon which frowned the woods; and night and a moaning wind were rising all round about him.

CHAPTER II

Ramon Alonzo Comes to the House in the Wood

Ramon Alonzo had travelled all day, and was twenty-five miles from his home; and now alone amongst darkness and storm and rocks he saw yet no sign of the house he sought, or any shelter at all. He had come past the sentinel oaks to the gloom of the wood, and neither saw light of window anywhere nor heard any of those sounds such as rise from the houses of men. He was in that mood that most attracts despair to come to men and tempt them; and indeed it would soon have come, luring him to forsake illusion and give up ambition and hope, but that just in that perilous moment he met a ragged man coming down through the wood. He came with strides, cloak and rags all flapping together, and would have passed the young traveller and hastened on towards the fields and the haunts of men, but Ramon Alonzo hailed him, demanding of him: "Where is the house in the wood?"

"Oh not there, young master, not there," said the ragged stranger, waving his hands against something upon his left and up the slope a little behind him. "Not there, young master," he implored again, and shuddered as he spoke. And no despair came near Ramon Alonzo then, to tempt all his aspirations down to their dooms, for he saw by the stranger's unmistakable terror he had only to keep on upward and a little more to his right to come very soon in sight of the house in the wood.

"I have business with the magician," replied Ramon Alonzo.

"May all such blessed Saints defend us as can," said the stranger. He wrapped his cloak round him with a trembling hand and went shuddering down the slope drivelling terrified prayer.

"A fair night to you, señor," called out Ramon Alonzo.

"Clearly not far," he added, thinking aloud.

And once more he heard struggling feebly against the eerie voice of the wind those plaintive words imploring: "Not there, young master, not there." And pressing on in the direction against which those feeble hands had waved so earnestly, he had gone some while against wind and slope and branches when a feeling came dankly upon him, as though exuded from the deep moss all around him, that he came no nearer to the house in the wood. He halted then and called out loud in the darkness: "If there be a magician in this wood let him appear."

He waited and the wind sang on triumphantly, singing of spaces unconcerned with man, blue fields of the wind's roving, dark gardens amongst the stars. He waited there and no magician came. So he sat on a boulder that was all deep with moss, and leaned back on it and looked into the wood, and saw nothing there but blackness and outlines of oak-boles. There he pondered how to come to his journey's end. And then it came to him that this was no common journey, to be guided by the rules of ordinary wayfaring, but, having a magician as its destination and in an ominous wood, it were better guided by spell or magic or omen; and he meditated upon how he should come by a spell. And as he thought of spells he remembered the scroll he bore, with the ink of the magician upon it written eighty years agone. Now Ramon Alonzo's studies had not extended so far as the art of writing; the good fathers in their school on the high hill near his home had taught him orally all that is needful to know, and much more he had learned for himself, but not by reading. Script therefore in black ink upon a scroll was in itself wonderful to him and, knowing it to have been penned by a magician, he reasonably regarded it as a spell. Arising then from his seat he waved this scroll high in the night and, knowing the liking that secret folk oft show for the number three, he waved it thrice. And there before him was the house in the wood.

It seemed to have slid down quietly from the high places of night, or it quietly appeared out of darkness that had hidden it hitherto, but the silence that cloaked its appearance almost instantly glided away, giving place to Arabian music that haunted the air overhead and plaintive Hindu love-chants that yearned in the dark. Then windows flashed into light, and there just in front of the mossy stone that the young man had made his seat was an old green door all studded with old green knobs. The door was ajar.

Ramon Alonzo stepped forward and pushed the green door open, and the magician came to his door with that alacrity with which the spider descends to the spot in his web that is shaken by some lost winged traveller's arrival. He was in the great black silk cloak that the young man's grandfather knew, but he wore great spectacles now, for he was older than he had been eighty years ago, in spite of his magic art. Ramon Alonzo bowed and the master smiled, though whether he smiled for welcome, or at a doom that hung over the strangers who troubled his door, there was no way for unlearned men to know. Then quickly, though still without fear, Ramon Alonzo thrust out the scroll that he bore, with the magician's own writing upon it all in black ink, saying, word for word as his father had bade him say, "I am the grandson of him that taught you the taking of boars nigh eighty years ago." The magician received it, and as he read his smile changed its nature and appeared to Ramon Alonzo somewhat more wholesome, having something in common with smiles of unlearned men that they smile at what is pleasant in earthly affairs. With a tact that well became him the master of magic made no enquiry after the young man's grandfather; for as the rich do not speak of poverty to the poor, or the learned discourse on ignorance to the unlearned, this sage that had mastered the way of surviving the years spoke seldom with common men on the matter of death. But he bowed a welcome as though Ramon Alonzo were not entirely a stranger; and the young man expressed the pleasure that he felt at meeting a master of arts.

"There is but one Art," answered the Master.

"It is the one I would study," replied Ramon Alonzo.

"Ah," said the magician.

And with an air now grown grave, as though somewhat pondering, he raised his arm and summoned up a draught, which closed his green door. When the door was shut and the draught had run home, brushing by the loose silk sleeve of the magician to its haunt in the dark of the house, which Ramon Alonzo perceived to be full of crannies, the host led his guest to an adjacent room, whence the savour of meats arose as he opened the door. And there was a repast all ready cooked and spread, waiting for Ramon Alonzo. By what arts those meats were kept smoking upon that table ready for any stranger that should come in from the wood, ready perhaps since the days of the young man's grandfather, I tell not to this age, for it is far too well acquainted already with the preservation of meat.

With a bow and a wave of his arm the magician appointed a chair to Ramon Alonzo. And not till his guest was seated before the meats did the magician speak again.

"So you would study the Art," he said.

"Master," the young man answered him, "I would."

"Know then," the magician said, "that all those exercises that men call arts, and all wisdom and all knowledge, are but humble branches of that worthy study that is justly named the Art. Nor is this to be revealed to all chance-come travellers that may imperil themselves by entering my house in the wood. My gratitude to your grandfather however, for some while now unpaid (I trust he prospers), renders me anxious to serve you. For he taught me a branch of learning that he had studied well: it was moreover one of those studies that my researches had not yet covered, the matter of the hunting of boars; and from this, as from every science that learning knows, the Art hath increase, and becometh a yet more awful and reverend power whereby to astound the vulgar, and to punish error, not only in this wood but finally to drive it out of all worldly affairs."

And he spoke swiftly past his mention of Ramon Alonzo's grandfather, lest his guest should have the embarrassment of admitting that his grandfather had shared with all the unlearned the vulgar inability to withstand the flight of the years. For himself he kept on a shelf in an upper room a bottle of that medicine philosophers use, which is named elixir vitae, wherein were sufficient doses to ensure his survival till the time when he knew that the world would begin to grow bad. He took one dose in every generation. By certain turns in the tide of life in those that he watched, a touch of grey over the ears, a broadening or a calming, he knew that the heyday of a generation was past and the time had come for his dose. And then he would go one night by resounding stairs, that were never troubled by anything human but him, whatever the rats might dare, and so he would come with his ponderous golden key, for an iron one would have long since rusted away, to the lock he turned only once every thirty years. And, opening the heavy door at the top of the stairs and entering that upper room, he would find his bottle grey with dust on its shelf, perhaps entirely hidden by little curtains that the spiders had drawn across it, and measuring his dose by moonlight he would drink it full in the rays, as though he shared this secret alone with the moon. Then back he would go down those age-worn steps of oak with his old mind suddenly lightened of the cares of that generation, free from its foibles, untroubled by its problems, neither cramped nor duped by its fashions, unyoked by its causes, undriven by its aims, fresh and keen for the wisdom and folly of a new generation. Such a mind, well stored with the wisdom of several ages and repeatedly refreshed with the nimble alertness of youth, now crossed in brief conversation the young mind of Ramon Alonzo, like a terrible blade of Toledo, sharpened in ancient battles, meeting a well-wrought rapier coming fresh to its first war.

"My grandfather unfortunately came to his death," said Ramon Alonzo.

"Alas," said the Master.

"Our family is well used to it," said the youth with a certain pride, for poverty has its pride as well as wealth, and Ramon Alonzo would not be abashed by his forbears' lack of years even though he should speak with an immortal.

"Is that so?" said the Master.

"I thank you," said Ramon Alonzo, "for the noble senti-
ments you so graciously felt for my grandfather and shall
greatly value such learning as you may have leisure to teach
me, for I would make gold out of the baser metals, my
family having great need of it."

"There are secrets you shall not learn," replied the magician, "for I may impart them to none; but the making of gold
is amongst the least of the crafts that are used by those skilled
in the Art, and were only a poor return for the learning I had
from your grandfather concerning the hunting of boars."

"Beyond this wood," said Roman Alonzo, "we set much
store by gold, and value it beyond the hunting of boars."

"Beyond this wood," replied the Master, "lies error, to ex-
tirpate which is the object of my studies. For this my lamp is
lit, to the grief of the owls, and often burns till lark-song. Of
the things you shall learn here earliest the prime is this, that
the pursuit of the philosophers is welfare. To this gold often
contributes; often it thwarts it. But it was plainly taught by
your grandfather that the hunting of boars is amongst those
things that bring pure joy to man. This study must therefore
always be preferred to such as only bring us happiness in-
completely, or that have been known to fail to bring it at all,
as the hunting of boars never failed, so I learned from your
grandfather."

"I fear that my grandfather," said the young man depre-
catingly, "was but ill-equipped for discourse with a philosopher, having had insufficient leisure, as I have often been
told, for learning."

"Your grandfather," answered the Master, "was a very
great philosopher. Not only had he found the way to happiness but of that way he was a most constant explorer, till
none may doubt that he knew its every turning; for he could
track the boars to the forest all the way from the fields

where they rooted, knowing what fields they would seek and the hour at which they would leave them, and could hearten his hounds while they hunted, even through watery places, and when scent was lost and all their cunning was gone he still could lead them on; and so he brought them upon many a boar, and slew his quarry with spear-thrusts that he had practised, and took its tusky head, which was his happiness; and rarely failed to achieve it, having so deeply studied the way.

"I also have followed the pursuit of happiness, studying all those methods that are most in use amongst men, as well as some that are hidden from them; and most of these methods are vain, leaving few that are worthy of the investigation of one holding the rank that I now hold amongst wizards. Of these few that have stood the test of my laborious analysis is this one that I owe to the researches of your grandfather, and which, seeing how few are the ways of attaining happiness, is certainly among the four great branches of learning. Who knows these four great studies hath four different ways of approach to the goal of mankind, and hath that might that is to be got by complete wisdom alone. For this cause I give great honour to your grandfather, and extol his name, and bless it by means of spells, and in my estimation place it high amongst the names of those whose learning has lightened the world. Alas that his studies gave him no time for that last erudition which could have ensured his survival to these days and beyond them."

The young man was surprised at the value the Master placed upon boar-hunting for, having as yet learned nothing about philosophy, he vaguely and foolishly believed it to be concerned with mere intricate words, and did not know in his youthful ignorance that its real concern was with happiness. Such folly is scarce becoming to young heroes, yet having sought to lure my reader's interest towards him I feel it my duty to tell the least of his weaknesses, without which my portrait of him would be a false one. And so I expose his ignorance to the eyes of a later age; he will not be abashed by it now; but seated beside the meat at that magic table he felt the triviality of his schoolboy's scraps of learning before every particle that the magician chose to reveal from his lore. And with all the intensity that trifles can summon up in youth he regretted his disparagement of his grandfather, not on account of his own reverence for him, but because he now perceived him to have been one that the Master held in honour. To cover his confusion he poured himself out some wine from a beaker at his right hand, partly bronze, partly glass, the bronze and glass being intermingled by magic; and, having filled his cup, a clear hollowed crystal, he hastily drank it before he spoke again.

And the wine was a magic wine with a taste of flowers, yet of flowers unknown to Earth, and a flavour of Spices, yet of spices ungathered in any isles Spain knew; and it had in it a memory and a music, and came to the blood like one that was closely kin, and yet of a kinship from ages and ages ago. And all of a sudden the young man saw his folly, in deeming that philosophy prefers the way to the end, and so for a moment he saw his grandfather's wisdom; but that wonderful wine's inspiration died swiftly away, and his thoughts were concerned again with the making of gold.

The magician had silently watched him drink of that magic vintage.

"It comes not from these vineyards," he said. And he waved his arm so wide that he seemed to indicate no vineyard of Spain, nor the neighbouring kingdom of Portugal; nor France, nor Africa, nor the German lands; Italy, Greece, nor the islands.

"Whence?" asked Ramon Alonzo, leaning forward in earnest wonder.

And the Master extended his arm, pointing it higher. It seemed to point towards the Evening Star, that low and blue and large was blinking beyond the window.

"It is magic," said Ramon Alonzo.

"All's magic here," said the Master.

CHAPTER III

The Charwoman Tells of Her Loss

As Ramon Alonzo supped that tall figure of magic stood opposite without moving, and spoke no more; so that the young man ate hastily and soon had finished. He rose from the table, the other signed with his arm, and passed out of the room, Ramon Alonzo following. Soon they came to a lanthorn which the Master of the Art took down from its hook on the wall; he turned then away from his green door and led his visitor on to the deeps of his house. And it seemed to Ramon Alonzo, with the curious insight of youth, as he followed the black bulk of the Master of the Art looming above the wild shadows that ran from the lanthorn, that here was the master of a band of shadows leading them home into their native darkness. And so they came to an ancient stairway of stone, that was lit by narrow windows opening on the stars, though to-night the Master brought his lanthorn to light it in honour of his guest. And it was plain even to Ramon Alonzo from the commotion of the bats, though he had not the art to read the surprise in

21

the eyes of the spiders, that the light of a lanthorn seldom came that way. They came to a door that no spell had guarded from time; the magician pushed it open and stood aside, and Ramon Alonzo entered. At first he only saw the huge bulk of the bed, but as the lanthorn was lifted into the room he saw the ruinous panels along the wall; and then the light fell on the bed-clothes, and he could see that blankets and sheets mouldered all in one heap together and a cobweb covered them over. Some rush mats lay on the floor, but something seemed to have eaten most of the rushes. Over the window a draught flapped remnants of curtains, but the moth must have been in those curtains for ages and ages. The Master spoke with an air of explanation, almost perhaps of apology: "Old age comes to all," he said. Then he withdrew.

Left alone with the starlight, to which the work of the moth allowed an ample access, Ramon Alonzo considered his host. The room was ominous and the house enchanted and there might well be spells in it more powerful than his sword, yet if his host were friendly it seemed to him he was safe amongst his enchantments, unless some rebel spirit should trouble the night, who had revolted from the spells of the magician. He generously accepted the Master's explanation of the state of the room, shrewdly considering him to be a man so absorbed in the perpetuity of his art that he gave no attention to material things; so trusting to his host's expressions of goodwill, and of gratitude to his grandfather, he lay down on the bed to sleep, untroubled by fear of spells or spirits of evil, but he took off none of his clothes, for against the risk of damp he felt there was none to guard him.

Either he slept or was in that borderland where Earth is dimmed by a haze from the land of sleep, and dreams cast shadows yet on the shores of Earth before they glide afar, when he heard slow steps come up the stairway of stone. And presently there was a knock, to which he answered, and a crone appeared in the door, holding the lanthorn that the magician had lately carried. Age had withered her beyond pity; for whatever pity there be for sickness and hurts, youth feels little pity for age, having never known it, and the aged have little pity to give to their fellows, because pity is withering in them with many another emotion, like the last of the flowers drooping all together as winter nears the garden. She stood there feeble and wasted, an ancient hag.

And before the young man spoke she quavered to him, with an earnest intentness the fervour of which not even her age could dim, stretching out a withered right hand to him as she spoke, the left hand holding the lanthorn: "Young master, give him nothing! Give him nothing, whatever he ask! His prices are too high, young master, too high, too high!"

"I have little money to give," said Ramon Alonzo.

"Money!" she gasped, for her vehemence set her panting. "Money! That is naught! That's a toy! That's a mousetrap! Money indeed! But his prices are too high: he asks more than money."

"More than money?" said Ramon Alonzo. "What then?"

"Look!" she cried lamentably, and twirled the lanthorn about her.

The young man saw first her face, and a look on it like the look on the face of one revealing a mortal wound; and then, as she swung the lanthorn round, he suddenly saw that the woman had no shadow.

"What! No shadow?" he blurted out, sitting suddenly up on his heap of cobwebs and sheets.

"Never again," she said, "never again. It lay over the

fields once; it used to make the grass such a tender green. It never dimmed the buttercups. It did no harm to anything. Butterflies may have been scared of it, and once a dragon-fly, but it did them never a harm. I've known it protect anemones awhile from the heat of the noonday sun, which had otherwise withered them sooner. In the early morning it would stretch away beyond our garden right out to the wild; poor innocent shadow that loved the grey dew. And in the evening it would grow bold and strong and run right down the slopes of hills, where I walked singing, and would come to the edges of bosky tangled places, till a little more and its head would have been out of sight: I've known the fairies then dance out from their sheltered arbours in the deeps of briar and thorn and play with its curls. And, for all its rovings and lurkings and love of mystery, it never left me, of its own accord never. It was I that forsook it, poor shadow, poor shadow that followed me home. For I've been out with it when the evenings were eerie and all the valleys haunted, and my shadow must have met with such companions as were far more kin to it than my gross body could be, and nearer to it than my heels, folk that would give it news direct from the kingdom of shadows and gossip of the dark side of the moon, and would whisper things that I could never have taught it; yet it always came home with me. And at night by candlelight in our cottage in Aragona it used to dance for me as I went to bed, all over the walls and ceilings, poor innocent shadow. And if I left a low candle to burn away he never tired of dancing for me as long as I sat up and watched: often he outtired the candle, for the more wearily the candle flickered the more nimbly he leaped. And then he would lie and rest in any corner with the common shadows of humble trivial things, but if I struck a light to rise before dawn, or even if I should light my candle at midnight, he was always there at once, erect on the wall, ready to follow me wherever I went, and to bear me that companionship as I went among men and women, which I valued, alas, so little when I had it, and without which now I know, too late I have learned, there is no welcome for one, no pity, no sufferance amongst mankind."

"No pity?" said Ramon Alonzo, moved deeply to pity, himself, by the old crone's sorrow, though unable to credit that her loss could matter so much as she said.

"No pity! No sufferance!" she said. "The children run from me screaming. Those that are large enough to throw, throw stones at me; and their elders come out with sticks when they hear them scream. At evening they all grow angrier. They come out with their long big faithful shadows, if I dare go near a village, and stand just beyond the strip where my shadow should be, and jeer at me and upbraid and there is no pity. And all the while they jeer there's not one that loves his shadow as I love mine. They do not gaze at their shadows, or even turn to look at them. Ah, how I should gaze at mine if it could come back, poor shadow. I should go to a quiet place alone in the open country, and there I should sit on the moss with my back to the sun, and watch my shadow all day. I should not want to eat or drink or think; I should only watch my shadow. I should mark its gentle movement that it makes in time with the sun, I should watch till I saw it grow. And then I would hold up my hand and move every finger, and each joint of my arm; and see the shadow answering, answering, answering. And I should nod to it and bow to it and curtsey. And I would dance to my shadow alone. And all this I would do again and again all day. I would watch the colour that every flower took, and each different kind of grass, when my shadow touched them. And this is not telling you one hundredth part of it. It is this to love one's shadow!

"And what do they know of their shadows? What do they

care whether their shadows lie on green grass or rock? What do they know what colours the flowers turn when their shadows go amongst them? And they won't let me live with them, speak with them, or pass them by, because forsooth I have been unkind to my shadow. Ah, well, perhaps the days will come when they too will love something too late, and love something that is gone, as I love my shadow; cold days and long days those."

"How did you lose it?" asked Ramon Alonzo, all wonder and pity.

"He took it," she said. "He took it. He took it away and put it in his box. What did I know of the need one has of a shadow: that they would not speak to me, would not let me live? They never told me they set such store by their shadows. Nor do they! Nor do they!"

The young man's generous feelings were moved by this wrong as though it had been his own.

"I will go there with my sword," he exclaimed, "and they shall speak with you courteously."

For the first time that night the old woman smiled. She knew that jealousy united with fear could not be made to forgive such a loss as hers. She had not known at first that it was jealousy, but had learned it at length by her lonely ponderings. The villagers saw that in some curious way she had stepped outside boundaries that narrowed them, and had escaped from one rule from which they had never a holiday. They could never be rid of the hourly attendance of shadows, but one that could should not triumph over them. She knew, and she smiled.

"Young master," she said, more than ever moved to help him by his outburst of generosity, "give him nothing."

"But you," he said, "did you give it to him?"

"Fool! Fool that I was!" she said. "I did not know I needed it."

"But for what did you give it?" he asked.

"For immortality of a sort," she said, and said so ruefully, with a look that told so much more, that the young man saw clearly enough it had been the gift of Tithonus.

"He gave you that!" he exclaimed.

"That," she said.

"But why?" asked Ramon Alonzo.

"He wanted a charwoman," she said.

CHAPTER IV

Ramon Alonzo Learns a Mystery Known to the Reader

When the crone had revealed the mean and trivial purpose for which the Master of the Art had cast her helpless upon the ages, she voiced her regrets no more; but, once more warning the young man against the magician's prices, she turned about with her lanthorn and went shadowless out of the room. Ramon Alonzo had heard and disregarded tales of men that had paid their shadows as the price for certain dealings with the scope of the Art; but he had never before considered the value of shadows. He saw now that to lose his shadow and to come to yearn for it when it were lost, and to lose the little greetings that one daily had from one's kind, and to hear no more tattle about trivial things; to see smiles no more, nor to hear one's name called friendly; but to have the companionship only of shadowless things, such as that old woman, and wandering spirits, and dreams, might well be to pay too much for the making of gold. And, well warned now, he decided that come what may he would never part with his shadow. In his gratitude he determined to ask the magician for some respite for that poor old woman from scrubbing his floors through the ages.

And then his thoughts went back to his main purpose, to what metals were suited best for transmutation, and whether he could turn them into gold himself if the magician's price were too high: other men had done it; why not he? And, led towards absurdity by this delightful hope, his thoughts grew wilder and wilder till they were dreams.

The sun coming through the upper branches of trees fell on that spidery bed and woke Ramon Alonzo. He perceived then a great gathering of huge oaks, seemingly more ancient than the rest of the forest, and the house was in the midst of them. It was a secret spot. He saw, now, that there was in his room a second window, but the little twigs had so pressed their leaves against it that no light entered there but a dim greenness; it was like hundreds of out-turned hands protesting against that house.

By such light as came through the southeastern window he tidied himself, brushing off with his hands such cobwebs as he could. He did not draw back the curtains, deeming that if he took hold of a portion of one it would come away from the rest; nor did enough material remain to obstruct much of the light that came in through the trees. Then, being dressed already, he opened his door and descended the stairs of stone. Every narrow slit that lighted those dim stairs continued to show vast gathering of oaks that pressed close on the house, so close that Ramon Alonzo saw now, what he had faintly heard overnight and not understood, that here and there great branches had entered the tower and been shaped as steps amongst the steps of stone, making two or three hollower sounds amongst the tapping footsteps of such as used that stair. Upon stormy nights the wooden steps swayed slightly.

When Ramon Alonzo had descended those steps he came to passages amongst a darkness of rafters which were like such nooks as children find under old stairs, only larger and stranger and dimmer, running this way and that; and, guided by glimmers of light that shone faintly from a far window, he came at length to the hall, at whose other end was the old green door to the forest. And there in his black silk cloak in the midst of the hall the magician awaited him.

He was standing motionless, and as soon as the young man saw him the Master of the Art said: "I trust you slept in comfort." For his studies allowed him leisure for courtesies such as these, but were too profound to permit of such intercourse with common material things as lifting the cobwebs to see the state of the bedclothes that had mouldered so long upon his visitor's bed. As for the charwoman, she had sorrows enough watching the ages beating upon her frame to trouble what a mere thirty or forty years might do to the sheets and blankets.

"I slept admirably, señor," Ramon Alonzo said, with a grace in his bow that is sometimes only learnt just as the joints and the muscles have grown too stiff to achieve it.

"I rejoice," said the magician.

"Master," said Ramon Alonzo, "would you deign to show me some unconsidered fragment of your wisdom, some saw having naught to do with the deeper mysteries, some trifle, some trick of learning, perhaps the mere making of gold out of other dross, that I may learn to study now, and so in time be wise."

"For this," said the magician, pointing the way with a gesture, "let us go to the room that is sacred to the Art. Its very dust is made of books I have studied, and is indeed more redolent of lore than any dust in this wood; and if echoes die not at all, as some have taught (though others urge finality for all things), the spiders in its corners, whose ears are attuned to sounds that are lost to ours, hear still the echoes of my earlier musings whereby I unravelled mysteries that are not for the ears of man. There we will speak upon the graver matters."

He led, and the young man followed. And again he was amongst beams of age-darkened oak, and twisty corridors leading into the gloom, which the shape of the magician before him rendered unnaturally blacker. They came to a black door studded with wooden knobs, upon which the magician rapped, and the door opened. They entered, and Ramon Alonzo perceived at once that it was a magician's work-room, not only by the ordinary appliances or instruments of magic, but by the several sheets of gloom that seemed to come down from the roof through the midst of the air, across the natural dimness of the room. The appliances of magic were there in abundance; stuffed crocodiles lying as thick as on lonely mud-banks in Africa, dried herbs resembling plants that blossom in wonted fields, yet wearing a look that never was on any flowers of ours, great twinkling jewels out of the heads of toads, huge folios written by masters that had followed the Art in China, small parchments with spells upon them in Persian, Indian, or Arabic, the horn of a unicorn that had slain its master; rare spices, condiments, and the philosopher's stone.

These Ramon Alonzo saw first as he came through the doorway, though what their purposes were he scarcely wondered, and these were the things that always came to his memory whenever in after years he recalled that sinister room. As his eyes became accustomed to the dimness, more and more of the wares and tools of the magical art came looming out of the dusk, while the magician strode to a high-backed chair at a lectern, on which a great book lay open showing columns of Chinese manuscript. In the high-backed chair the magician seated himself before the Cathayan book, and taking up a pen from an unknown wing, he looked at Ramon Alonzo.

"Now," he said, as though he came newly to the subject or brought to it new acumen from having sat in that chair, "what branch of the Art do you desire to follow?"

"The making of gold," responded Ramon Alonzo.

"The formulæ of all material things have been worked out," said the magician, "and they have all been found to be vanity. Amongst the first whose formulæ failed before these investigations, revealing mere vanity, was gold. Yet should you wish to study the Art from its rudiments, from the crude transmutation of mere material things to the serious and weighty matter of transmigration, I am willing to give you certain instruction at first upon the frivolous topic of your choice. And it is not entirely without value, for by observing the changes in material things we chance sometimes on indications that guide us in graver studies. But the whole of the way is long, even as the masters count time. Would you therefore begin from these earliest rudiments?"

"I would," said Ramon Alonzo.

"Know then," said he, "that my fees are never material things, but are dreams, hopes, and illusions, and whatever other great forces control the fortune of nations. Later I will enumerate them. But while we study the mere transmutation of metals I will ask no more than that which of all immaterial things most nearly pertains to matter, at one point actually touching it . . ."

"My shadow," cried Ramon Alonzo.

The magician was irked by his guest's discovery of his fee, though he was indeed about to tell him; but he had a few more words to say first about the worthlessness of shadows, and the sudden disclosure of the point was not in accordance with his plans for conducting a bargain; and, as many a man will do in such a case, he denied that he was about to ask precisely that. He soon however came round to it again, saying: "And even so it were little enough to ask for my fee, which might well be larger were it not for my gratitude to your grandfather; for a shadow, of necessity, shares the doom that overtakes matter, and is commoner far than faith if all were known, and is of the least account of all immaterial things."

"Yet I need it," said Ramon Alonzo.

"For what purpose?" asked the Master of the Art.

"I shall need it when I go among the villages," he answered, "or whenever I meet with men."

"Learn," said the magician, "that aught that has value is to be treasured on that account, and not for the opinion of the vulgar; and that which has no value is foolishly desired if its purpose be but to minister to the fickleness of the idle popular eye."

"Is my shadow valueless?" asked Ramon Alonzo.

"Utterly," said the Master.

"Why then does your Excellency demand it?"

"Address me rather as your Mystery," said the magician to gain time.

Ramon Alonzo apologized with due courtesy and conformed to the correct usage.

"I need it," said His Mystery, "because there are those that serve me better when equipped with a shadow than when drifting vapidly in their native void. They have no other connection with Earth except these shadows I give them, and for this purpose I have many shadows which I keep here in a box. But you who were born on Earth have no need at all of a shadow, and lose none of our mundane privileges if you should give it away."

And for all the wisdom of the magician the young man

remained less moved by his well-reasoned arguments than by the grief and garrulity of the charwoman.

So he held to his shadow and would not part with it; and the more the magician proved its uselessness the more stubborn he became. And when the magician would not abate his fee the young man determined to stay and study there rather than to return home empty-handed; and to bide his time, perhaps to come one day on the secret of transmutation, perhaps to grow so learned through his studies that he might work out its formula for himself. Therefore he said: "Are there no other mysteries that I may learn for a different fee?"

The Master answered: "There are many mysteries."

"For what fees?" asked Ramon Alonzo.

"These vary," said the magician, "according to the mystery. Your faith, your hope, half your eyesight, some illusion of value: I have many fees, as indeed there are many illusions."

He would not give his faith, nor yet his hope, for that would be nearly as bad; and he had ever clung somewhat tenaciously to his illusions, as indeed we all do.

"What mystery," he asked, "do you impart for half my eyesight?"

"The mystery of reading," answered the Master.

Now Ramon Alonzo had such eyesight that he could count the points on a stag's head at five hundred paces, and deemed half would well suffice him. The magician moreover explained that it was not his custom to take that fee in advance, but that the length of his sight would diminish appreciably as he mastered the intricacies of the mystery.

This well suited Ramon Alonzo, for he had ever wondered how the thoughts of men could lie sleeping for ages in folios, and suddenly brighten new minds with the mirth of men centuries dead; for the good fathers had not taught him this in their school, perhaps fearing that they would make their wisdom too common if they recklessly made the laity free of its source. And, believing as many do that wisdom is only a matter of reading, he thought soon to be on the track of the lore of those philosophers who in former ages transmuted base metals to gold, and so come by what he sought without losing his shadow.

"Master," said Ramon Alonzo, "I pray you teach me that mystery."

The magician shut the book. "To read Chinese," he said, "I do not teach for this fee, for the Chinese script hides secrets too grave to be learnt at so light a cost. For this fee I teach only to read in the Spanish language. Hereafter, for other fees . . ."

"Master," the young man said, "I am well content."

And then, with sonorous voice and magnificent gestures, the magician began to expose the secrets of reading; one by one he stripped mysteries, laying them bare to his pupil; and all the while he taught in that grand manner, that he had from the elder masters whose lore had been handed down. He taught the use of consonants, the reason of vowels, the way of the downstrokes and the up; the time for capital letters, commas, and colons; and why the "j" is dotted, with many another mystery. That first lesson in the gloomy room were well worthy of faithful description, so that every detail of the mystery might be minutely handed down; but the thought comes to me that my reader is necessarily versed in this mystery, and for that reason alone I say no more on this magnificent theme. Suffice it that with all pomp and dignity due to this approach to the prime source of learning the magician began to unfold the mystery of reading to the awed and wondering eyes of Ramon Alonzo. And while they taught and learned they heard outside in the passage the doleful sweeping of the shadowless woman that minded that awful house.

CHAPTER V

Ramon Alonzo Learns of the Box

Before that day had passed Ramon Alonzo had learned the alphabet. He did not master it in one lesson; yet when the magician ceased all in the midst of his wonders, in order that Ramon Alonzo should have the mid-day meal, he felt that the pathway was already open that led to the boundless lands made gay by the thoughts of the dead. And in those lands what spells might he not unravel, and amongst them the formula for the making of gold. If the magician ate he ate secretly. But Ramon Alonzo, going by his bidding to the room in which he had eaten and drunk overnight, found hot meats once more that awaited him.

As he entered the room he heard a small scurry of feet near the far door, but saw nothing. He ate; then, guided by an impulse of youth, which is always curious until it is sure it knows everything, he began to roam through the darknesses of the house in order to find who it was that served those meats. And the further he went, the lower the corridors ran, till he had to bend low to avoid the huge dark beams above him.

Sometimes he came on towering doors in the darkness, and opened them and found great chambers, wanly lit by such daylight as came through the leaves of the forest, which everywhere were pressed against the windows. In these chambers were tapestried chairs set out for a great assemblage, with ancient glories carved upon their frames, and dim magnificencies; but the cobwebs went from chair to chair and covered all of them over, and, descending in huge draperies from the roof, cloaked and festooned the splendours that jutted out from the wall. He went from door to door, but found no kitchen. And all his quest was silent but for the sound of his own feet.

At last, as he turned back by the wandering corridors, he heard in the distance before him the work of the charwoman. She had ceased her sweeping and was scrubbing on stone. He walked to the sound of the scrubbing, and so found her, the only living thing that he had met since he left the magician. She was in a passage scrubbing at one stone, upon which, as Ramon Alonzo could see, she had often worked before, for it was all worn with scrubbing. There was blood on the stone, but though years of scrubbing had hollowed it, the blood had gone deeper than the hollowing, so deep that Ramon Alonzo asked her why she toiled at it.

"It was innocent blood," she answered.

The young man did not even ask for that story; the house was so full of wonder. He asked instead what he had sought to find: "Who serves the dinner?"

"Imps," she said.

"Imps?" said Ramon Alonzo.

"Imps that he catches in the wood," she said, looking up from her work on the floor.

"How does he catch them?" he asked.

"I know not," she said. "With his spells, like as not. He says they are no use in the wood, and so he catches them."

"Are there imps in the wood?" asked Ramon Alonzo.

"It is full of them," she said.

Turning to a more profitable matter he said: "I am learning a mystery from the Master."

"For what price?" she asked quickly. "What price?"

"Only half my eyesight," he told her.

"Oh, your bright eyes!" she sighed.

"I can see so far," he said, "that that is a little matter. One must needs pay something for learning."

But she only looked wistfully at his eyes.

"When I have learned that mystery I can find others for myself," he said cheerfully. "You know those jars of dust on his shelf with their names in writing upon them: I shall be able to read what dust they are." And he would have told her many of the mysteries that seemed to lie open to him. But she interrupted him when he spoke of the jars, saying: "I know nothing in that room. He has put a spell against me across the lintel, so that I may not enter."

"Why?" he asked, remembering the cobwebs and the great need of tidying.

"He has my shadow," she said, "in a box in that room."

"Your shadow!" he said, perturbed by the grief in her voice.

"Aye," she said, "and he'll have yours there too!"

"Not he," said Ramon Alonzo.

"And the light of your eyes," she said sorrowfully.

But Ramon Alonzo, who already knew half the alphabet, was far more concerned with the unravelling of new wonders than he was with any price he should have to pay, and he turned from the charwoman's talk with a certain impatience to be once more engaged upon serious things. She sighed and went on with her work on the blood-stained stone.

When Ramon returned to the room that no charwoman ever entered he saw the magician awaiting him, standing beside a book that made light the secrets of reading. Once more the young man toiled at the mystery, and by evening the alphabet was clear to him. That which a day before held twenty-six secrets for him, and was as a barrier to roving thoughts, was now as an open path for them, leading he knew not whither. To him it seemed, as he finally mastered Z, that here was the very first and chiefest of mysteries, since it opened a way for the living to hear the thoughts of the dead, and enabled the living in their turn to talk to unborn generations. Yet he shrewdly foreboded that if the magicians should spread their power too widely it might not be well for the world. With evening a natural darkness blending with the gloom of the room covered up all the mysteries, and the secrets of reading hid themselves; and with those secrets the glories of former days withdrew themselves further off, and lurked in dim nooks that they had in the dark of the ages.

Then the Master of the Art bowed, and with a wide sweep of his arm, which both opened the door and indicated the way to it, he showed Ramon Alonzo out, and followed and closed the door as magically as he had opened it. They came then once more to the room where the baked meats waited, and once more Ramon Alonzo was seated alone. It seemed as though the Master of the Art would not permit himself to be seen, at least by Ramon Alonzo, engaged on any work so mundane as that of eating. The young man expressed his great satisfaction at the wonders already revealed to him.

"It is but the due," said the Master, "of any sprung from

your grandfather. Yet the whole art of reading is naught compared with the practise of boar-hunting: so I was once assured by that great philosopher."

He then withdrew, leaving the young man all alone with his plans. But the more he planned to make gold, the more another plan came jutting into his mind, perpetually pushing away his original purpose; a plan fantastic enough, a sentimental, generous, youthful plan, no less than a plan to find the magician's box, and open it and get the charwoman's shadow, and give it to her to dance once more at her heels or float away over the buttercups. Yet it was all too vague to be called a plan at all: he had not yet seen the box.

He rose then and went out to call her, but standing in the doorway remembered he knew not her name. So he went to the blood-stained stone, and she was not there, but nearby he found her pail. Awhile he wondered; then he went to the pail and kicked it noisily, knowing that folks' fears for their own property are often a potent lure, and deeming this to be wellnigh all the property the poor old woman had. Soon she came running.

"My pail!" she said, clasping her hands.

"How shall I find your shadow," he said, "to give it back to you?"

"My shadow," she wailed. "It is in a box."

And she uttered the word box as though boxes never opened, and anything put in a box must remain for ever.

"Where is the key?" he asked.

"The key?" she said, bewildered by such a question. "It opens to no key."

She said this so decisively that Ramon Alonzo felt he got no further here but must bide his time till some opportunity should come to that dark house. Meanwhile he must know her name, and asked her this.

"Dockweed," she said.

"Dockweed?" he answered. "Did your god-parents call you that? They were ill disposed towards your parents."

"My god-parents," she cried. "Poor innocent souls, they did not call me that. My god-parents, no: they called me by a young and lovely name, they gave me one of the earliest names of Spring. But that was long ago; I am Dockweed now."

"Who calls you Dockweed?" he asked.

"He does," she said.

"But it is not your name."

"He is master here."

"But what is your own name?" he asked.

"It was a young name," she said.

"I will call you by it."

"It is of no use now."

"But what name did your god-parents give you?" he asked again.

"They called me Anemone," she said.

"Anemone," he said, "I will get your shadow."

"It is deep in a box," she wailed.

Shadowless then she walked away from the lanthorn that he had brought from its hook on the wall and left on the floor near her pail; and he began to contemplate that it was easier to utter his gallant confident words than to overcome the secrets of that dark house. Then he made many plans, which one by one appeared to be unavailing, and he was driven again to await the coming of opportunity. As he made and discarded his plans he ascended the ancient stairway of stone and branches, and so came to his room.

What tidying was possible in such a room had been done. The great cobweb had been taken away from the bed, and the bedclothes had been smoothed as far as was possible when sheets and blankets had mouldered into one. But the cobwebs amongst the curtains had not been touched, for if these had been torn away the curtains would have come with them; the great rents, however, were partly filled with light flowers; more than this the remnant of fabric could not have supported.

He found a jug and basin of crockery with clear spring water in the jug, and knew that Dockweed, who had once been Anemone, had drawn it for him in the cool of the wood. He washed with such washing as was customary near the close of the Golden Age, then with loosened clothes lay down on the mouldering bed. He did not extinguish the lanthorn, because the candle in it was down to its last half-inch. Instead he watched the shadows dancing with every draught, and making huge bold leaps when the wick fell down and the flame was fluttering over a pool of grease. He watched their grace, their gaiety, and their freedom, and thought of Anemone's shadow, forlorn in the dark of the box.

Surprisingly soon the blackbirds called through the wood, and Ramon Alonzo saw that the night had passed.

That day as Ramon Alonzo sat at his work his mind was full of his plans to rescue the shadow, yet he worked hard nonetheless, for he thought to be a better match for the powers of the magician when he knew at least one of his mysteries. He felt at first a momentary compunction at thus arming himself with one of his adversary's weapons, but considered that the Master was getting his price. Indeed the gloomy room seemed unmistakably lighter than it had been the day before, and the thought came to Ramon Alonzo that this slight brightness, if brightness it were, might be some of the light that was gone from his own eyes, with which the magician might be lighting his room. Yet not for this brightness could he see among the dim shapes on the floor, under cobwebs, behind the crocodiles, any sign of such a box as seemed likely to hold a shadow. So he bided his time and learned the mystery all day, and the Master taught him well.

That day he sought out the charwoman again, who was scrubbing still at the stone.

"Anemone," he said, "how shall I know the box in which he has hidden your shadow?"

"It is long and thin," she said.

Then she shook her head and went on with the scrubbing, for she despaired of him ever finding her shadow. He would not consult her despair, but went away to build plan after plan of his own. And next day he discerned more closely; but even if the room were again a little brighter he could not distinguish such a box as she said amongst the lumber that ran all round the wainscot; the gloom on the floor was still too thick, and there were too many crocodiles.

He worked hard during those days, and soon was able to read the short words that had only one syllable; and still he worked on to unravel the whole of that mystery, and lesser wonders gradually became clear to him from things the magician said or from what he learned from Anemone: he learned how his food was baked by imps at a fire in the wood, little creatures of two feet high that could gambol and jump prodigiously; and he knew how the Hindu chants that haunted the air above the magician's house had been attracted from India, a wonder signifying little to us, who can hear those chants in Europe at the very moment men sing them upon the Ganges, but curious at that time, even though it took many years to lure them from India; so that all the songs that Ramon Alonzo heard had been sung in youth by folk now withered with age, or by men and women long gathered to Indian tombs. He learned that the Master's gratitude to his grandfather was genuine; and yet he thought he taught him the mystery of reading not so much

from gratitude as from a desire to lure him to further studies, and so to further fees, luring him on and on till he got
his shadow!

And so the days went by; and now to read the words of
only one syllable needed no more than a glance, while the
many-syllabled words gave up their mysteries after little
more than a brief examination, till it seemed to Ramon
Alonzo that the past and the dead no longer held secrets
from him. In such a mood he sought avidly for writing, beyond the big black script in the Master's book, for he
yearned to solve his own mysteries; but book there was
none in the house, outside the gloomy room that was sacred
to magic. And then one day as he worked at some great
four-syllabled word, there came a timid knock on the door
to the wood, and the Master passing out of his sacred room
like a great black shadow driven along dim walls by a
draught, came with long strides to his door. And there was
one Peter, who worked in the garden of the Tower and
Rocky Forest (sweeping the leaves in autumn and trimming
the hedge in spring), with a letter for Ramon Alonzo from
his father. And with stammered apologies, and even tears,
for thus disturbing his door, he handed the parchment at
arm's length to the magician.

CHAPTER VI

There Is Talk of Gulvarez

To the Tower beside the forest rumour came seldom, for it was the last house that stood in the open lands: on the one side the forest cut it off entirely from converse with other folk; on the other only the strongest rumours that blew over the fields of men ever came so far as the Tower. But many rumours from over the fields were reaching the Tower now, and every one of them brought the name of Gulvarez.

Gulvarez was a small squire of meagre lands, twelve miles away from the Tower, where he dwelt in a rude castle and kept two men-at-arms. They knew his name at the Tower and knew that his pigs came sometimes to market at Aragona, and that their price was good, for the pigs of Gulvarez were noted.

But now they heard that the Duke of Shadow Valley, being upon a journey, would rest a night at his castle with Gulvarez. Nor did this rumour fade, as such often did that came so far over the fields, but others came to verify it. They told how the Duke had sent messengers to Gulvarez, praying him to receive him in ten days' time, when he would pass that way on his homeward journey.

This was that very potent Magnifico, the second Duke of Shadow Valley, of whose illustrious father some tale was told in the Chronicles of Rodriguez. He ruled over all those leafy lands that of late were held by his father, and had amongst many honours the perpetual right to stop any bull-fight in Spain whilst he went to his seat, if it should be his pleasure to arrive late; and this he did by merely holding up his left hand, after one of his men-at-arms had sounded a call upon a small trumpet. So rare a privilege he exercised seldom, but it was his undoubted right and that of his heirs after him for ever. The news that so serene a prince was to visit Gulvarez spread over the countryside as fast as gossips could tell it, and came like the final ripple of a spent flood, lapping at its last field, to the walls of the Tower that stood by the Rocky Forest.

"Gonsalvo," said the Lady of the Tower, addressing her lord, "it is surely time that Señor Gulvarez married."

"Gulvarez?" he said.

"He is past thirty-five," she answered.

"But his castle is small and dark," said he, "and much of it bare rock. Who would live there with him?"

"The Duke of Shadow Valley," she said, "is to stay with him on a visit."

And so said everyone who spoke of Gulvarez, and many spoke of him now who had thought little about him hitherto.

The Lord of the Tower and Rocky Forest reflected one silent moment. "But he is a greedy man," he said, "and will demand a dowry such as a man cannot give."

"It is not for us to punish his greed," she said. "Those that cannot pay his dowry must go without him."

"But the coffer," he explained, "that I have set apart for Mirandola's dowry is empty. I saw it only lately."

"Ramon Alonzo will fill it for us," she answered with as much faith in her husband's scheme as he himself had had when it was new to him. And her hopefulness set him pondering as to whether all was wholly well with his scheme. And in the end of his pondering, although he said nothing to her, he decided that the time was come to renew his exhortations to his son.

For this purpose he sent Peter, from the garden, with a message to a certain Father Joseph, who dwelt not far away, asking him to come to the Tower. For he needed Father Joseph in order to write a letter to Ramon Alonzo, not deeming this to be a suitable occasion on which to employ his own skill with the pen, the art of which he had learned a long while ago. And before Father Joseph came he called Mirandola, and spoke with her in the same room as that in which he had had the long talk with his son, the room on the walls of which he hung his boar-spears.

"Mirandola," he said, "you must surely one day marry, and are now well past fifteen, and it not seldom happens that those that marry not when they may, come soon to a time when none will marry them, so that they are spinsters all their days. What now think you of our neighbour Gulvarez, whom some have called handsome?"

A look like one of those flashes from storms too far for thunder lit for one moment Mirandola's eyes. Then she smiled again.

"Gulvarez?" she said to her father.

"Yes," he said. "He tends a little perhaps toward avarice," for he thought he had seen the look in his daughter's eyes, "but there are many worse sins than that, many worse, if it be a sin at all, which is by no means clear; but I will ask Father Joseph about that for you, I will ask him at once. For myself I believe it to be no sin, but a fault. But we shall ask, we shall ask."

"As you will," she said.

"You like him then," said her father. "He is not ill to look on; two women not long since have called him handsome. And he is a friend of the Duke of Shadow Valley."

"I like him not yet," she said. "But haply if he come . . ."

"Yes," said he, "he shall come to visit us."

"If he come with his friend," said she.

"We cannot ask that," he said in gentle reproof. "He could not bring the duke to visit us."

"Then he is not his friend," said Mirandola.

Thus lightly was brushed away the claim of Gulvarez to the excited interest of all that neighbourhood.

The Lord of the Tower held up his hand to check her hasty utterance while he thought of appropriate words with which to reprove her error. And when he found no suitable words at all with which to show his daughter she was mistaken, and yet felt the need to speak, he said that he would consult Gulvarez on this, which he had not intended to say. And afterwards, conferring with his wife, they did not find between them a ready reason for refusing this curious whim of their dark-haired daughter; and in the end they decided to humour her, judging it best to do so at such a time, though both of them feared the arrival, if indeed he should ever come, of that dread Magnifico and illustrious prince, the serene and potent Duke of Shadow Valley.

Then Father Joseph came. He had walked scarce a mile, but he had hurried to do the Lord of the Tower's bidding, and, being now slender no longer, he panted heavily; and his tonsure shone warm and damp so that there was a light about it. He held that before all else are the things of the spirit, and in many ways he sought their triumph on earth, and for this purpose was ever swift to do the behests of the Lord of the Tower, who in that small neighbourhood at the edge of the forest had such power as is permitted on Earth, which Father Joseph hoped to turn toward heavenly uses. Therefore he came running.

"In what can I serve you?" he said.

The Lord of the Tower motioned him to a chair.

"Long ago," he said, "I learned the art of writing in case that the occasion should ever arise on which it should be needful to use the pen."

"It is indeed a noble art," said Father Joseph. "You did well to acquaint yourself with it."

"The occasion however," said the other, "did not arise. My pen hath therefore had but little practise, save for such strokes as I may have sometimes made in idleness to see the ink run. In short, for want of this practise my manner of writing is slow, while you, putting your pen daily to many sacred uses, have a speed with it that is no doubt swift as thought."

" 'Tis but a poor pen, and an aged hand," said Father Joseph, "but such as it is . . ."

"Now I have need of a letter to be written in haste," continued the Lord of the Tower, "for which I deemed your pen to be suited beyond the pens of any, and if you will write what I shall say the work will be speedily accomplished."

"Gladly will I," answered Father Joseph, his breath already beginning to come more easily from the rest he had had in the chair. "Gladly will I," and he brought forward an ink-horn that hung at his girdle, and drew from under his robe a roll of parchment that was curled round a plume, for he had all these things upon him; and as soon as the Lord of the Tower had lent him a knife he had shaped the end of the quill for a pen in a moment, and pared it and all was ready. These things he took to a table and dipped the pen, and was readier to write than Gonsalvo was to think. For there was this difficulty about the letter that he desired to send to his son: he wished to exhort him to continue his studies with a redoubled vigour, such a message as Father Joseph would smile to hear, glowing for some while after with an inner satisfaction; but then again those studies were nothing less than the Black Art, and the produce of them no ordinary lucre, but a dross that might well seem to Father Joseph to come hot from the hands of Satan. How was he to ask that some of this dross should be sent full soon for the righteous purpose of settling his daughter comfortably in the holy bonds of wedlock, without shocking the good man by too open a reference to the method of its manufacture? It cost him some moments of thought and nigh puzzled him altogether. Then he began thus, and the pen of Father Joseph scurried behind his words:

"My dear son, I trust that you apply yourself diligently to your tasks and that you are already well advanced in your studies, and, in especial, in that study which I most commended to you. That coffer which I showed you the day before you left is in no better state than it was then. We urgently require somewhat that will cover the satin lining, which is in such ill repair. Your studies will have acquainted you with what material is best suited for this purpose, and you will be able to acquire some of it more easily than we and to send us sufficient. We have a neighbour shortly coming to visit us, and he will doubtless see the coffer, and, should he see the satin lining (in its present state of ill repair), it would shame us and Mirandola. Hasten therefore to send us some of that material that will best cover it. And the covering will need to be thick, for this neighbour has shrewd eyes. Your mother sends her love, and Mirandola. Your loving father, Gonsalvo of the Tower and Rocky Forest."

"What studies does your worthy son pursue?" said Father Joseph.

"He is studying to take his proper place," said Gonsalvo; "learning to be a man. He is being taught such things as concern his sphere in life; fitting himself for such responsibilities as will fall on him; learning to take an interest in the proper things; studying to concern himself with the things that matter."

"I apprehend," said Father Joseph.

But still the Lord of the Tower felt that more phrases yet were required of him, and he poured out all those he knew which, although having no meaning, could yet be introduced into conversation. There were far fewer of them then than there are now, so that he soon came to an end of them, but then he quoted proverbs and popular sayings and such circumlocution as had come down to him after serving various needs in former ages.

"I apprehend," said Father Joseph.

Then the Lord of the Tower took the parchment and sealed it up with his seal. And Father Joseph sat there rubicund, affable, blinking, a study for anything rather than thought. Yet years of familiarity with incomplete confessions had given him a knack with the loose ends of parts of stories that enabled him to unravel them almost without thinking. This he had done already with the story now before him, but he desired to be sure, for he was a careful man.

"I have myself," he said, "some material that might line a coffer, a very antique leather, or some damask that . . ."

"No, no," said the Lord of the Tower, "I should not think of depriving you of these fair things."

And Father Joseph knew from his haste to refuse this offer, and his eagerness to send the letter quickly, that he had indeed unravelled the story of Ramon Alonzo. Behind that beneficent smile that lingered after his speaking he pondered somewhat thus, so fast as thoughts may be overtaken by words: "The Black Art! An evil matter. The earning of gold by dark means, perhaps even the making of it. Let us see to it that it be put to righteous uses, so that it be not entirely evil, both end and origin."

And he began to plan uses for some of the gold that Ramon Alonzo should so sinfully earn, blessed and holy uses, so that not all should be evil about this wicked work, but that good should manifestly arise from it, like the flower blooming in April above the dark of the thorn; and the Powers of Darkness should see and be brought to shameful confusion.

CHAPTER VII

Ramon Alonzo Follows the Art

So fast the magician came striding back to his room with the letter he had from Peter, that Ramon Alonzo's eye had scarce time to rove, and had not found the long thin box for which it began to seek. One thought alone, to rescue the charwoman's shadow, was filling his generous young mind, when the magician gave him the letter that came from his father. The letter he read alone though the magician proffered his aid, but Ramon Alonzo was eager to use his new learning; the magician therefore watched his face as he read, and learned thereby as much of the letter as Father Joseph had guessed of its purpose, for the thoughts of men were much the concern of them both.

When Ramon Alonzo had read the letter he sighed. Farewell, he thought, to his shadow. He began to think of it as he had never thought before. A mood came on him such as comes on us sometimes at sunset, when shadows are many and long; yet we never think of shadows as he then thought of his: wistful pictures of the slender intangible thing were brooding in his mind: he too was learning how one may love one's shadow. Such fancies as we may sometimes have for swallows when we see them gathering to leave us, such feelings as men may have for far-off cliffs of a native land they are losing, such longings as schoolboys have for home on the last day of holidays, all these Ramon Alonzo felt for the first time for his shadow.

And then he thought of his sword and reflected that it could not be for him as it was for that poor old woman; men had not the need, as women had, of the protection of common things that the vulgar set store by; if any would not speak with him because he had lost his shadow the matter could be argued courteously with the sword; and, as for stones, he esteemed that none would dare to throw them, nor he care if they threw. So he looked up at the magician and, with some echo of sorrow touching his tones, said: "Master, I fain would learn the making of gold."

The Master glanced at a magic book, for a moment refreshing his memory: "The fee is your shadow," he said.

And once more Ramon Alonzo thought of the grace of his shadow, and the years they had been together: he remembered its lightness, its pranks, its patient followings; he thought of long journeys together returning at close of day, he growing wearier at every step and the shadow stronger and stronger. He hesitated and the magician saw him. Then, to close his finger and thumb upon that young shadow, and add it to the band of which he was master, the Master of the Art made a sudden concession, and so closed the bargain. "Out of the gratitude I bear to your grandfather," he said, "I will give you a false one to wear at your heels in its place."

One shadow were as good as another, thought Ramon Alonzo, unless it had any evil or sinister shape.

"Will it be even as mine?" said he.

"I will shape it exactly so, as artists make their pictures."

It was enough: who would not have made such a bargain? How could he have guessed the truth of that duplicate shadow?

"Before I receive my fee," said the magician, "I will make the copy. Stand now in the light of the window that the copy may be exact."

And Ramon Alonzo stood where he was told.

Then the Master, with eyes intent on the young man's shadow, cut a copy from out of the gloom that hung in the air, using a blade that he held between finger and thumb, too tiny for earthly uses; while with his left hand, by tense signs and beckonings, he held Ramon Alonzo rigid so that his shadow might make no stir. Then he cut from the gloom a shadow so like to the human one that when he carefully laid it out on the floor side by side with the true one none could have guessed which was which, except that the new one's heels as yet were attached to nothing mortal. A space of light like the shape of Ramon Alonzo hung for a while in the dark of the air from which the shadow was cut; then the gloom fell gradually in on it.

"See," said the magician, pointing to the two shadows, and the young man turned his head: certainly no one that wished to part with his shadow could have desired a better copy.

"The likeness," said Ramon Alonzo, "is admirable."

Then the magician went to the young man's heels and severed his shadow with the same curious instrument with which he had cut the other out of the gloom; and, holding it tight in one hand, he picked up the copy in the other and placed it nearer; and as soon as the false shadow came near Ramon Alonzo's heels it ran to them.

He moved from his place and the false shadow moved

with him; there was no appreciable change; and yet he had paid his fee to the magician, and was about to receive that learning that had been the goal of so many philosophers. And now the magician, still holding the shadow tight, leaned over a crocodile, and after a moment's rummaging, picked up a long thin box from the dark of the cobwebs. By its great length and narrowness and lightness, for the magician lifted it easily with one hand, Ramon Alonzo knew it for the shadow-box. It was padlocked, but in the padlock was no keyhole. He watched the Master go to his lectern and put down the box and turn over several pages of the great Cathayan book; he saw upon which page his eye rested, a page with one spell upon it in three black Cathayan characters; then the Master closed the book and said a spell to the padlock, but in so low a voice that Ramon Alonzo heard never a word. The padlock opened, the Master raised the lid, and in went his shadow. For a moment the young man saw in the box a mass of wriggling greyness, then the lid shut down and the keyless padlock snapped.

Then the Master took down from a shelf the philosopher's stone, an object no larger than a small bird, and of texture and colour similar to what we call fire-clay, but of a slightly yellower tint; its shape resembled the shape of the lumps of pumice we use. This he took to his lectern and put down beside the book, but before lecturing upon its use he explained to Ramon Alonzo that many had sought it, as the world knew; and many had found it, as the world knew not. With this the philosophers made gold by touching certain metals, upon which he would afterwards discourse, in a certain manner, which he would later explain; and when they had done with the gold they usually buried it in the extremes of Africa, or in a continent that there was to the south, or in other places beyond the possessions of Spain, so that the object of their experiments should not corrupt men. He then discoursed on the power of gold to corrupt the unlearned; but this Ramon Alonzo had already studied in the school of the good fathers, so he let his thoughts roam far from the gloomy house, whither his body had not gone since first he had entered it so many days ago. He thought of the village of Aragona, its flowers, its merry houses, the trees with their deep-leaved branches bending over its happy lanes, and its simple mortal people following their earthly callings. So that soon he had planned to see that world again, with its sunlight, movement, and voices, of which he had only known for some days now through the black letters of books.

As the magician ended his lecture on the corrupting power of gold the young man through force of habit murmured Amen. The magician stepped sideways, and made, swift as a parry, a sign to guard himself that was not the sign of the Cross. And then Ramon Alonzo felt again that confusion that had troubled him once when he inadvertently swore, while the Bishop of Salamanca rode near on his mule. The bishop had not heard him and all had been well.

The brief silence was broken by the Master of the Art, who said: "To-morrow I will discourse on those metals, whose structure most nearly resembling the structure of gold, are therefore most adaptable to the changes of transmutation."

"Master," said Ramon Alonzo, "I pray you to give me half a holiday."

"For what purpose?" asked the magician.

"To see the world," said Ramon Alonzo, "as far as Aragona."

"There is nothing," replied the magician, "to be learned in the world that is not taught in this house. Moreover there is no error in this wood; but fare beyond it and you shall meet much error, to the confusion of true learning."

"All error that I meet beyond the wood I hope to correct by your teaching," said Ramon Alonzo.

The ancient mind of the magician, perpetually refreshed through the ages, and stored with wisdom that few have time to acquire, perceived the ring of mere flattery in this statement, and yet he was not immune from this earthly seduction. He let Ramon Alonzo go.

"Go in the morning," he said, "and be back before the sun is westering."

Ramon Alonzo rejoiced. But the magician only cared that he had got the young man's shadow. For his power was chiefly over shadowy things, and he lusted for shadows as others lust for the substance, having learned by ages of learning the utter vanity of substantial things. And he counted the secret of gold well yielded up in exchange for a shadow; for he knew how men set their hearts and hopes on gold, and how it failed them, and wot well that these hopes could not be built on a shadow.

And Ramon Alonzo went, light of heart, to find the charwoman, to let her see how little, as he supposed, he had lost by giving away his shadow. The magician returned to his box and took all his shadows out, and enjoyed amongst them awhile that absolute power that ancient monarchs had, who had no laws to control them or hostile neighbours to fear.

And while the magician was revelling in his power, in the quiet and gloom of his room, Ramon Alonzo, guided by his more human sympathies, was telling the charwoman that he had seen the shadow-box, and knew where it lay in the cobwebs behind a crocodile, and hoped somehow to coax it open and rescue her shadow. While she sighed and shook her head he walked often up and down before a window so that she saw the shadow, and could see she never suspected the price he had paid for the sight he had had of the shadow-box. And he, as he saw that perfect copy running so nimbly behind him, believed with the blindness of youth that he had paid nothing.

CHAPTER VIII

Ramon Alonzo Shares the Idleness of the Maidens of Aragona

Next morning Ramon Alonzo descended blithely the steps of timber and stone, and soon he was listening to the magician's lecture with his thoughts away in the village of Aragona. The magician explained that there was but one element, of which all material things were composed, but that the fragments of this element that made all matter were variously and diversely knit together. When these elemental fragments were closely associated he explained that their bulk was heavy and often smooth; when more loosely knit, the material they formed was lighter and of a rougher surface. To change therefore the mere arrangement of its fragments was to change one metal to another, at least in the estimation of the vulgar, who knew not that there was but one element and that no true change was possible, all matter being only the varying aspects of an element eternally unchangeable. Even water was made of it and even air.

"Hence," said the Master of the Art, "we see the superiority of spiritual things, which are of a vast multiplicity, while matter is but one. Moreover, spirits have much control over matter; while matter has neither the will nor knowledge nor power to affect one spirit, even though it may chance, upon a journey, to come close to a whole world." And the magician continued his theme, so that never was the cause of the spirit so ably pleaded, nor matter more humbled, nor all its pretensions more completely exposed. But Ramon Alonzo's day-dreams were in arbours of Aragona, and they did not return thence until the magician, looking out carefully at the height of the sun, said: "Now you may go down to the haunts of error until the sun is westering. And now this lesson concludes. Be sure that you have learned a greater wisdom in learning the oneness of matter than is to be found in the changing of its manifestation out of its leaden form to that form which is held in greater esteem by the vulgar."

Once he warned the young man against lateness, who then sped blithely away, passing out through the old green door through which he had come only once, and seeming to see in his shadow a sprightly merriness that was as eager as he to be out in the summer morning away from the gloom of the house. The young man and the still younger shadow went laughing and leaping together down the slope; and soon between trunks of the trees came glimpses of Aragona, a village sunning itself in the merry glint of the golden Spanish air. Blithe in that glittering air as they came from the wood, the shadow revelled over the flowers and grass, and felt the soft touch of small leaves that it had not known before.

It was in the afternoon that they came to Aragona, but a little before the hour at which the Master had made the shadow; it was nearly one day old. Ramon Alonzo turned then and looked at it carefully to see if it had paled in

twenty-three hours: it was as strong a grey as ever. Untroubled then by any lingering anxiety, he strode manfully into
the village and his shadow strode beside him. He glanced at
it once or twice to see that it still was there, until, finally re-
assured, he forgot it entirely.

And soon he saw a gathering of maidens who had come
out to be merry together, lest there should be a hush in the
little street while all the men were working in the fields.
They laughed when they saw him come by the way from
the wood, for so few came that way. He halted a little way
from them and doffed his hat, and the blue plume floated
from it large and long. And they all laughed again.

"Who are you?" said one, and laughed to hear herself
speak out thus to a stranger.

"Don Ramon Alonzo of the Tower and Rocky Forest,"
he answered simply.

"That's over there," said one, "but you come from the
wood."

"I am studying there with a learned man," he said.

"The Saints defend us," cried another, "there's no learned
man in the wood."

"You know the wood, señorita?" he asked.

"The Saints forbid!" she said. "None goes to the wood.
There may be aught there; but there's no learned man."

And at a look of alarm that he saw on their faces he
added: "His house is beyond the wood, upon the other
side."

And the fear went from their faces and they were merry
again.

Long after he confessed to Father Joseph that he had
made this statement that fell short of the truth or, to be exact, went over it; and Father Joseph put the matter away
with a wave of the hand and the words, "A geographical er-

ror": he had heavy work to do that day giving absolution for traffic with the Black Art.

And then one or two called out to him: "What do you study?"

"The different branches of learning," said Ramon Alonzo.

And then they all cried out such questions as "What is three times twenty-seven?" "What is nine times ninety?" "Can you divide a hundred and eighty by seven?"

"That is arithmetic," answered Ramon Alonzo. And they were a little awed by his learning, though they did not cease to laugh.

Then he sought to make some remark that would be pleasing to them, and many a happy phrase came fast to his mind; and yet he said none of them, for there were so many maidens, and if they should all laugh together he feared for his tender phrases, which were such as should have been said softly at evening when all voices are low and laughter has all been hushed by the rise of a huge moon.

Instead he asked them some question as to what they did, without even wishing an answer.

"We are watching for strangers," said the tallest.

"Why?" he asked, for she stood there waiting for him to speak.

"For our amusement," she said.

There was no evading their laughter.

But when they had laughed enough they turned again to their former occupation, which had been to watch a beetle that crawled on the road, leaving tracks on the thick white dust; and they let Ramon Alonzo watch it with them, for during the ordeal of laughter not one of those frivolous eyes but had been watching him shrewdly, and now he was judged and favourably. Had they been less frivolous, even very learned; had they worn robes and wigs; had they called evidence and employed counsel, and taken days or weeks instead of moments, that judgment would not have been wiser.

Bells were heard now and then, high over them, their echoes lingering drowsily; hawks rested on the heavy summer air; bright insects shone in it; the idleness that charmed those southern lands and blessed the Golden Age was theirs to toy with, and they let the young man share it.

When the novelty of the beetle and his tracks was lost they turned to other interests, and when they wearied of these they changed again, following novelty yet. And so the afternoon wore on, and the sun went slanting over their happy idleness, when Ramon Alonzo suddenly saw that it soon would be westering, and all at once remembered the warning of the magician. So he made swift farewells, meeting laughing words with words as light as them, and strode away towards the wood. A glance at his shadow seemed to show that it was not so late as he feared; and then he came into the shade of the trees.

To find the house in the wood was not easy even though he knew the way. The closer he got the harder it seemed to become. And when he knew that he was within a few paces of it he could see no sign of any house at all. Then he stepped round the trunk of an oak-tree, and there it was. The green door opened to him and, walking into the house, he soon saw the darker form of the magician standing amongst the dimness.

"You are late," said the Master of the Art.

Ramon Alonzo made courteous apologies.

"Did anything happen?" asked the magician.

"No," said the young man wonderingly.

"It is well," said the magician.

"To what had the Master referred?" pondered Ramon Alonzo. "What should have happened?"

Throughout his supper he wondered. Then he drank of that magical wine, which so illumined the mind in the brief while of its power; but the wine only filled him with fear of the strange new shadow.

When the fear faded, as it rapidly did, he had one more matter to ponder, for he had promised that band of maidens that he would join them again in two days' time, for some purpose that they had named, too trivial for record. He was pondering some way of asking His Mystery for leave to go once more to the frivolous fields that lay beyond that wood, and looking for reasons for his request that might not appear too flippant when exposed to the scrutiny of the magical wisdom that the Master of the Art had gleaned from the ages. And, as he pondered, night came down on the wood, and the unnatural gloom of the house grew naturally deeper.

He would have found the charwoman then to gladden her with the talk of his gay outing, and tales of the frivolous fields, and news of her Aragona; but he knew not where she was: whatever room she frequented lay beyond his explorations. Then it was bedtime for him, and soon he was asleep in his spidery room, dreaming of Aragona. And in all dreamland he saw not that band of maidens with whom he had toyed in the golden afternoon, but always only a face far fairer than theirs, which he had never seen before, and yet knew with the knowledge of dreams to be the face of the charwoman.

CHAPTER IX

The Technique of Alchemy

In the glittering morning that came even to that wood, through layers and layers of leafiness, Ramon Alonzo arose; and first he found the charwoman, at work where she mostly worked, on that deep-stained stone.

"Anemone," he said, "I have been to Aragona."

"Ah, Aragona," she answered wistfully. "Was it very fair?"

And he spoke of its beauty, resting amongst its lanes and arbours; and the wide plains dreaming around it, lit with a myriad of flowers; and its spires rising above the trees and the houses, taking the sunlight direct from the face of the sun, like planets out in ether. He spoke of the gladdening voices of its bells—like merriment amongst a band of grave old men—wandering through summer air. It was not hard to praise Aragona's beauty.

And then he told her such names as he had heard of the folk that dwelt in the village, and little tales of some of the older ones that he had got from the maidens' prattle; but to all this she shook her head mournfully and would hear more of the lanes and the arbours. So he told of these, and the pomegranate groves; but even then there often came over her that mournful look again, and she drooped her head and murmured: "Changed. All changed." Only when he spoke of the hills far off, and of the tiny valley of the stream that tinkled through Aragona, did content descend on her like an old priest's blessing given with outstretched hands on some serene evening, as she listened beside her pail, overfull of a calm joy.

And when he saw her face as she knelt by her work, sitting back on her heels, arms limp, hands lightly folded, listening with quiet rapture to every word that he told of the old Aragona that lived in her ancient memories, he determined that she should go to her village again and should take a shadow to show in the face of all men.

So he said: "I will get you a shadow. The Master shall make you a false one."

He had youth's confidence that the magician would do this for him as soon as he asked it, and if not he should do it because of his grandfather who taught him boar-hunting.

But she cried out: "A false shadow! That is of no avail. A mere piece of darkness. He has my own good shadow: of what use are his strips of gloom?"

And all the while his own shadow lay full on the floor beside her, as good a shadow as any man's. He smiled quietly and said nothing.

Then the young man hastened away to the room that was sacred to magic, for he knew the magician awaited him. And the first thing he said when he reached it, and saw the blacker mass of the magician out-darkening the gloom of the room, was, "Master, will you make me a shadow for me to give to the charwoman?"

"What should she do with a shadow?" he said.

"I know not," said Ramon Alonzo, "but I would give her one."

"Idleness comes of such gifts," the magician replied. "She will go to the villages with it and flaunt it there amongst common mundane things. It will lead her towards all that is earthly, for what is commoner or more vain than a shadow?"

The young man knew not how to answer this. "I would give her a present," he said, "of some such trifle."

"Brooches and earthly gauds are for these uses," replied the Master; "but the wisdom that I have drawn from so many ages is not for such as her."

"I pray you give it to me," said Ramon Alonzo, "for the sake of what my grandfather taught you of boar-hunting."

"The teaching that I had from that great philosopher," said the magician, "is not to be mentioned beside the vanity of a charwoman's shadow. Yet since you have invoked that potent honoured name I will make the shadow you seek. Bid her therefore come and stand before my door that I may copy her shadow even as artists do."

At once Ramon Alonzo left the room that was sacred to magic to bring the good news to the charwoman, and found her still at that stone.

"He will make you a shadow," he cried, "a fine new shadow."

But none of his eagerness found any reflection in her wan worn face, and she only repeated with sorrowful scorn: "A piece of common darkness. I know his strips of gloom."

Then said Ramon Alonzo: "Is my shadow common darkness? Is my shadow mere gloom?"

And he pointed towards it lying beside her pail.

"Yours!" she cried. "No! Yours is a proper shadow. A fine lithe shadow; beautiful, glossy, and young. A good sleek shadow. A joy to the wild grasses. Aye, that is a shadow. God bless us, there are shadows still in the world."

And he laughed to hear her.

"Then this shadow of mine," he said gaily, "is no more than what you shall have. He made it."

"He made it?" she cried out, all with a sudden gasp.

"Yes," he laughed. "He made it two days ago. And you've seen it many a time, and never knew till I told you."

"O your shadow!" she wailed. "And I warned you. Your sweet young shadow in his detestable box. O your grey slender shadow! And I warned you. I warned you. Oh, why did you do it? I warned you. So proper a shadow. And now it drifts about beyond the world or wherever he sends it when he takes it out of his box, doing his heathen errands and hobnobbing with demons."

"But this shadow," he said, pointing to the one that lay now at his heels, a little pale in that house, but grey enough, as he knew, in the sunlight and on the grasses, "is not this shadow slender and grey enough? You have just said so."

"I did not know," she wailed. "I did not know."

"Is any shadow better?" he asked.

But she was weeping, all bent up by her pail. He waited, and still she wept.

"Come," he said. "The Master will make you a shadow."

But she only shook her head, and continued weeping. And when he saw that, for whatever reason, she was weeping over his shadow, and that nothing he said could solace her, he left at last with the shadow that only made her weep. As he entered the room again that was sacred to magic he saw the magician standing all in the midst of the gloom.

"She will not come," said the young man.

And somewhat hastily the Master of the Art passed from that topic. "We will then examine," he said, "the differences and the kinship of various metals with gold, in order that we may choose those that with least disturbance can be transmuted to that arrangement of the element which forms the rarer metal. And this, as all men know, is accomplished by means of the philosopher's stone, in the proper handling of which I will instruct you to-morrow, together with all spells that pertain to it; for there is a special dictology, or study of spells, belonging only to the use of this stone."

He then lay on his lectern, in view of Ramon Alonzo, several angular pieces of metals of different kinds, of a convenient size for handling. About these he lectured with all that volume of knowledge that, in his long time on Earth, he had learned concerning the rocks that compose our planet.

"The arrangement of the element," he said, "is most near in lead to that which it takes in forming the structure of gold. And this arrangement, the fitting together of particle into particle, is easy to be expounded, were it not for one thing; and but for one thing lead were transmuted to gold with facility. This one thing is colour. For in the final arrangement of the particles, when all else is understood, there is a certain aspect of them which produceth colour, that of all mundane things is the least to be comprehended."

"Colour?" said Ramon Alonzo, his roving youthful fancy called back to that gloomy room by hearing the Master attribute a wonder to colour, with which he had been familiar through all the years of his life.

"Aye," said the Master, "the outward manifestation of all material things that come to our knowledge, and yet the nature of it has baffled, and is still baffling, the studies of the most learned amongst mankind. For this reason alone there are those that have discarded the study of matter, caring little to struggle with difficulty in so trivial a business as to seek for the meaning and use of material things. To other branches of study, whatever their difficulty, we are lured by the chance of prizes beyond estimation; these however concern you not, having chosen the humble study whose lore we now consider. Colour then depends upon the arrangement of the element in its most subtle form. Were there only one colour we should esteem that it was the natural manner in which light affected surfaces. Yet are there four, and these must therefore depend on a variation of surface profoundly intricate.

"Now it is the nature of gold that wherever and however it be cut, or powdered or melted or broken, the surface presented is yellow; and the delicate arrangement of particles that in other metals presents other colours than this needs to be overcome; for, without this, transmutation is not accomplished. And but for this colour the changing of lead into gold were amongst the easiest of all the traffickings men have with material things. And if the vulgar would accept as gold what is truly gold in its essence, although it be black, the business were easy enough; but it has been ascertained that in regard to this they are stubborn."

Then, taking up a piece of iron pyrites, he explained how by mingling various metals together the student could acquire the colour of one, the hardness or softness of another, and so blend them that the weight of the whole mass should be what was desired; and it should be in all respects most suited to undergo those changes that were to be caused by the use of the philosopher's stone.

The lecture that he delivered that day, with all the metals before him, upon the preparations for transmutation, has probably seldom been surpassed; for he had for the material of his discourse the wisdom of those ages that had preceded him, while a few centuries later the study of the philosopher's stone fell much into desuetude. Yet who shall estimate the relative excellence of lectures on transmutation, seeing that they have ever been given in gloom and secrecy to classes of ones and twos?

And Ramon Alonzo listened docilely; not, as might have been thought, because to learn transmutation was the object of his sojourn in that dim house, but because he awaited a favourable opportunity, an amiable mood in the magician, when he might ask for leave once more to return to the fields of frivolity. And not till evening came and the magician banished him from his sacred room, in order that, as Ramon Alonzo knew, he might play some secret game with his captive shadows, did the young man learn, with shrewd intuitions of youth, that he cared far more for the fee that he had in his box than for any learning he might impart as his part of the bargain.

He did not look for Anemone that evening, for he saw that the sight of his shadow troubled her, believing her overwrought by the loss of her own, and deciding to renew the magician's offer in a few days when she was calmer. That she should have a shadow again he was determined, and walk without hurt or taunt in her Aragona.

As he went to his room that night up the stairway of stone, with a candle all blobs of tallow and ragged wick spluttering within a lanthorn, he had an idea for a moment on one of the steps that there was something wrong with his shadow; but he looked again, holding the lanthorn steadier, and the idea or the fear passed.

CHAPTER X

The Exposure of the False Shadow

The work of the morning was to learn the correct application of the smooth philosopher's stone to the surfaces of metals that had been already so blended that they approached in texture and colour to the texture and colour of gold, and were thus already prepared to receive the changes to be given their element by the touch of the stone. "Without this preparation," the magician warned his pupil, "the change in the element is too violent, and has in former times not merely wrecked, but entirely transmuted, the houses of certain philosophers; whereby the world has lost such store of learning as may in no wise be estimated.

"Nor is it well to attempt the change of the element in too great a bulk at one time, as men have done when too greatly drawn by the lure of material things, seeking to change whole mountains, which, far from bringing them gold, has been the cause of volcanoes.

"Now the application of the philosopher's stone is made in this manner: having chosen suitable metals to avoid too enormous a change, in such bulk as will cause no calamity, pass this stone over the surface with the exact rhythm that there is in the spell you use. There are many spells, as there are many metals." And he brought from a box in two handfuls a bundle of small scrolls.

Ramon Alonzo, who had believed he was about to be shown the secret, saw then, as the magician slowly sorted the scrolls, that there was still much to be taught. He had been patient all the day before; but now the light that shone through the volume of leaves, coming down cliffs of greenness, called to his inner being with so imperious a call, that it almost seemed as though Spain and the musical summer, and the mighty sun himself and the blue spaces of ether, all longed for Ramon Alonzo to wander to Aragona to toy with the idle maidens through empty hours of merriment. And a bird called out of the wood, and Ramon Alonzo felt that he must go.

"Master," he said, "may I go once more to the fields of error? I have some business there not worthy for your attention; yet to myself it is pressing."

The magician made a certain show of reluctance, to conceal the truth that he cared for little but his fee of the young man's shadow, and meant soon to send him away, content with the vain acquirements of transmutation, for so it seemed to the magician. And then he gave him leave; but, with an earnestness far more real and a vehemence that seemed genuine, he warned his pupil again to be back before evening. And swift as dust on draughts that sometimes moaned in those chambers, and gay and light as the leaves, away went Ramon Alonzo. And once more the golden morning was before him as he came down from the wood, and Aragona twinkled in the distance. And partly his heart was full of a frivolous laughter and partly a wistful feeling all grave and strange, for the spires of Aragona moved even youth to solemnity; and none knew how this was, for the spires were bright and glad.

He gave one glance at his shadow to see that all was well with it, then strode over glittering grass with the shadow striding beside him: and so he came untired to the edge of the village, and saw there the band of maidens where they had promised to be. Blithe on the idle air came the merriment of their welcome.

And not a levity that blew their way all in the azure morning, and not a vanity that reached their thoughts, going from mind to mind, but they welcomed and toyed with and acclaimed as new. So they passed the morning, and when the heat of the day began to increase they loitered to a lane that had one long leafy roof, and there they sat in the shade and ate fruit that they had in baskets and listened while each in turn recounted the idlest tales. And the meed of every tale that pleased was laughter, and not a learned conceit nor studious fancy was allowed to intrude in any tale they told. After the wisdom that burdened the house in the wood, and the learning with which its very gloom was laden, its ancient store of saws and sayings and formulae, Ramon Alonzo rejoiced at every quip that they uttered and every peal of laughter that followed each quip, as the traveller over Sahara welcomes the pools in the mountains and the bands of butterflies that gather about them.

In the heavy leafy shade they laughed or talked continually, while all round them Spain slept through the middle hours of the day. And many a tale they told of surpassing lightness, too light to cross the ages and reach this day, even if they were worthy, but lost with all the little things that founder in the long reaches of Time, to be cast on the coasts of Oblivion, amongst unrecorded tunes and children's dreams and sceptres of unsuccessful emperors.

But when shafts of sunlight slanted, and voices from

beyond their lane showed that Spain was awaking, and the grandeur of the sun was past and he grew genial again, then they loitered out into the light, straying towards the hills. And, as they wandered there, other young men joined them, leaving their work till the morrow, for morrows they said would be many—young dark-skinned men with scarlet sashes flashing around their waists. Then the party drifted asunder as shallow streams in sunny sandy spaces when the water takes many ways, all of them gold and light-laden. And a tall dark maiden drifted with Ramon Alonzo, and one more slender than she; and the first was named Ariona and the second Lolun. And sometimes fair fancies came to Ariona, by which that band of maidens was often guided because they were strange and new. But the slender form of Lolun was driven by any fancy, in whatever mind it arose: a song would guide her, or any merriment lead her, as though she had less weight than these invisible things, as the thistledown has less weight than the south wind.

And as they drifted slowly towards the low western hills Ramon Alonzo saw that the sun was westering, and remembered the warning of the magician.

"I must go," he said.

"Go?" said the two maidens, as though to leave that low sunlight to go alone through the wood were some monstrous imagination.

"I must return to the learned man with whom I study beyond the wood," he said. "He desires me to be back with him this evening."

"Oh!" said Lolun. She was shocked to hear of such a demand.

"He wishes to investigate with me one of the branches of learning."

Then the two girls' laughter on the mellow air rang out against learning, and trills of it floated as far as the hills, and echoes came back to the fields, and went wandering fainter and further; and in all the ways that heard them there was no thought of learning. And Ramon Alonzo's plans were laughed away, as in later days the Armada was broken by storm, and so he forsook his intention to return to the house in the wood. He long remembered those trills of merry laughter, for not for long was he free of care again.

Driven then by those gusts of laughter as small ships are by light breezes, he came with the girls to the hills when the sun was low. And drifting all aimless on, they went up the slope, prattling and laughing and straying, led by whatever fancy led Ariona. And her fancy was to see the willowy lands that lay beyond the hill, with their trees and the shadowed grass looking strange in the evening. At such a place and at such a time, she felt, whatever there was of faery in our world would show clear hints for any girl to guess. And the further they got the eagerer grew Lolun to find whatever it was for which Ariona was searching. And, these impulses holding fair, Ramon Alonzo still went on before them.

And so they came to the ridge of the hill and saw the willowy lands. The low sun glittered in their faces, no longer a flashing centre of power avoided by human eyes, but a mystery, an enchantment, almost to be shared by man; and wholly shared by solitary trees, and bands of shrubs, far off on the wild plain, which now drew a mystery about them, as men in the tended fields began to draw their cloaks. They gazed some while in silence at those strange lands, which none saw from any window in Aragona, seeking their mystery, which was almost clear and was coming nearer and nearer, and finding it, but for the tiniest shrubs and shadows amongst which it hid, though barely, its secret enchantment. And as they looked at that strangeness, part spell and part blessing, descending on all those acres out of the evening, not a ripple of laughter shook the calm of their wonder. And then a cold wind blew for only a moment, rising up from its sleep in nowhere and moving to distant sails; and they stirred as the wind went by, and their search was ended.

They turned round then to look back at Aragona, with the late light on its spires, and its windows flashing, and saw men drawing toward it home from the fields. They stood there wondering to see how far they had come; waiting in idleness for the next whim to guide them, a little band of three with the young man in the middle. The slope they had just climbed lay golden below them.

Then Ariona screamed. Again she screamed before Lolun had followed the gaze of her terrified eyes. Then scream after scream went up from Lolun also.

Ramon Alonzo stood silent in sheer amazement between them. Then they sprang away from him making the sign of the Cross. But just as they sprang away Ramon Alonzo saw for a moment, amidst the shining grass, his shadow between their shadows; theirs lying so far along the golden slope that they ran a little way out to the level fields, his only five feet long.

CHAPTER XI

The Chill of Space

"So it does not grow," said Ramon Alonzo bitterly.

He was all alone on the hill and the girls had fled. Alone with a mere strip of gloom; a thing refused by the charwoman. So this was the shadow he had received so confidently, believing he had obtained from magic something without payment. A mere patch of darkness that neither dwindled nor grew. In a flash his memory went back to the suspicion he had suddenly had on the stair, and recalled how the shade of the trees in the heat of the day had hidden the evil secret a little longer. He remembered how two evenings ago it had seemed not so late as it was; that was his lying shadow. But he no longer thought of it as a shadow at all; it was mere art, and the Black Art at that. It counterfeited what his own shadow had been in the middle of that fatal afternoon, and could no more grow than shadows in pictures grow.

What should he do? A chill came into the evening, depressing all his thoughts, and his fancy roamed to the long thin magical box, in which his young shadow lay. He pictured it locked in the gloom with other lost shadows, fallen a slave to magic. He thought of its blitheness at dawn, on dewy hills in Spring; and then he looked at the sinister thing beside him, an outcast amongst the lengthening shadows as he was now an outcast amongst men. At that moment he would sooner have been shadowless like the charwoman than to have that mockery there looking ludicrous in the landscape, and seeming to taunt him with the folly he had committed after warning enough. He turned his back on it and his eye fell then on the willowy lands a little to the left of the sun, and he saw the great trees far off with a new jealousy. Almost silvery their great shadows looked, slipping over the grass in the evening; and he saw the beauty of shadows as he had not seen before, and saw with envy. It had come to this already, that the man was jealous of trees.

From the grand substantial forms of the distant trees, and those dark comrades that vouched for them as being material things, he bitterly turned away, and looked once more to the spires of Aragona, with his gaze held high to avoid the mockery at his feet. But not by lifting his gaze could he escape the thought of his folly, for now he saw Lolun and Ariona hastening home over the fields, and knew he had lost his part in material things.

Some slight regret, some reluctance, Lolun showed as she went, which Ramon Alonzo was not able to see. He only felt all tangible things were against him.

"Must we leave him?" said Lolun after they had run for a while.

"He is not earthly," cried Ariona.

"We might stay for only a little," said Lolun.

"It were sin," said the other, "though for only a moment."

"Must we never sin?" sighed Lolun.

"Sin? Yes," said Ariona, "where there is absolution. But this . . ." and she shuddered.

"This?" whispered Lolun, half terror, half curiosity.

"He has had traffic with what we may not name."

And, as Ariona said this, the last of the sun's huge rim disappeared from the hill, and a chill came into the air; and their doubts all turned to fears in the hour of bats. So they hurried on and did not stop to rest, and came all weary into Aragona; and there the news spread quicker than their tired feet could carry it that Ramon Alonzo had trafficked in the gaudy wares of damnation.

And he, with that pitiable ware he had got, that tawdry piece of gloom, stood all alone on the hill in the deepening gloaming, making helpless human plans that he hoped to set against magic. There was his sword, that he had never used yet on any serious business; he would confront the magician with its slender point and make him open the shadow-box; its purpose was to rescue the oppressed, then why not those hapless shadows that lay with his own in the box? And then there was the spell he had seen in the book, with which the Master opened the lock of his shadow-box. But he could not read the spell, which was in Chinese, and did not know with what art from his stores of magic the Master would meet the passes of his merely terrestrial sword. Vain plans that melted away as fast as he formed them.

Then the sun set; and in the sudden loss of gladness that all things felt, the faint melancholy that tinged wild grasses and tended gardens, Ramon Alonzo had comfort. For a little while he seemed to have lost nothing that all nature had not lost: he did not know that the word had gone out "The man is shadowless," and that he would have to travel far, and faster than that rumour, to find any kindly human welcome again. And now it was the hour when all things sought their homes, and Ramon Alonzo turned towards the wood.

He came to the wood before the gloaming faded, but amongst those oaks it was as dark as night. Once more he pried for the house; once more its dark door was before him all of a sudden as he picked his way round a tree. It stood ajar as though tempting whatever was lost in the wood to enter that sombre house and be robbed at least of its shadow.

Again as Ramon Alonzo went in through that door he saw the magician's presence increasing the gloom of the hall.

"You are late," said the magician.

"I am late," said Ramon Alonzo, and strode on to pass the magician, his left hand resting lightly on his sword-hilt. When the Master of the Art saw Ramon Alonzo's humour he lost some of his ease, and stood there pondering answers to what his guest should say; for he saw that the great defect in his artificial shadow had by now been detected, and was ever anxious that nothing mortal should guess aught of his dealings with shadows. But Ramon Alonzo said nothing. He walked on silently into the deeps of the house, and presently the magician turned away and went somberly back to the room that was sacred to magic, and unpadlocked his shadow-box; and soon in a riot of power exerted on helpless shades, he forgot all the irk he had felt at having one of his crooked dealings discovered.

But the young man called Anemone through the house; and she heard him and came from the nook in which she was resting, and met him in one of those dark passages, and led him back to the nook. It was a space beneath a wooden stair that ran whither she knew not; once in every generation she would hear the steps of the magician resounding above her head, going gravely up the stair upon which she was not permitted, and coming blithely down. One side of the space was open to the passage, but in the part that was sheltered by the stair she had a heap of straw to lie on, and all her pans and pails. Old brooms against the wall seemed to add to the darkness. She led him silently there before they spoke, seeing his attitude full of trouble if it was too dark for her to see his face; and there they sat on the floor on patches of straw, and she began to light a candle, a thing she had saved up out of old pieces of tallow.

"I have found out about his shadow," he said.

"Ah yes," she said, "a mere piece of gloom." She knew he must have discovered it when she saw how late he was out.

"It will not grow," he said.

"Never an inch," she answered.

"You warned me," said Ramon Alonzo.

She only sighed. She had known that the magician was after his shadow, but knew not all his tricks. Had she dreamed that he would have dared to offer one of his wretched pieces of darkness even in part exchange for a good human shadow she would have warned Ramon Alonzo of the specious imitation. And now she regretted she had not. And as she sighed a sudden tremor shook her. And shook the wretched candle she had just lighted, and convulsed her again and again, till the straw upon which she sat rustled audibly with her tremblings. And Ramon Alonzo suddenly trembled too, as he had trembled once before in that strange house, and previously he had put his tremors down to the draughts and the damp, but now they were more violent.

"It is our shadows," said the charwoman, leaning towards Ramon Alonzo and speaking with chattering teeth.

"Our shadows?" said he.

"They are out on dreadful journeys," she replied.

"Whither?" said he.

"Who knows?" she said. "And we are feeling their terror."

"Has he that power?" he gasped.

"Aye," she said. "He is sitting there now over his shadow-box, taking them out and driving them off by the dreadful spells he uses, to carry messages for him to spirits far from here. And their misery and terror touches us, for so it is with shadows."

Ramon Alonzo was shivering now with a fear that was strange to him. The charwoman watched him a moment.

"Yes, yes," she said, "he has our shadows out."

"Are they far from the house?" he asked between chattering teeth.

"Beyond Earth," she answered.

This he could scarcely believe. But now a gust of more dreadful shivering shook her, and he too felt the touch of a sudden chill.

"They are beyond the paths of the planets now," she said. "I know that cold. It is the chill of Space. Yes, that's Space sure enough. It's little warmth enough that they get from the planets; just a little from some of the larger ones, and that's something. But this is Space: I know it. They're right out there now."

She huddled her hands almost into the flame of the candle, but that did no good, for the shudders that come from lost shadows go deeper than skin or bones. They chill not merely the blood but the very spirit.

And the chill and the awe of Space gripped also Ramon Alonzo.

"Why does he send them there?" he whispered to her, for his voice had sunk to this.

"Ah, we don't know that," she said. "He's too deep and sly. But he has friends out there, and he's likely sending them, poor shadows, to one of them, to bow before one of them and give it a message, and dance to it and then come back to the shadow-box."

"He'll bring it back?" asked Ramon Alonzo quickly.

"Oh yes," she said, "he always brings them back. He won't part with his shadows."

"What spirits are they?" he asked.

"Evil spirits," she answered.

And then they sat silent awhile, trembling and wan, while their nerves were numbed by an unearthly cold. And if the charwoman's aged frame was more easily shaken by tremblings, yet the young heart of Ramon Alonzo seemed to feel more vividly his shadow's distress.

"Often the spirits pass close to Earth on a journey, and he sends his shadows a little way out to greet them. But they are right beyond that now, poor shadows," she said.

"Why does he send them so far?" he asked.

"Lust of power," she said. "Cruel savagery. I know his piques and his ways. He doesn't like your finding out the trick that he played you. I've known him make the shadows dance for hours because I haven't worked hard enough for him. And I've been all tired after that, worn out and years older."

Somehow her courage in speaking at all when racked by those terrible tremors, and in speaking against the grim man to whose tyranny they were subject, brought a warmth to Ramon Alonzo.

And soon she said: "They are turning homeward now."

Then they sat silent, both waiting. And now the terror had gone, and gradually some slight thawing, too faint to be called a glow, touched the unearthly cold that had gripped them so sorely. Whether it was some warmth that the shadows got from Jupiter, or from the sun itself, neither Ramon Alonzo nor the wise old charwoman knew; and at last the charwoman leaned back against the wall with a certain content again on her worn old face: "They are back in the box," she said.

And suddenly he stood up, his left hand dropping upon his sword-hilt, a fine figure there in his cloak, even in that dim light.

"I will take your shadow," he said, "and he shall torment it no more. My own must stay in the box because of the bargain I made with him and the need that I have for gold, but I will bring back yours to you and he shall torment it no more."

He had said the same before, and she had smiled it away; but he was so vehement now that, if resolution could have accomplished it, she saw the thing had been done. And yet she shook her head.

"I have my sword," he said.

But she looked at it pityingly.

"He has more terrible things," she answered sadly.

And at that he realized that in that dark house more store must be set by immaterial things than by those that men can handle. And he thought of the spell.

"Then I will open the box while he is away," he said. "And you shall have back your shadow and mine will stay in the box."

And again she warned him that the shadow-box opened to no key.

"I have seen the spell in his book," he said, "unto which the padlock opens!"

"Can you utter it?" said she.

"No, it is in Chinese."

Now there was at that time no Chinaman in all the lands of Spain. And the ships of Spain had no traffic with Chinese lands. Yet Ramon Alonzo pondered this most faint hope, and leaving the pails and brooms went thoughtfully thence.

CHAPTER XII

Mirandola Demands a Love-Potion

When Ramon Alonzo appeared next day in the room that was sacred to magic the magician was there before him.

"You have a fine strong shadow," said the magician.

Certainly it lay black and bold on the floor; and, since it was then as many hours before noon as the making of the shadow had been after it, it was just as long as the shadows of other men. But not a word did Ramon Alonzo answer. He went instead to his seat, and there sat waiting to receive more of the learning for which he had paid so much. The gold must needs be got for his sister's dowry, even at the cost of those tremors and terrors, against which fortitude that endured the ills of the body seemed of so little avail; and after that, if other plans failed, he might become so wealthy with the gold he should make that he would buy back his shadow, or if the magician paid no heed to gold he might find those who did, and arm them and go against the house in the wood and capture the spells and the shadow-box. But his head was too full of plans for any one to ripen; and then the voice of the magician came breaking across them suddenly. "When by blending the metals," he said, "till their texture is nearest to the texture of gold, we have made the preparation that is meet, the philosophers choose from amongst such scrolls as these a spell that is best suited to the material to be dealt with. And having read it aloud in its own language, whatever language it be; for these spells are ever written in the tongue of whatever sage has been first to compose them; and the Persians have for long been adept at this, as well as some few of those that adore Vishnu," at which name he paused and bowed; and, as he bowed, one knocked on the door to the forest, and the echoes went roaming uncertainly, as though lost, through the house.

At the sound of the knock the magician swept out of the room, once more reminding the young man of a spider when some lost thing touches his web. And, left alone in the room that was sacred to magic, Ramon Alonzo again considered his dark master, whom he regarded henceforth as his opponent, from whom the charwoman's shadow must yet be won. The Master was keeping to his bargain, thought Ramon Alonzo, and it was a hard bargain, and in the matter of the false shadow a sly one, and the Master knew that he had found this out.

Suddenly his eye fell on the great book, and he left his speculations, which, considering the depths to which the magician's character ran, had gone but a little way; and he rose up, led by a more practical thought, and turned the Cathayan pages, and came again to the three great syllables of the spell that opened the box. Alas that they were in Chinese.

A swift idea came to him. The padlock knew Chinese, for he had seen it open. He seized the book and carried it to the shadow-box and, leaning over a crocodile, showed the open page to the padlock, holding it still before it; and the padlock never stirred. He rose up then from the dust and gloom and replaced the book on the lectern, and only just in time, for the steps of the magician came resounding back to the door and he came again to his room that was sacred to magic. He gave one scornful glance at the book on the lectern, knowing it had been moved; and in the scorn of that look Ramon Alonzo's disappointment grew, for he saw not only that he had failed but that the attempt had been hopeless.

"A yokel is at the door of the forest," he said. "He has a message to you that the oaf will give only to you."

Ramon Alonzo went in silence, still heavy with failure, and came to the door to the wood. And there outside was Peter, who had knocked on the old green door and had then run back a little way into the wood. Thence he had spoken with the magician. And now to the door that he dreaded, while his fears expected anything that they were able to guess, there came his young master.

"Young master," cried Peter, "young master. I have brought you a letter from Donna Mirandola. And does he treat you well? Does he feed you well? You'll be very learned now, master. The big boar-hound is eating well."

"Is he strong?" asked Ramon Alonzo.

"As strong as ever," said Peter.

"Now the Saints be praised," said Ramon Alonzo, reverting to an old way of speech that he did not use in that house.

"Here is the letter, master," said Peter, drawing it out from his cloak. "But, master, there is a word with blots upon it; that word should be 'love-potion,' and not the word that is writ under the blots."

"Love-potion," repeated Ramon Alonzo.

"Aye, master; and not the word under the blots. Donna Mirandola bid me to say it."

"That is well," said Ramon Alonzo.

The letter was written in the same clear hand as the one that had come from his father, and was short, as the young man saw with joy, for he wished to read not too slowly before Peter, and fast he could not go.

It said: "To Don Ramon Alonzo. Do not send gold, but send me a prayer-book. Your loving sister, Mirandola."

Over the word "prayer-book" were the marks of small fingers that had been dipped in ink.

"Say I will send that prayer-book," said Ramon Alonzo.

"Aye master," said Peter, "and is there any more?"

"Feed the big boar-hound well," said Ramon Alonzo.

"Aye, indeed, master," said Peter.

"Farewell."

"Farewell, young master, farewell. Please God we'll hunt boars in the winter."

And Peter turned slowly away and walked a few paces slowly, then faster and faster till he got away from the wood.

Ramon Alonzo pondered bitterly: he had sold his shadow for gold, and now gold was not needed.

He had not yet learned the whole art of transmutation. Would the magician give back his shadow?

And Mirandola must have her love-potion, and the charwoman have her shadow out of the box. He had much to do if his plans were to come to fruition.

Back he went to the gloomy room that was sacred to magic. "I have no need of gold," he said.

"It is a worthless metal," replied the magician. "The philosophers sought it for the interest they took in rearranging the element. But the stuff itself was nought to them. They buried it where I have said, and have often warned man of its worthlessness; in testimony whereof their writings remain to this day."

"I would learn no more of it," said Ramon Alonzo.

"No?" said the magician.

"I pray you therefore give back my shadow," he said.

"But it is my fee," said the magician.

"I would learn other things," said the young man, "for other fees. But this fee I pray you return."

"Alas," said the magician, "you have learned much already."

"Of this matter nothing," said Ramon Alonzo.

"Alas, yes," replied the magician. "For you have learned the oneness of matter, and that there is but one element. And this is a great secret to the vulgar, who believe there are four. And doubtless they will, in their error, discover even more than these four before ever they come to learn that there is but one, which you have learnt already, and this is my fee for it." And he stooped and rapped the shadow-box somewhat sharply.

"You gave me a shadow to wear in its place," said the young man.

"I will make you a longer one," replied the magician.

Ramon Alonzo saw that words would not do it, and that whatever he said would be verbally parried with skill.

"Then give me a love-potion," he said.

"I do not dispense these things," said the magician haughtily.

"Then teach me how they are made, and not the making of gold."

The magician pondered a moment. It was all one to him. He had his fee safe in the shadow-box. He despised equally gold and love, and cared not which he taught. Some etiquette he had learned from some older magician seemed to prompt him to give something for his fee.

"Gladly," he answered briefly.

Then Ramon Alonzo sat down without a word, thinking of Mirandola.

He had never enquired the reason of anything that she

asked for. It was Mirandola, with eyes like a stormy evening. Thoughts passed behind those eyes such as never visited him. Mirandola knew. It is hard to say how the flash of those eyes swayed him. He never sought to know, and never questioned Mirandola's demands.

"By the admixture of crocodile's tears with the slime of snails," came the voice of the Master, "the basis of all love-potions is constructed. Unto this is to be added a powder, obtained by pounding the burned plumage of nightingales. Flavor with attar of roses. Add a pinch of the dust of a man that has been a king, and of a woman that has been fair two pinches, and mix with common dew. Do this by light only of glow-worms and saying suitable spells."

Ramon Alonzo, following the gestures that the Master made as he spoke, saw on the shelves the ingredients that he mentioned. He saw a jar holding attar of roses beside one named "Dust of Helen." He saw two jars side by side called "Dust of Pharoah" and "Dust of Ozymandias," one of them probably Rameses. He saw a vial labelled "Crocodile's Tears." All that he needed seemed there; outside in the wood the glow-worms burned, and there were plenty of snails.

The lesson went on drearily, the magician intoning various spells that the young man learned by heart or believed he learned, and naming alternative ingredients that had of old been used in more torrid lands. Of the ingredients Ramon Alonzo was so sure that no mistake was possible; if ever he erred at all it was with the spells.

CHAPTER XIII

Ramon Alonzo
Compounds the Potion

Next morning Ramon Alonzo rose full early, all impatience to do Mirandola's errand, all eagerness to exercise his new skill. That day the magician was to teach him more spells and alternative ingredients; doubtless with quips at the expense of Matter, scoffs at the vanity of the ambitions of Man, quotations from ancient philosophers, and lore of his own seeking. An opportunity not given to every young man; for this master had gathered and stored with his own hands the fruits of many ages, besides the lore he was heir to from former philosophers.

When Ramon Alonzo entered the room that was sacred to magic he saw with a sudden joy that this opportunity was not yet to be his. For he had come down the spiral stair of timber and stone by the palest earliest light, and the magician was not yet about. But with his new learning glowing bright and fresh in his mind he ran a sure eye over the Master's shelves and saw the ingredients he needed. Then he took from a jar some dust of Ozymandias and mixed it in right proportions with some of the dust of Helen. His shrewd young mind guessed well the aphorisms that the Master would have uttered over these pinches of dust; for, secure with his doses of elixir vitæ, he neglected few chances to mock the illusions of Man. Attar of roses and crocodile's tears were close by in their vials, and the dried skin of a nightingale hung on a nail near. He procured a flame and burned some of the feathers and pounded them into a powder, and mixed it up with the rest. Then he hastened towards the wood, anxious to gain the door before the magician came, and to do the work unaided; for he knew that the aged had often ideas of their own, setting undue store by ritual and unprofitable quotations, and hindering eager work that the young would do in a hurry. He came to the door to the wood and listened a moment acutely. Not a sound came from the corridors; the magician was not yet afoot. The dew was yet in the wood, and of this he got a small cupful, gathering it drop by drop from the bent blades of grass; and here he found large snails and, after a while, a glow-worm. And these he carried into a hollow oak where the darkness was deep enough to be lit by the glow-worm; and in the light of that he put all his mixture together, saying the while a spell that had great repute in Persia. The viscid substance he poured into a vial, out of the common mortar in which he compounded it, and carefully corked the vial and turned back towards the house in the wood. And, attracted by the croon of the curious Persian spell, or else by the scent of the love-potion, small things of the wood were lured to follow him. He heard the pattering of their feet behind him; but if he turned they were away on the other side of the oak-boles, and if he went back to a tree behind which one hid and walked round to the other side, he heard small finger-nails scratching, always on the far side from him, and knew the small creature had gone up the tree and slipped round it whenever he moved, so as to keep the trunk between it and anything human. They were only imps, light creatures composed of the idleness and mystery of the wood, and led now by curiosity, which was their principal motive. Soon the pattering of footsteps ceased, for they dared come no nearer to the magician's house, but sat down behind their trees uttering little cries of wonder.

When Ramon Alonzo returned to the house in the wood he sought at once for the charwoman, and found her in her nook amongst all her pails.

"Anemone," he said, "I am going back to my home, for my sister has need of a love-potion."

"For what purpose needs she that?" said the charwoman.

"I know not," said Ramon Alonzo, "but she desired one."

"Is she not young?" said the charwoman.

"Aye," said Ramon Alonzo, "but perhaps she wished to make sure."

"Aye, they are sure, those potions," said the charwoman, for she knew much of magic, having minded that house for so long. "Only let him see her first after he hath drunk of the potion, or even be nearest to her at that time, and he hath no escape after that from magical love. You have the potion there?" For Ramon Alonzo had the vial in his hand.

"Aye," said he, "I made it myself in the wood."

"He taught you how?"

"Yes," said Ramon Alonzo.

"And for that you gave your shadow," she said sorrowfully.

And he would have explained to her that he had learned more than this, but she would not heed him, only sitting on the straw with dejected head, and mourning to herself over his shadow.

Then seeing her sorrowful face, and the gloom of that

dark nook, and the sombre melancholy of all things round her, he sought to persuade her to flee from the house in the wood, and he would escort her into Aragona. But she only said: "The world is harder than his house."

He reasoned with her, saying suave things of the world; but she only answered: "There is no place for me there."

And then he said: "I will come back for you, and when I come I will get back your shadow."

And she shook her head sorrowfully as she always shook it whenever he spoke of that.

"But I have a plan," he said.

And when she only shook her head again he told her what his plan was.

"I saw the spell," he said, "when he opened the shadow-box, and have seen it again since. It is in Chinese and I cannot speak it, but now I remember it well, each syllable; and I will learn the art of the pen and then I will make the likeness of one of those syllables upon parchment. There are three syllables, but I will make the likeness of only one at first, and with it I shall write words of my own imagining, making them square and outlandish. And I shall say to him: 'Master, I was given this writing by a heathen man that I met. I pray you read it for me.' "

She listened at first, but when he spoke of writing words of his own imagining she turned again to her melancholy.

"But hearken," he said, and his eagerness gained her attention. "Oft as he reads he mutters, and if the room be dark and the script small then he will mutter surely, and I hear the words he mutters. Now when all the script is strange to him but one word, he will surely mutter that one and then stop and ponder; and I shall hear that word and remember. And then some days must go by, and many days; and then one day I will bring him another script, with the second syllable, and long afterwards the third, and then I shall have the spell."

She was listening now with a look on her face that seemed to be like hope; but hope had been absent from her face so long that if it now shone in her eyes its image there was too faint for Ramon Alonzo to be quite sure what it was. And after a while she said: "Learn not the art of the pen from him. There are good men that can teach that art, and not only he."

"Why?" said Ramon Alonzo.

"Because," she said, "if he deems that you have not the art he will not suspect you wrote it."

And then Ramon Alonzo knew that she hoped, for she had taken a part in his plan. And for a long while they talked of it. And all the while the faint hope of the charwoman grew, and her eyes shone now with a bright unwonted light in the haggard withered face.

One thing she warned him which Ramon Alonzo remembered, and that was to give up his false shadow to the magician before he opened the shadow-box, if ever he should be able to open it. For the magician could cut off the false shadow, having the necessary tools; but if this were not done he would never be able to rid himself of it and would always have two shadows, a true and a false. Thus they plotted together; but Ramon Alonzo thought nothing of his own shadow, planning only to rescue hers, with his thoughts as they roved to the future fixed on nothing but the picture of her old face lit up by some feeble smile from a wan happiness when she should have her old shadow again.

And now the morning was wearing on to the hour when the magician would be astir, and Ramon Alonzo desired to be gone before he appeared. For he had acquired a lore in his youth which taught him ever to avoid the aged when merry plans were afoot; for the aged would come with their wisdom and slowness of thought, and other plans would be made, and there would be, at least, delay. So he was impatient to go, and yet he dallied, reluctant that any word should be the last, reluctant to leave the new plan that they had made between them, and reluctant to leave the old woman, who somehow held his sympathy in such a way as he had not been taught that it could be held by the aged.

Then they spoke of trifles as folk often do that are at the moment of parting. He told of the imps in the wood, that he had never seen, but whose feet he had heard following. And she told him how to see an imp, which was easy. For a man can see three sides of a tree, and whatever comes the imp will go to the fourth side; and there he will wait till he is sure of being able to peep round without being seen. "But throw your hat past the right side of the tree," she said, "and he will clamber round at once on to the left side, and you will see the imp."

Of such trifles they spoke. But fearing now to see at any moment the dark form of the Master, or to hear his stride along the booming corridors, Ramon Alonzo made his farewells; and one last message of good cheer he gave her before striding away with his cloak and his sword to the wood.

"When I have rescued your shadow," he said, "I will take you away from this house, and you shall be charwoman at my father's tower, and the work will be light there and you may do it slowly, and none shall molest you and you may rest when you will and you shall have long to sleep."

Some glance of gratitude he looked for; but a smile so strange lit her face and haunted her eyes, that he went from the sombre house and into the wood, and all the way to the open lands, still wondering.

CHAPTER XIV

The Folk of Aragona Strike for the Faith

When Ramon Alonzo came out of the wood he saw that the shadows were already shortening. He saw then that he had delayed too long with the charwoman, and should have started while shadows were long, and so gone through the dark of the wood while his own was unnatural, and come to frequented ways while it was as other men's. And he felt ashamed of his dalliance. For had he been delayed by some radiant girl her beauty would have so dazzled him that he could not have seen his folly; but to come under the fascination of a most aged charwoman seemed a thing so unworthy of his knightly ambitions that he hung his head as he thought of it, and yet all the while remained true to his chivalrous plan to rescue her poor old shadow.

A little way he went; but soon seeing men in the distance in the fields, he thought it better not to go beyond the last of the oaks that stood outside the wood until other men's shadows should be a little longer, and so avoid the ill-informed foolish pother that folk seemed to make when all shadows were not exactly evenly matched. Already he had come to feel a vigorous scorn for the absurd importance that others attached to shadows. For youth argues rapidly, and—in a way—clearly, from whatever premises it has, not often tarrying to enquire if more premises be needed. These were some of the premises from which Ramon Alonzo argued: a shadow is of no possible value to anyone, nor does anyone ever suppose that it is; and, if it were, the poor old woman that lost hers should have been pitied; and he himself actually possessed a shadow, and, if it were too short, their own shadows had all been just as short an hour or two ago; and the same folk that called it too short in the evening would doubtless call it too long at noon. There is indeed a great deal of futility amongst the human race which we do not commonly see, for it all forms part of our illusion; but let a man be much annoyed by something that others do, so that he is separated from them and has to leave them, and looks back at what they are doing, and he will see at once all manner of whimsical absurdities that he had not noticed before; and Ramon Alonzo in the shade of his oak, waiting for the noon to go by, grew very contemptuous of the attitude that the world took up towards shadows.

Nobody passed him and, if any saw him far off, they only saw him keeping a most honoured observance of Spain, which is the siesta, or pause for the heat of the day to go by.

And, when shadows had grown again, he left the shade that had sheltered him against the heat of the sun and the persecution of men and walked boldly down the road, protected by as good a shadow as was to be found in attendance on any man. He had little thought to set such store by so light a protection, or to consider at all the attendance of a thing so slight and vain; but he was learning now the value that the world attached to trifles, and that there were some the neglect of which had no more toleration than sacrilege.

And then, before he had come to Aragona, a glance at the landscape showed that the hour had come when shadows were longer than material things. It was not by any measurement that he saw this, but by a certain eerie look that there is over all things when shadows have become greater than their masters, so that shadowy things seem to influence earthly affairs instead of good solid matter. This eerie hour he had known of old, and often felt the influence of it, yet never before had his conscious thoughts noted it, or told him as they did now that this was the turn of shadow-tide, when each shadow surpassed the stature of its master; so much do our own affairs sharpen our observation. Had he gone on perhaps none would have noticed; but there was growing fast in him the outcast's feeling, and, however much he scorned the importance folk attached so vainly to shadows, he not only felt his defect but intensely exaggerated it, until impulses came to him to slink and to hide, and he began to know the natural avoidances that are part of the habits of the forsaken and hunted. Therefore he went no nearer to Aragona than where he saw a small azalea growing a little way ahead; and there he sat down, protected by its shadow, which was only just enough to conceal his deficiency. If any noticed him he pretended to be eating, though he had forgotten to bring any food with him. At times small clouds passed over the face of the sun, but they did not stay long enough to take him through Aragona, so he stayed in the protection of that humble growth that had what he lacked, and wished he had never had to do with magic. Something was making the evening pass very slowly, and making it very cold, and Ramon Alonzo did not know it was hunger.

And at last the sun drew near to the horizon and all the shadows stretched out dark and long; and Ramon Alonzo, more than ever conscious of his own wretched strip of grey darkness, felt amongst these unbridled shadows much as he might have felt on some gala evening had he gone to a glittering fête, where men and women were dressed in all the silks of festival, and had moved amongst them himself in tawdriest oldest cloth. And then the sun set and his buoyant spirits arose and, feeling himself the equal of any material thing, he left the humble protection of the azalea and strode on towards Aragona.

No sooner had he come to the fields and gardens that lay about the village than idlers saw him and stood up at once and called aloud to warn the village folk, as though their idleness had been a perpetual guard whose purpose was triumphantly fulfilled. "The man with the bad shadow," they all cried out; and he saw that his story had been noised about, and that this was become his name. Answering voices called from the little streets and out of small high windows, and there was the noise of feet running. And then some ran to the tower where the ropes hung down from the belfry, to ring the bells that they rang against magic or thunder, and those mellow musical voices went over the fields to protest against Ramon Alonzo. They seemed to be flooding all the gloaming with memories, as they carried to Ramon Alonzo there in his loneliness vision on vision of times and occupations from which he was now cut off and debarred by a shadow. He felt a wistful love for their golden voices, calling out to him from this land he had lost, where dwelt the happy men that had not touched magic; but when the bells rang on and on and on a fury came on him at the narrow folly of the folk that made all this fuss about a shadow, and he flung his arm impatiently to his sword-hilt. But when he saw, amongst the crowd that was hastening to gather against him, women and even children, and the protestation of the bells still filled the air with outcry, he perceived that there was an ado that it was beyond his sword to settle. So he turned back along the way he had come; and soon his shape was dim on the darkening hill-side to the eager crowd that watched and talked in the village, and soon their excited voices reached him no more, and he heard no sound but the bells warning all those lands against him.

For a while he paced the hill-side in the chill, full of all such thoughts as arise from hunger, and that thrive in the cold and fatigue that hunger brings—doubts, fears, and despairs. What was he himself, he wondered, now that his shadow had left him? Was he any longer a material thing? And he helplessly cast his mind over all known forms of matter. Were any of them without shadows? Even water and even clouds. And what of this sinister thing with which he associated, the magician's piece of gloom? How much was he a fellow conspirator with it? How much was it damned?

And his thoughts turned thence to the dooms of the Last Day. How much was a shadow necessary to salvation? Would the blessed Saints care for so light and insubstantial a thing? But at once came the thought that they themselves had renounced material things and were themselves immaterial and spiritual, and might set more store by a shadow than he could ever know.

And all the while as he walked on the darkening hill-side doubts asked him questions and despairs hinted replies, which might neither of them ever have spoken at all had he thought to bring some food with him in a satchel. And all the while the blue of the sky grew deeper, and moths passed over the grass, with a flight unlike the flight of whatever flies by day, and little queer cries were heard that the daylight knows not; and then, like a queen slipping silently into her throne-room through a secret panel of oak, bright over lingering twilight the first star appeared.

It was the hour when Earth has most reverence, the hour when her mystery reaches out and touches the hearts of her children; at such a time if at all one might guess her strange old story; such a time she might choose at which to show herself, in the splendour that decked her then, to passing comet or spirit, or whatever stranger should travel across the paths of the planets. Ramon Alonzo, cold and lonely while star after star appeared, not only drew no happiness from all that mellow glow, but saw in it a new horror. For looking closely with downcast eyes on the moss and grass of the hill he noticed now that the piece of gloom that the magician had given him was a little darker than the natural darkness of that early starry hour; so that he alone, of all things in the night, had a shadow creeping beside him. And again he brooded bitterly, trying to guess the end of it. Must he share the obvious doom of this false shape? Must he lose salvation because he had lost his shadow? And as he mournfully pondered the night darkened, and soon was darker than that piece of gloom. When Ramon Alonzo saw that it had gone, and that he was for the moment like all other men and things, shadowless in the night, he soon forgot the future, and turned again towards the village of Aragona, thinking to pass through its streets like any other traveller.

When he reached the village it was full night and all the stars were shining, not only those that had stolen into sight, one by one, where no eye watched, but the whole Milky Way. The bells long since had ceased, and a hush held all the village as Ramon Alonzo strode through. But it was a hush of whisperings; the strained hush of watchers. All the upper windows were open; men were gathered in the darkened rooms. Women peered behind curtains. Even in lofts there were watchers. And for all their eagerness they did not see Ramon Alonzo till he was well within the village. Perhaps they expected some more stealthy approach than his honest, confident stride; perhaps they whispered too earnestly amongst themselves; most likely they thought that not just at that moment would the event for which they waited occur. But when one sharp angry cry was heard from an upper window all the watchers saw him at once. Then the hush broke in a tumble of feet descending wooden stairs, and a clatter of scabbards, and a noise of doors flung open, and sudden voices, and the sound of feet in the street.

"For the Faith," they cried; "for the Faith! Where is he?"

Behind him Ramon Alonzo heard many voices; before him he saw four men, one of whom carried a lantern. A few paces more and he was half-way through the village. And these few paces brought him close to the four men. Behind him a confusion in the voices showed that they were not certain where he was. Ahead of him there seemed no more than these four. He went quickly up to them; and they no less eagerly, and even gladly, hastened towards him. His sword was out, and theirs.

"For the Faith!" they cried.

"One at a time, señors," said Ramon Alonzo with a sweep of his hat; for they were all coming on him together. And at these words one hung back a little, but another turned to him.

"It is for the Faith," he said. Then they all came on together, three upon Ramon Alonzo while the fourth stood beside them with drawn sword, holding the lantern high.

"That for St. Michael!" cried the first to cross with Ramon Alonzo. But the stroke was well parried.

"That for all archangels!" the same swordsman cried,

making another blow at Ramon Alonzo. But he had taken off his cloak and folded it on his left arm, and the cloak took that blow. With his sword he parried a thrust from one of the others.

But one man cannot fight against three for long; and the stationary lantern and the clear sound of steel had told the crowd in the street where the young man was, the man with the bad shadow, as they called him, and they were pouring that way. Ramon Alonzo therefore pushed past his antagonist, muffling his sword's point with his cloak and so passing him that he was for a moment between himself and the other two swordsmen. Then he passed round and attacked the man with the lantern.

The four men had their plan, and it was evidently planned that the man with the lantern should not join in the attack but should light the others. This they had probably long talked over and settled while they waited for Ramon Alonzo. And the man with the lantern would surely have been the least skillful swordsman. But that Ramon Alonzo should attack him they none of them had considered.

As Ramon Alonzo passed round behind the backs of the three, each of them turned and stood on guard for a moment, for it is well known to be dangerous to have an armed man behind you in the dark. In that moment Ramon Alonzo launched himself upon the man with the lantern. There was no more than a pass and a parry and then again a thrust.

"That for the mother of St. Anne," said the man with the lantern, aiming his last stroke. And then Ramon Alonzo's point entered his ribs.

The strange magical shadow spun weirdly about as Ramon Alonzo grabbed the fallen lantern; and, holding it with the arm that had the cloak, his own eyes were protected by a fold of the cloth from the light that somewhat dazzled the eyes of the three. But it was not only the three; there were twenty or thirty more pouring up the street only now a few paces away. With a flourish of cloak and lantern in their faces, and an always watchful sword-point, he now disengaged from the three, and turned and ran as the crowd came pouring up.

He had suddenly gained a few paces, but the light of a lantern is easy to follow at night; and, keeping to the road, he was soon approached by the swiftest of the runners. For a while they raced, but when Ramon Alonzo saw that in the end he would be overtaken he stopped and put down the lantern in the road. The other came up, not one of those three with whom he had already crossed swords. Ramon Alonzo flung his whole cloak at his head, and picked up the lantern and ran on. Time enough to fight him later, he thought, if he overtook him again. But the cloak had completely covered the man's head and his sword had gone through it, and the crowd came up with him before he was able to start after the lantern again. And Ramon Alonzo at once ran lighter without his cloak, and sped on with a certain pleasure such as comes to athletes in youth. The crowd now cursed the lantern that they saw bobbing on before them, confusing it with lights of hellish origin, and forgetful or ignorant that it was the respectable lantern of a good kitchen-grocer of their own village.

Ramon Alonzo they abjured to stop, calling him by the names of certain famous devils; but he no more heeded them than would these devils have done. Only he noticed that, though they fought or pursued, as their cries indicated, for the Faith, for St. Michael, for St. Joseph, for St. Judas not Iscariot, for all the Saints, for the King, they none of them cried "for a Shadow." And yet that was all that the fuss was about, he reflected irritably. There are always two views, even over a trifle.

He had been gaining a little ever since he dropped his cloak; but now one runner seemed to be ahead of the crowd again. He heard his feet above the sound of their shouts and their running. On his left ran a little lane among deep hedges, joining the wider road. And now was come the time to put the lantern to the purpose for which he carried it. He ran down the lane till he found a gap in the hedge on his right, then he put the lantern high up on the hedge on his left and stuck it there still alight. He then crawled through the gap on his right and ran softly towards the road he had left, over a corner of a wild field.

They soon came to the lantern. They did not hear him run softly over the field, but gathered round the lantern, and pulled it down; and, finding he was not there, they pursued in every direction, some of them going across the field to the road and following Ramon Alonzo. But they had wasted too many moments and could no longer hear him running. Following that lantern had been too easy, and now that it guided them no longer they did not immediately use their wits and their ears.

For some while Ramon Alonzo heard voices behind him; then they dropped off and mingled with the far noises of night. He ran leisurely on. And presently the various parties turned back from their roads and lanes and gathered again in the village, and there was talk till a late hour of what they had done for the Faith. And many a guess there was of whence he had come, and many of where he had gone; and many a tale there was of the same thing differently seen, and these tales were checked by the wisdom of elder men who had not been there but could make some shrewd guesses. And when all was compared it was seen there had been more magic than one could easily credit if it had not actually happened. And a wise old man who had not spoken as yet was seen to be shaking his head; and when all were listening he spoke: "Well, it is gone," he said. "The Saints be praised."

"Aye, it is gone," said they all.

So they went to bed.

CHAPTER XV

Ramon Alonzo Talks of Technique and Muddles His Father

Ramon Alonzo ran on in the night, then dropped to a walk, and soon he no more than sauntered along the road, whose greyness before him seemed the only light on Earth. Above him the whiteness of the Milky Way seemed to suggest other roads, and his thoughts rambled awhile through the mazes of this idea until they were quite lost in it; then they came back bitterly to Earth. The charwoman had been right! All this ridiculous fuss about a trifle, and not a trifle that they even set any store by themselves; for who prizes his shadow, who compares it with that of others, who shows it, who boasts of it? A trifle that they knew to be a trifle, the least useful thing on Earth—a thing that nobody sold in the meanest shop and that nobody would if they could, and that nobody would buy, a thing without even a sentimental value, soundless and weightless and useless. Far more than this Ramon Alonzo thought, and believed he had definitely proved, to the detriment of shadows. No doubt he exaggerated a shadow's worthlessness. And yet the folk of that village that had turned out sword in hand had by their action exaggerated the other side of the argument, and extremes are made by extremes. Nor was Ramon Alonzo in any way checked in his furious exposure of shadows by any wistful yearning that he had often felt for his own since the day that he lost it, and was often to feel again. Logic indeed had been flouted upon either side in this business, and it is for just such situations as these that swords are made. Ramon Alonzo had used his well, and he wiped it now on a handful of leaves and returned it to the scabbard.

How late it was he did not know, but it was full time for sleep, so he lay down by the road; but without his cloak he found it too cold, even in the summer night, so he rose and sauntered on. On the way he met a stream and drank from it, and noticed the vivifying effect of water, perhaps for the first time.

Neither his lonely walk nor his lonely thoughts are worth recording, until a faint colour from the coming dawn began to brighten his journey, and the approach of another day turned his thoughts to the future, and a memory that he had the vial that his sister needed came to brighten his mind.

And then the false shadow appeared again on the ground, scarce noticeable had he not chanced to see it the evening before at a time when his eyes were downcast, less noticeable than the faintest of earthly shadows that will sometimes fall from a small unsuspected light, but enough to warn Ramon Alonzo that he must hide and slink and follow the ways of outlaws. Not far from him now was the forest that sheltered his home, and above a dark edge of it he could see a gable upon his father's house beginning to gleam in the morning. Yet not now could he seek his home: he must wait till the long shadows that were about to roam the fields had shrunk to a length that was somewhat less than man's. He hastened on to reach the nearest part of the forest before the sunrise should expose his deficiency to whomever might be abroad in the clear morning. So he left the road and took his way to the forest.

The sun rose before he gained the shade of the trees, but no man was yet abroad, and only a dog from a sleeping cottager's house saw the man with the short shadow hurrying over the grass upon which no other shadow was less than its master. Among shadows more enormous than the sound solid rocks the dog came up with him, its suspicions well aroused, probably by the queer unearthly appearance that the short shadow gave Ramon Alonzo rather than by any exact observation that his shadow was not the right length; but this we cannot know, for neither the wisdom of dogs nor the wisdom of men is as yet entirely understood by the other, though great advances have already been made: one has only to mention such names as Arnold Wilkinton, Sir Murray Jenkins, Rover, Fido, and Towser.

The dog followed at first sniffing; then he came up close and took one long sniff at Ramon Alonzo's left leg, and stopped and sat down satisfied. Presently he thought to bark, and gave four or five short barks as a matter of duty; but that human scent that he got had been enough, and he showed none of that fury of suspicion and anger that men had shown in the village of Aragona. Ramon Alonzo was enormously heartened by this, for he saw that whatever magic there had been, and although he was able to cast no natural shadow, yet his body was still human: he trusted the dog for that. And then the dog, feeling that he had not perhaps quite given warning enough against this stranger that strolled by his master's house so early, barked three or four times again. But this in no way checked Ramon Alonzo's newly found cheerfulness; for the dog might have howled.

The young man went on and came to the shade of the forest, while the dog got up and walked slowly back to his barrel, whence he had first been attracted by the curiously spiritual figure that Ramon Alonzo cut in the landscape at that hour, which had not seemed at first sight satisfactory.

Through the forest Ramon Alonzo hastened towards his home; and yet haste was of no use to him, for he came as near to the garden's edge as it was safe to come long before he dared show himself. Hungry, though watching the windows of his own home, in hiding even from his own parents and sister, he lay on some moss in the forest near the end of the white balustrade, waiting for the hour in which all human shadows would be a little bit shorter than men. And as he waited he saw Mirandola coming into the garden: he saw her walk by paths and shrubs that they both knew so well, and past small lawns on which they had played, as it seemed to him, almost for ever. He longed to call to her to come to the forest; and yet he would not, for he knew not what to say, and would not let her know the price he had paid to obtain the vial she needed. And he durst not come to her, so he stayed where he was, and the slow shadows shortened.

Not enough light reached him in the forest by which to judge the length of other shadows, so he tried to watch the length of Mirandola's, still walking in the garden. But when Mirandola came to the end of the garden that was nearest the edge of the forest he could not raise his head to look without causing dried things in the thicket to crackle, so that she might have heard him; and when she turned back in her walk he was soon unable to see her shadow clearly, even when he stood up. So he watched a small statue that there was on the lawn, in marble, of a nymph, such as haunted the brake no longer, as men were beginning to say; and he saw its shadow dwindle. And when the time was very nearly come that the shadows of all things else would be as his, and already the difference was not to be easily noticed, Ramon Alonzo walked from the wood. Mirandola saw him at once coming over the open between the balustrade and the dark of the forest, and ran down one of the paths of the garden towards him. But all things are not shaped towards perfect moments; and, as they ran to meet, their father and mother appeared, coming towards that part of the garden.

"I have the potion," said Ramon Alonzo.

And without a word Mirandola took the vial, and secreted it. So swiftly passed her hand from his to her dress that he scarcely saw her take it; and he looked to her face, where all human acts are recorded, to see her recognition of his gift, but there was nothing there to show that she had just received anything. Then she smiled in her beauty and turned round to her parents. "Ramon Alonzo is home," she said.

Then there were greetings, and questions to Ramon Alonzo, which he did not need to answer, for there were so many that he could not have answered one without interrupting the next. And when there began to be fewer, and the time was come for answers, he was able to choose the questions to which answers were easiest made. And he thought that Mirandola sometimes helped him when difficult questions were asked of the making of gold: certainly her own questions were sometimes frivolous, though whether they came of her frivolity or her wisdom he was not quite sure.

His mother asked him: "Is magic difficult?"

His father said: "Have you as yet made much gold?"

And Mirandola asked: "Can you bring up a rabbit from under an empty sombrero?"

But there were too many questions for record, and most

of them were but a form of affectionate greeting and did not look for answers.

Soon, however, the Lord of the Tower and Rocky Forest sought to detach his son from the rest of the little group in order to talk with him precisely upon the matter of business. And this he achieved, though not easily, because of Mirandola. And even then Mirandola chanced within hearing, so that at last he had to say to her: "Mirandola, we speak of business."

And to definite questions of the making of gold Ramon Alonzo found it difficult to reply now that his sister was no longer nigh to help him. He trusted her bright perceptions so much that he well believed the love-potion she had sought would better avail her than the gold that their father demanded, but he could not reveal her secret, and so found it difficult, without a sound training in business, to give exact accounts of gold that was not actually in existence. Chiefly he sheltered behind the technique of magic, withholding no information from his father on the matter of transmutation, on the contrary giving him much, yet shrewdly perceiving that these learned technicalities confused the matter in hand, and led as surely away from it as the paths in a maze that run in the right direction soon lead their followers wrong. For some while this talk continued, and though Ramon Alonzo had no skill to write a prospectus he none the less evaded the absence of gold and protected his sister's secret. And as they spoke they drew toward the house, and it was not long before they entered the little banquet-chamber. And there, while Ramon Alonzo ate to his heart's content, the Lord of the Tower told him of Gulvarez. "Somewhat a greedy man, I fear," he explained. "And one that will bargain long and subtly in the matter of Mirandola's dowry, for which reason the gold is urgent."

Ramon Alonzo said nothing, thinking of the gross man whom he had once seen and of whom he had often heard.

"Yet if we refuse to close with him," continued his father, "whom shall we find in these parts for Mirandola? Will one come from the forest? No. And we are not such as can go to Madrid. The worst of Gulvarez's demands will cost us less than that."

And he laid his hand thoughtfully on the empty silver box that he now kept in the room with him, into which they had come from the scene of Ramon Alonzo's repast, the room where his boar-spears hung.

"Could we not wait awhile?" said Ramon Alonzo.

"No, no," said his father, smiling and shaking his head. "It is too easy to wait awhile in youth. It is thus that the greatest opportunities pass. Even as you wait youth passes. Ah well, well."

No more said Ramon Alonzo; and his father fell to contemplating the future silently and with quiet content; and from this, the day being warm, he grew somewhat drowsy and scarcely noticed his son, who thereupon went back again to the garden while the state of the shadows allowed him to walk abroad without yet attracting notice.

There he spoke some while with his mother, unable to get away to Mirandola; and all the while the shadows were wasting. And at last his mother turned to the cool of the house and he made hasty farewells, pleading the urgency of work, and promising to return soon, and leaving her before he had quite explained why he had come; while she warned him not to set too much store by magic, beyond what would be required to please his father. Then he went to Mirandola in another part of the garden. And the shadows grew shorter and shorter.

As he spoke with Mirandola he hastened with her to the

edge of the forest to gain the protection of the oaks, whose mighty shadows he had come to envy. And as they went he said to her: "Our father has arranged that you marry Señor Gulvarez."

"He hath," she said.

"Mirandola," he said, "is he not a trifle gross, Señor Gulvarez? Might he not, though pleasing at first, grow however slightly tedious when he grew older, and become, though never irksome, yet of less charm, less elegance, as the years went by?"

But Mirandola broke into soft peals of laughter, which long continued, until they said farewell, and Ramon Alonzo walked alone through the forest.

CHAPTER XVI

The Work of Father Joseph

Mirandola came back from the edge of the forest wondering, over wild heath to the garden. It had been her wont to know what her brother did, and even what he thought. But now he had some thought that she did not know, and it was at this that she wondered. She considered all the events that she thought might touch her brother—love first of all; and awhile she thought this was his motive, and then she thought it was something else. But she had not spoken with him long enough to guess that he went away so soon and so fast through the forest, with a packet of meat in his satchel, because he had lost what all material things have in attendance upon them whenever they face the light, and that he durst not show while other shadows were shorter his miserable strip of five feet of gloom. She had indeed heard tales of men who had sold their shadows, and knew that her brother had daily dealings with magic, but she had not guessed the fee that the Master took. She had told him not to bring gold. For what purpose then was his haste? Wondering, she returned to the garden.

Who could tell her? Only one. One only, amongst the few Mirandola knew, was able to work out such puzzles, and that was the good Father Joseph. And just as she thought of him she saw his plump shape coming smiling across the garden. It was by a path through the garden he was wont to come from his house whenever he came to see the Lord of the Tower; and he came now to help make ready for that event, now near at hand, of which all the neighbourhood talked, the visit of the serene and glorious hidalgo, the Duke of Shadow Valley.

And before he entered the house to take part in the preparations upon which the Lord of the Tower had long been occupied, except for the brief interruption of Ramon Alonzo's visit, Mirandola greeted him and turned him aside to another part of the garden, hoping to find from him the clue of her brother's sudden departure. That he would discern it she had no doubt, that he might tell her she hoped; for these two were good friends, almost one might say comrades in spiritual things. Mirandola's confessions were the most complete of any that dwelt at the Tower, perhaps the most complete the good father heard, and indeed they were a joy to him. Often from these confessions he gathered such knowledge as it was right that he should have of the little earthly events that befell in that neighbourhood, which might not otherwise have come his way. He came much to rely on them; and so it was that he and Mirandola had a certain comradeship in the wars that the just wage ever against sin.

"My brother came to-day," she said as they walked.

"He did?" said Father Joseph.

"But he only stayed a short space and then went away."

"Oh. That is sad," said Father Joseph.

"He spoke with all of us and ate a dinner, and then he left at once."

"I trust he ate well," said the good man.

"Very well," answered Mirandola.

"Very well?" repeated Father Joseph.

"Yes. He ate a large dinner."

"More than usual with him?"

"Yes."

"Ah," said the good man, "then he had travelled fast."

"I suppose so," said Mirandola.

"For what purpose did he come?" asked Father Joseph.

Mirandola looked at him and smiled gently. "He came to see us," she said.

But Father Joseph had seen from that smile and from her eyes, before she spoke, that he would not get an answer to that question.

"Very right. Very proper," he said.

"But he would not stay," she said.

"Ah. He should have stayed awhile," said Father Joseph.

"He went away very fast through the forest," she said.

"By what road did he come?" he asked.

"Through the forest," she said.

"Ah. Hiding," said Father Joseph.

Not only was Father Joseph ready at all times with help for those who sought it, but one good turn deserved another, and he joyously used his wits for Mirandola. He argued thus with himself: a man hides either from enemies or from all. A man sometimes hid from the law; but the law came seldom to these parts, and in summer never, for la Garda slept much in the heat. From enemies then or from all. Now in all the confessions he had heard from men that had enemies he had noticed that none went back from their journeys by the same way by which they had come, as Ramon Alonzo had done. Did he then hide from all, except from his family? That would argue some change in him that he wished to conceal, or even in his clothing, for he had known young men as sensitive about their mere clothes as about the very form God had made, or—alas—about even the safety of their souls. But what change then? It would not have escaped the eyes of Mirandola.

"I trust he was well," he said.

"Yes," she said.

"He looked as he ever looks?" he asked.

"Oh, yes."

"Quite the same as ever. Yes, of course. And he was dressed the same?"

"Yes," she said. "All but his cloak."

"Ah, his cloak was different," said Father Joseph.

"It was not there," she said.

"No," he said, and thought awhile. And now his thoughts ran deeper and stranger, touching the ways of magic, of which he knew much, but as an enemy.

"My child," he said, and he took her hand and patted it, lest his words should alarm her, "had he a shadow?"

She gave a little gasp. "Yes, his shadow was safe."

That was as near as Father Joseph came with his guesses. He thought much more but strayed further away from the truth, and then he decided that more facts were needed, small things observed, short phrases overheard, which he knew so well how to weave; and determined to bide his time.

"That is all now," he said to soothe her, lest she should fear another question probing such dreadful things. "We shall find why he left."

They turned back then to the house to take part in the preparations.

There Father Joseph found all the old repose gone. Comfortable chairs that stood in quiet corners had been moved, chairs that his body loved when a little wearied perhaps by spiritual work; and the corners that had seemed so quiet now glared with a harsh light with all their old cobwebs gone, and stared with a strange emptiness because their chairs had been taken away to the banquet-hall. The quiet old boar-spears, that had seemed a very part of lost years, no longer rested soberly on the wall, but flashed and sparkled uneasily, for they had been newly polished and seemed to have become all at once a part of the work-a-day present, and to have lost with their rust all manner of moods and memories that they used to whisper faintly to Father Joseph whenever he saw them there. And, though the moods that the dimness and rust of the old things brought him were always edged with sadness, yet he gently lamented them now. But news had just come that the morrow was the day when Gulvarez would bring the Duke of Shadow Valley, with four chiefs of the Duke's bowmen and his own two men-at-arms. So Father Joseph was soon moving chairs with the rest; and, though somewhat lethargic of body, yet his great weight moved the chairs as the torrents swollen with snow move the small boulders. And by the middle of the afternoon nothing seemed left of that mysterious harmony that is the essence of any home: had Penates been set up there as in Roman days they would not have recognized the rooms that they guarded. But before the sun had set a sudden change came over the confusion, and there was a new orderliness; and a tidiness that the Lord of the Tower had quite despaired to see was all at once around him. And Peter, who had come in from the garden to help, attributed this to the aid of all the Saints, and in particular to the aid of that fisherman from whom he had his name; but likely as not, it was but the result of mere steady work. Then Father Joseph sank into one of the chairs and rested.

And then the Lord of the Tower and his lady began to

discuss the reception of the Duke— where they should meet him, who should go with them, and the hundred little points that make an occasion. And here a nimble power came to their aid from where the large man in his chair rested heavily, for the mind of Father Joseph was bright and agile, and the making of plans never tired it as pushing chairs tired his body. He it was that suggested that the two maids from the dairy and the girl that minded the house should go with Mirandola and strew the road with flowers. And he planned, or they planned under his encouragement, that Peter and three men from the stables should take each a boar-spear and stand two each side of the door like men-at-arms. And it was Father Joseph's thought that another man should ride down the road till he saw the Duke arriving, and then spur back and tell them so that all should be ready. And the chamber that the Duke should have was prepared, and a room appointed by the Lady of the Tower for each of his four bowmen, and last of all they thought of Gulvarez. Lo, it was found that there was not room for him. But they thought of a long dark loft there was over the stables, where the sacks of corn were kept, longer than any room and nearly as warm: this they set apart for Gulvarez and his two men-at-arms.

CHAPTER XVII

The Three Fair Fields

The day dawned splendidly, and air and fields glittered all the morning with sunlight, which welled up over the world and was only stopped by the forest. Her mother called Mirandola to the room in which the draughts and the tapestries upheld their age-old antagonisms, and spoke with her of Gulvarez. She spoke awhile of his merits, and often paused, for it was her intention to answer her daughter's objections, but Mirandola made no objections at all. It was of these objections that the Lady of the Tower had been better prepared to speak than of such merits as might be attributed to Gulvarez, and when there were no objections to answer, her pauses grew longer and longer; and soon she said no more at all, but sat and looked at her daughter. And that was a sight for which many would gladly have travelled far; yet the Lady of the Tower was puzzled as she looked, seeing no doubts in her daughter's face, no hesitations, only a quiet acquiescence, and beyond that the trace of a smile that she could not fathom.

Then Mirandola went from her mother's room back to her own, with a quick glance, as she went, through every window she passed that looked to the road. And she took the vial that she had had from her brother from the place in which she had hidden it overnight, and once more placed it secretly in her dress. And as she passed through a corridor, leaving her room, she saw from a sunlit window the horse-man they all awaited hurrying home.

At once there was a stir of feet in the Tower. The four men with the boar-spears ran to the door; and Father Joseph came out and blessed their gathering, and showed them where to stand and how to hold the spears; and all the while a certain flash in his eye showed them that blessing was not his only work. And the three maids ran to their baskets, that were all full of wild flowers gathered by them in the dew; and Mirandola came with them carrying a basket of rose-petals. As the maidens came through the door Father Joseph blessed the baskets. Then they went slowly up the road all four, strewing the way with flowers.

Once more Father Joseph had seen in Mirandola's face a look of wonder and awe and joy, as though something had come to her that was new and strange. What should it be but love? And yet he deemed that it was something else, but knew not what it was. It was that she carried in the vial that her brother brought her a magical thing, the first she had ever owned.

As Father Joseph mused and failed to find an answer, there began to arrive the folk from neighbouring cots, com-ing across the fields: they gathered a little way off from the door and began to talk of Gulvarez. They were a folk much as other folk are, and yet they were as it were maimed of half their neighbourhood, for none dwelt in the forest. It may be because of this they gossiped more eagerly of what neighbours they had: it may be that all gossip everywhere runs to its limit, and is nowhere more or less. They spoke of Gulvarez, who was so strangely honoured; and some said that the only cause of the visit was that his castle chanced to stand by the Duke's journey, while others said nay, arguing that in his youth there must have been some sprightly quality that Gulvarez had had, some excellence of mind or limb, for the sake of which the Duke remembered him now. How else they said would this exquisite hidalgo, the mirror of all that followed the chase whether of wolf, stag, or boar, whose mind was brightly stored with the merriest songs of the happiest age Spain knew, whose form, when mounted on one of his own surpassing horses, was the form of a young centaur, how else would he tolerate the gross Gulvarez? Thus merrily flew the gossip, passing backward and forward lightly from mouth to mouth.

And suddenly, where a hump of the road appeared white against the blue sky, all saw two horsemen. At once Father Joseph called sharply to the improvised men-at-arms in a voice unlike the one wherewith he was wont to bless. They stiffened under it and became more like the guard they were meant to be. The Lord of the Tower and his lady came out and stood before their door. The girls went on strewing flowers. And then was seen the velvet cloak and cap of the Duke, and the great plume, and the clear thin face, and his peerless chestnut horse aglow in the sun, and the plump figure and coarse whiskers of Gulvarez. These two were seen and recognized by all before one of the chiefs of the bowmen had yet been discerned. But two of these were nearer to the Tower than anybody knew; they slipped quietly from bush to bush and went carefully over horizons; two were far before the Duke and two close behind him: it was the way of the bowmen. And then, a little way behind the riders, straggled Gulvarez's two men-at-arms. At first they had marched in front, but the horses of the Duke and Gulvarez ambled rather than walked, and the two men-at-arms in their green plush and cuirasses, with the heat of the sun on the iron helmets they wore, soon fell a little behind. And now a bowman coming into sight hailed the group of gazers near the door of the Tower; and they saw two of those green bowmen that were so seldom seen, and were so famous in fable and gossip: a little thrill of wonder ran through the crowd. And presently these two halted one on each side of the road, and the Duke beside Gulvarez rode on between them and came to where the girls were scattering flowers. As soon as Gulvarez perceived Mirandola he bared his head and smiled at her. It was a huge grimace. Mirandola curtseyed to him; perhaps she smiled, but it was not easy always to trace exactly every expression that passed over her face. And then she gravely continued strewing the rose-petals. Then the Duke doffed his hat of dark blue velvet, and the great plume, of a brighter blue, curved through the summer air; and a glance of the Duke's blue eyes met a flash from the darker ones of Mirandola.

So passed the Duke and Gulvarez by Mirandola, riding over the flowers and rose-petals, and not a word was said. She had seen the eyes of the Duke and the teeth of Gulvarez, and both men saw her beauty; and so that instant passed. There came a wavering cheer from the group of gazing neighbours, a shot of anger from Father Joseph at some clumsiness of the improvised guard, and the Lord of the Tower and his lady were welcoming the Duke as he dismounted on flowers. The neighbours, clustering a little closer, appraised the Duke's great blue cloak; the jewels in his sword-hilt; his easy seat upon that splendid horse, a certain indolence redeemed by grace; the strong gait of his walk; his face; his youth. Aye, they praised his youth, as though any man could deserve credit for that; but there was such a way with him, so pleasant a grace, that they gave praise out of their thoughtless hearts to everything that formed it. Then the horses were led away by the men of Gulvarez, and host and hostess and guests and Mirandola all passed into the Tower.

The Lord of the Tower walked with the Duke, exchanging courtesies with him, his lady walked with Gulvarez after them, and Mirandola followed behind. And so they came through the hall and towards the banquet-chamber, the host watching opportunity all the way; and not until they arrived where the banquet was ready, and the maids that had strewn the wild flowers had brought a silver bowl to wash the hands of the Duke in scented water, did the Lord of the Tower note and take his opportunity. He went then to Gulvarez past Mirandola, speaking low to her as he passed: "You shall see him presently," he said to her. "Yes, presently," said the Lady of the Tower, just hearing, or, if not, divining what her lord had said to his daughter. Both thought she smiled obediently. And to Gulvarez he said: "I have a pretty tusk that I would show you before we banquet. A boar we took last season."

Gulvarez well understood; for there had been a bargain not in clear words, and without seals or parchment, inscribed only upon those two men's understanding, that if he brought the Duke to visit the Lord of the Tower the hand of Mirandola should go to Gulvarez. And the time was come to ratify it. Gladly then Gulvarez went away with his host.

The bringing of the Duke had been none of Gonsalvo's bargain; he had come to a time of life when events and occasions seemed but to disturb the placidity of the years: it had been forced on him by some whim of Mirandola. They came to the room that the host most often used, in which there were indeed boars' tusks to show; but this both men soon forgot.

"I have begun to think somewhat of late," said the Lord of the Tower, "concerning my daughter's future."

"Indeed?" said Gulvarez.

"Somewhat," replied his host.

No more instants passed than are needed for a heavy mind to move; and then Gulvarez said: "I take then this opportunity to express my ready willingness to marry your daughter should this have your approval. I trust that my castle may be an abode not unworthy of one of your honoured house."

Gladly then the Lord of the Tower expressed his approval in phrases not unfitted to that occasion: many such phrases he uttered, fair, courteous, and flowery, and still invented more, though the arts of perfect speech were some years behind him now; but he feared the next words of Gulvarez and seemed to wish to delay them: perhaps he blindly hoped to stave them off altogether.

"You will doubtless," said Gulvarez, "give her a dowry in keeping with the lustre of your name."

"I shall indeed give her a dowry," said Gonsalvo. "Indeed the coffer that I set aside for this very purpose is here." And he laid his hand on the coffer of oak and silver.

Gulvarez lifted the box a few inches with one large hand, that could span the box and hold it, and put it down again. The Lord of the Tower waited for him to speak, but Gulvarez said nothing. It seemed to the owner of the box that it would have been better had Gulvarez depreciated it than that he should have thus weighed it in silence. And as Gulvarez did not speak, his host continued.

"It is not as if I had not the coffer," he said. "It is here. I have set it aside. But it has not been convenient to plenish it lately, or indeed as yet to put anything in it at all."

Still Gulvarez said nothing.

"The coffer is there," said Gonsalvo. Gulvarez nodded.

"I had intended to fill it later," Gonsalvo continued, "if it should not be ready by the day of the wedding; and one day to send it after Mirandola."

Gulvarez was slowly and heavily shaking his head. It seemed to the Lord of the Tower that the stubbly growth of Gulvarez's chestnut whiskers almost shone as he shook his head, as the skin of a horse when he is in good fettle.

"That would be too late?" said Gonsalvo.

"Somewhat," replied Gulvarez.

Gonsalvo sighed. It must then be the three fair fields, the pastures that lay at evening under the shade of the forest. Perhaps two; but, no, Gulvarez would ask for all three; and how could he find a husband for Mirandola if he rejected Gulvarez's demands? Time was when he could have done so, for he had known somewhat of the world once. But the world had changed.

"My son, Ramon Alonzo," he said, "is studying to learn a livelihood, from which we have great hopes."

Never a word from Gulvarez helped him out; merely a look of interest that compelled him to go on. "In case he should be delayed," he continued, "in assisting me to set aside the dowry that I should wish to offer, my fields, my two fields, should be given, until the money was sent."

"Two fields?" said Gulvarez.

"Nay, nay," said his host. "All three."

"Ah," said Gulvarez.

"So we shall be agreed," said Gonsalvo.

"How much money, señor, are you pleased to give on the day that it shall be convenient?"

"Three hundred crowns of the Golden Age," replied the Lord of the Tower.

Gulvarez smiled and shook his head as though in meditation.

"Five hundred," said the Lord of the Tower.

"My respect for your illustrious house," said Gulvarez, "and my friendship for you, señor, that I deem myself honoured to have, holds me silent."

"Five hundred?" said the host with awe in his voice, for it was a great sum.

Gulvarez waved something away with his hand in the emptiness of the air. "Let us speak no more, señor," he said. "Our two hearts are agreed. It is a great honour, and I am dumb before it."

The Lord of the Tower sighed. He had known, whenever he thought, that he should do no better than this; and yet he had thought seldom, but hoped instead. Now it was over, and the three fields gone. They never seemed fairer than now. "Come," he said, "we must return to Mirandola."

So back they went, and jauntily walked Gulvarez, though in no wise built or planned for walking jauntily; but a spirit, whether of greed or love or triumph, was exalted within him and was lifting his steps. Once more, as they returned to the banquet-chamber, his whiskers seemed to shine.

"Heigho," thought the Lord of the Tower, "my three sweet fields!"

And there was Mirandola standing near her mother, her left hand to her dress, about the girdle, as though armed. And a look was on her face that Father Joseph could not interpret, for he had come into the room and was watching her. It was as though she were about to enter a contest, and stood proud before an armed and doughty antagonist.

Her mother and the Duke were already seated: the maids were pouring wine into chalices from a goblet that stood on a small table apart. The host and Gulvarez seated themselves, and then Father Joseph. Then the four chiefs of the bowmen came in, and took seats lower down the table. Father Joseph said grace. And still that look in the eyes of Mirandola.

Then Mirandola went over to the maids that stood at the table apart, and took from them one of the chalices and carried it to Gulvarez. Her father and mother smiled at her mistake, for she should have carried it to the Duke first; but their smiles broadened into smiles of merry understanding as each caught the other's eye. Gulvarez would have strutted had he been standing; had he been a peacock he would have spread his tail-feathers and rattled them. As it was, smirks and smiles expressed all this and more. He was about to speak, but Mirandola left him to fetch another chalice. So far as Father Joseph was concerned it was unnecessary for Gulvarez to say anything, for the priest knew every thought that passed through his mind, but he had not yet fathomed the mood of Mirandola.

Then, returning, she offered a chalice to the Duke and went back and stood by her mother.

"Be seated, child, by Señor Gulvarez," said her mother.

But Mirandola still stood there awhile.

Gulvarez, though flustered with pride because he had been given the wine by Mirandola first, yet dared not drink it before his august friend drank. Now they both drank together. Still Mirandola stood beside her mother, between her and the Duke. A moment she watched him with those eyes that never saw less than keenly; then she turned from a glance of the Duke's blue eyes and answered her mother tardily, as though just returned from far dreams. "Yes, Mother," she said, and went to the chair beside Señor Gulvarez.

And now wine was carried by the maids to Father Joseph and the four chiefs of the bowmen, whereafter they placed the goblet before their master. And meats were set before all, and talk arose, and men's hearts were warmed and they spoke of hunts that had been and the taking of ancient boars. But silent and with a strange look sat the Duke of Shadow Valley.

CHAPTER XVIII

The Love-Potion

The look on the face of the Duke of Shadow Valley was gradually growing stranger. The outlines of his face were wearying; his quick glances roamed no more, but turned to his plate listlessly; and he was breathing faster. The Lady of the Tower thought his cheeks grew a little paler under the summer's tan and yet she was not sure, when a pallor swept over his face even to the lips suddenly. And all at once the Duke was very sick.

"Poison?" wondered Father Joseph. "Not the Lord of the Tower," he thought, "nor his lady, nor Mirandola." He looked quickly at the others, from face to face. "No. What then?"

So far Father Joseph was right; but no one had spoken and he needed more material to arrive at the truth. Then the Duke was sick again. All the bowmen stood up, irresolute.

Still no one spoke, unless the murmured anxieties of the Lady of the Tower were speech.

Mirandola was silent as a little sphinx long left by the earliest dynasty in a tomb of rock under sand. Gulvarez was thinking to himself that he had fulfilled his part of the bargain, whatever happened to the Duke when he arrived.

The Duke was sick again all in the silence.

Then suddenly there was speech. Suddenly there was a tempest of words stinging and fierce and hot, as when Africa rains sand through a silvery darkness. It was the Duke speaking. His courtly tongue, for whose grace he was known through Spain, shot forth the words as the long whip hurls the little lash at its end.

The Lord of the Tower seemed to be growing smaller as though shrivelling under the words; Father Joseph's eyes turned downward and he became absorbed with humility. I will not repeat the words.

Against his hostess the Duke said nothing, but his speech so blasted Gulvarez for bringing him there that she shuddered.

And the bowmen stood there ready, awaiting any command from their master. He accused none of poison: had he done so the hands of the bowmen would have been on that one's shoulders instantly; but he deemed himself insulted either with meat long dead, or with wine of so deadly a cheapness that when the gipsies brew it out of no honest berries they neither drink it themselves nor allow their children near it. It was this insult that the serene hidalgo felt more than the pains of the retchings. And these were severe. His anger raged as though from some magical source rather than any annoyance caused by mere earthly cares. And he would have still raged on till all but he had gone trembling out from the chamber; but another bout of retchings came upon him, and all pressed round him offering ministrations. None of these would he have, but only demanded of them the place of his bedchamber, desiring to rest awhile before he should ride away from the cursed house. And this the Lord of the Tower offered to show him, bent almost to his knees by contrition at the neglect of his duty as host and at the insult offered in his house to so serene a hidalgo. But the Duke of Shadow Valley would have none of him, and commanded his bowmen instead to find the way to his bedchamber. They therefore searched discreetly, two going on before, the Duke following slowly, supported by the shoulder of another, while the fourth marched menacingly behind, to guard his master against whatever new outrage might be meditated in this suspicious house. Behind the fourth bowman, and as near as they durst, followed the whole household, trying to tell the bowmen the way to the Duke's bedchamber, but not to a word would one of the four chiefs hearken. Yet, however much they disdained the cries of the maids and the ejaculations of Gonsalvo himself, these must have been clues in their search; and soon they came to a larger room than the others, which was clearly prepared for a guest: into this they led the Duke, who immediately banished them, to be alone on the bed with his sickness and anger.

And in the afternoon the Duke's sickness ceased, so far as the bowmen could hear who guarded the door, but his anger remained with him, and none could bring him food, not even his own bowmen.

And the evening wore away and the Duke was weak after his vomitings, yet none of his bowmen durst enter to bring him food, for he roared with anger whenever one touched his door, and any mention of food increased his fury. And at nightfall the Lord of the Tower himself brought food, but when he came to the door the Duke swore an oath to eat no food in that house nor even drink water there. So he went disconsolately away.

In the anxiety that hung over all that house the suit of

Gulvarez made but little progress. He talked to Mirandola, but there was a strange silence upon her, and she had spoken seldom since the Duke had drunk the wine that was in the chalice she brought him. He spoke awhile with her mother but, whatever words were said, all ears were only alert for any sounds that might tell or hint any changes in the Duke's health or his anger. And it grew late and none durst go again to the Duke's chamber with food. So they went to their own bedchambers, passing by the silent bowmen sternly guarding the door; and when midnight came it brought no hush to that house that was not lying heavily there already, for the whole house seemed to brood on the enormity of the insult that it had offered to that serene Magnifico the Duke of Shadow Valley.

But when morning came and still the Duke refused food, and still lay weak on his bed and his anger was strong as ever, and not even the bowmen durst bring to him food or drink, then a new and darker anxiety troubled the house. For if his weakness forbade him to ride away and his anger would not permit him to touch food or drink in that house, might not the Duke die? Then the Lord of the Tower told his lady that he would try once more; and he went with a savoury dish and a flagon of wine. But he returned so soon, so flushed and so ill at ease, that the anxieties of all that saw him were only increased. Of what had passed he said nothing, beyond saying to his lady and often telling over again, whether to others or muttering it low to himself, that he knew that the Duke had never meant what he said. Then Father Joseph, noticing his distress, went without a word to the savoury dish and the flagon and carried them from the room, and soon his suave phrases were heard outside the Duke's door by such as listened round corners in their anxiety; and none failed to hear the roar of the Duke's answers.

So Father Joseph sighed and returned to the Lord of the
Tower, who, wishful to conceal that he had heard what the
Duke had shouted, said to his guest: "How fared you?"

"The power of Holy Church is waning," said Father
Joseph. "It is not what it was in the good days."

"Alas," said Gonsalvo. And there were looks of commis-
eration towards Father Joseph.

"It is because of all this sin," Father Joseph continued,
"that there has been in the world of late." And the commis-
erating looks changed all of a sudden, for they knew that
Father Joseph knew all their sins.

Then the Lady of the Tower took the flagon, thinking
that perchance the Duke might drink if no word were said
about food.

"He will not touch it. He will not touch it," said her lord
as she left. Nor did he.

When the Lady of the Tower was gone Father Joseph
drew Mirandola a little apart.

"It is a strange and awful anger," he said to her.

"Is it?" she said, a little above a whisper, her eyes much
hidden under the dark lashes.

"Yes," said he.

And no more said Mirandola till in a little while he spoke
again.

"What was it?" said Father Joseph.

"A love-potion," said Mirandola.

Father Joseph thought for a moment, though his face
showed no more sign of thought than surprise.

"I fear your brother mixed it ill," he said.

"I fear so," said Mirandola.

And, his curiosity satisfied, he had leisure to turn to the
things of his blessed calling. "Nor does Holy Church com-
mend these snatchings," he added, "at the good things of
the world by means of the evil Art and the brews of magic."

"I have sinned," said Mirandola.

Father Joseph waved a hand. It was a small sin to bring to the notice of one of his years and calling; for there were enough men and women in his little parish for the study of every sin. Nevertheless he was thinking deeply.

Then Mirandola saw her mother return, and put down food and flagon with a sigh. And she knew that that splendid young man was lying there without food, and the thought of the harm she had done him touched her heart to a sudden impulse.

"I will take the food to him myself," she said.

Instantly Father Joseph laid a firm hand on her arm.

"When he is weaker," he said.

Mirandola looked at him, held back by his grip, while her impulse died away.

"Yes. Not till evening," said he, with that assurance that he was wont to use whenever he spoke of the certainties of salvation. And more than his heavy grip that tone held Mirandola.

She passed the long day anxiously, fearing what weakness and the want of food might do to that mirror of chivalry, the young Duke, at whom folk gazed in the glorious courts of Spain, when he came to visit the victorious King; what wonder then he stirred hearts when he rode through the little fields to such a tower as this in the lonely lands, where the forest ended all, and illustrious knights rode rarely and were gone by in a canter. She was ill at ease all day. Only once a sparkle of her own merriness came back to her. Her mother had asked her to walk in the garden with Gulvarez, and Mirandola spoke of the Duke's hunger, and thought that he might take food from his friend and would doubtless drink with him. So Gulvarez went, with a large plate full of food, and a flagon of wine and two glasses; and the voice of the Duke was heard, ringing out with that magical anger.

Back then came Gulvarez, denying all the things that were said the loudest, and that must have been clearly heard, and brooding upon the rest; and there was no walk in the garden.

And all that day went by, and none could bring food to the Duke. But when evening came and all was quiet but the birds; and light came in serenely, level through windows, with the flash of insects, silver across the rays; all in the calm Mirandola took the flagon, and past the bowmen went to the Duke's door, and opened it and stood there in the doorway. And for a moment his anger muttered, then stumbled, and was all silent, as though it had faded out with the fading of day, or had some magical cause whose power had waned, and he lay there looking at Mirandola and she stood looking at him. So passed a moment.

Then she came to him and poured into a chalice a little wine from the flagon. Once more she offered him wine; but it was all earthly now, the glory and the glow of southern vineyards, and distilled by no prentice hand such as Ramon Alonzo's. And he accepted the wine, lying weak on his bed. Awhile she spoke with him, until there came to him the thought of food, and when he spoke of it she went to bring it to him. She passed again by the bowmen, who questioned her in low voices. "He will recover," she said, and sighed as she said it, thinking of all the night and day he had lain there pale and weak. She went to the kitchen and gathered small savoury things such as might be lightly eaten by one that had been so strangely troubled, small earthly condiments of daily uses that had nought to do with magic. And a rumour, of things overheard from the mutterings of the bowmen, spread through the house and told that the Duke would eat again.

Then came Gulvarez to the kitchen offering to carry the

plates for Mirandola. And this she let him do. And when they were come to the door of the Duke's bedchamber he carried the plates in, Mirandola waiting without. But even yet the Duke's anger was not over, and the sound of it boomed down the corridor, as he swore that none in that house should bring him food, unless Mirandola; and least of all Gulvarez, who had brought him to those accursed doors within which he had suffered so vilely. And Gulvarez came out so swiftly that the food shook and slid on the plates; then Mirandola took them and went in; and Gulvarez remained awhile with the bowmen, explaining such things as men explain when sudden fault has been found with them unjustly or justly.

The Duke ate little for weakness; but Mirandola sat by his bed, and somehow her eyes strengthened him when he looked in the deep calm of them, as though he found a power in their gentleness: and often he stopped, overwrought by the wrong that that house had done him, but flashes from Mirandola's eyes seemed to beat across his wrath and seemed to parry it, and after a while he would eat a little again. And so a little of his strength came back, and for brief whiles he slept. Then Mirandola crept out and told the bowmen, and one by one they stole in on their soundless feet, and saw that his sleep was natural, and stole out again; and all the house was hushed, and the Duke slept till morning.

CHAPTER XIX

Father Joseph Explains How the Laity Have No Need of the Pen

Gonsalvo and Gulvarez went early to the Duke's bed-chamber to assure themselves that the hopes of last night were just and that the Duke would live. He still lay weakly upon his bed but his anger flamed up at once as soon as he saw them, and was the old enormous wrath they had known the last two days. Before it they backed away towards the door, and ever as they tarried fresh waves of it overtook them and seemed to sweep them further. Sometimes one would delay and stammer polite excuses, while the other backed away faster; then the rush of the Duke's anger would bear down on the one that was nearest and drive him back spluttering; and another swirl of it soon would overtake the other. So, breathless with protestations, they were both swept out, and behind the closed door the Duke's anger died into mutterings, like the croon of a tide along a deserted shore.

Descending, they joined the Lady of the Tower and Father Joseph in the room where the boar-spears hung. And in answer to the anxious enquiry in his lady's eyes as they entered Gonsalvo said: "He has slept and is no weaker. But the humours of sickness have not yet left him."

She turned then to Gulvarez, seeming to look for some clearer news from the stranger.

"He does not yet lucidly understand your hospitality," he said. "He comprehends where he is, but the fevers of his malady delude him concerning it. As yet he knows not his friends, or only sees them transmuted by the vain humours of fever."

At this moment Mirandola passed by the door carrying two dishes, one of meat and the other of fruit. The Lady of the Tower was about to call her, for she was perplexed between the Duke's weakness and the strength of his fevers; but Father Joseph laid a hand on her arm, and Mirandola went by. Then Father Joseph went to the open doorway and blessed the carrying of the dishes.

And much of that morning Mirandola sat by the Duke's bedside, and at whiles he spoke with her and at whiles ate a little from the two dishes; and while she was with him his great anger was lulled; but not yet would he take food or drink from any in all that household save only Mirandola, nor tolerate one of them at the door of his bedchamber. And the rumour went through the house that the Duke would live, but it passed through gatherings of doubts and fears that had haunted the house since first he was taken ill, and many a fear clung yet to the hopeful rumour. But Father Joseph, who had some familiarity with the ways of life and death, saw how it would be and, deeming that there would be no entertainings at the Tower, nor high doings, nor any need of him, his thoughts turned now to his own little house, and the humble folk that came there for many a work-a-day need and to be unburdened of their different sins. He therefore said farewell to his host.

"What?" said the Lord of the Tower. "You leave us already?"

"It is time," said Father Joseph.

"But you will help us to entertain the Duke?"

"Haply," said Father Joseph, "he will lie awhile in bed."

"But when he is recovered," said Gonsalvo, "we will give a banquet to celebrate his deliverance."

But Father Joseph was more sure of the passing of the illustrious visitor's illness than he was of the fading of his anger, in the heat of which he had himself stood once already.

"I must return to the village," he said.

Mirandola had entered the room.

"Then you will come again," said Gonsalvo, "to marry Mirandola to Señor Gulvarez."

For Gonsalvo had a small chapel in his house.

"Gladly," said Father Joseph.

"Thank Father Joseph," said the Lady of the Tower.

"Thank you," said Mirandola.

Then away went Father Joseph; and soon from the pinnacles of lofty plans his mind descended to the little sins that the folk of the village he tended would have been sinning while he was away. He tried to think as he walked of the sins that each would have done; sometimes some girl of strange or passionate whims would a little puzzle his forecast, but for the most part he guessed rapidly, and just as he named to himself the sin of his last parishioner he reached the door under the deep black thatch of the house he loved so well.

He turned the handle and entered; it was not locked, for none in those parts dared rob Father Joseph's house; nor was the sin of robbery much practised in houses there but rather on the road in the open air. He entered and was once more with his pleasant knick-knacks that he had not seen for two days; and for a while his eye roamed over them, going from one to another, as he sat in his favourite chair in deep content. For a long while he sat thus, drawing into his spirit the deep quiet of his house, which had never been broken by such events as trouble the calm of the world: no illustrious hidalgos sojourned there; rarely even they passed it by: the sound of a trumpet or the sight of a gonfalon came once, or at most twice, in a generation. His gaze was reposing now on an old mug shaped like a bear, which rested upon a bracket: sometimes he was wont to fill it with good ale and so pass lonely evenings when sunset was early. Gazing now at the mug those evenings came back to his memory and he thought of the joyous radiance that there seemed to have been about them, when, again and again till it interrupted his thoughts, came a very furtive knock on his back door. He imagined the timid hand of some penitent sinner, come there to be rid of his sin, and arose to open the door. When he opened the little back door that looked to the forest, who was there but Ramon Alonzo?

The young man was wearing a fine old cloak of his father's, which Mirandola had begged for him on the day that he had gone cloakless away from the Tower. She had told Peter to take it after him, but Peter's master had not allowed him to go until the Duke had been received at the Tower; but when the banquet came to that sudden end none thought any more of Peter except Mirandola, so he took the cloak and went; and quietly, as he left, Mirandola said to him, "Tell him all that you saw." So Peter had travelled all the rest of that day and all through the night, and had come on Ramon Alonzo in the magician's wood; for Ramon Alonzo going circuitously round Aragona, over fields and wild heath, by night, and in the daylight travelling cautiously at such times as his shadow looked human, arrived on the second night so late near the house of the Master that he decided to sleep in the wood and enter by daylight. There Peter found him about dawn with the cloak, and glad Ramon Alonzo was of it. But when he heard of the malady that had overtaken the Duke, the dreadfulness of which Peter told in all fullness, and learned that the Duke had just drunk of a flagon of wine, he knew at once with a guilty inspiration that it had been the love-potion, and supposed that by some mistake of the serving maids the flagon meant for Gulvarez had been changed with the one for the Duke. Then anger came on him against the magician, and a hatred of all his spells, and he determined to put his plan into instant practise. But this plan involved writing, for he meant to write the syllables of the spell that opened the shadow-box, one by one amongst other writings, and to trick the magician into reading them for him. Therefore he thanked and said farewell to Peter, and as soon as ever the man was out of sight he turned his back upon the house in the wood, and travelling fast but cautiously and going wide again round Aragona under cover of night, came secretly the next morning out of the forest to the little door at the back of the priestly house. And there, as Father Joseph opened the door, ready to give absolution for some small sin, the first words that greeted him were: "I pray you, Father, to teach me the way of the pen."

Truly now there is no sin in the pen itself, though it be a full handy tool in the fingers of liars, and the greater part of the cheating that there is in the world is done by the pen to this day. And whatever Father Joseph suspected of Ramon Alonzo's work, he could not easily refuse instruction in the proper handling of aught that was in itself so innocent. He therefore rather temporized.

"The pen," he said. "That is indeed, no doubt, a worthy

tool; yet of little use to the laity. Those things it is needful to know are written already, and, should more ever be necessary, are there not monks to write it? Or is it to be supposed that those most illustrious presences, our spiritual overlords, should have neglected some matter that it were well to write and should have failed to record it?"

"Indeed no," said Ramon Alonzo, lowering his head in a pose of appropriate humility.

"For what purpose then would you put your own hand to the pen?" Father Joseph asked of him.

"I would fain know the handling of it," replied Ramon Alonzo, "yet not from any wish to write upon parchment, for that is no knightly accomplishment."

"Indeed not," said Father Joseph; "yet to know the handling of a pen, as your father knows, and the way that it takes up ink, and sometimes to have essayed sundry marks with it, as he hath, upon parchment, are things that add credit to a knightly house. This much I will teach you. But deem not that there is aught to be written that hath not long since been well said, and committed to parchment, and given to the charge of those whose duty it is to watch and protect learning."

No more than this Ramon Alonzo needed. He therefore thanked Father Joseph courteously, who went and fetched a pen; and soon the young man was being taught the way of it, where the fingers go, the place of the thumb, the movement of the whole hand, the method of taking ink, and the suitable intervals.

"Here," said Father Joseph, "near the window, where you shall have the full light." For Ramon Alonzo had seated himself in a corner and dragged the little table to the darkest part of the room.

But Ramon Alonzo, as it drew near noon, shunned any

approach to light, and would go near no spot on which shadows fell. Whether Father Joseph noticed or not this strange avoidance of light, his intellect pounced at once on his pupil's trivial answer, excusing himself for keeping his seat in the dusk of the corner; and from that moment his old suspicions came on to the right trail, which they never left till the strange secret they followed had been tracked up to its lair.

As Ramon Alonzo came by the knack of the pen he began to copy one by one on the parchment those three syllables, clear in his memory, that were the key of the shadow-box. He rejoiced to think that by asking Father Joseph for never a letter of the Christian alphabct he persuaded him that he sought for no more than he said, a certain way with the pen that should be a knightly accomplishment. Far otherwise was it: for, as Father Joseph watched those sinister syllables that were no language of ours, he began to see a young mind given over wholly to magic, and as each syllable appeared on the parchment he muttered inaudibly, "The Black Art. Oh, the Black Art."

But with practise Ramon Alonzo made those syllables clearer and clearer, until they appeared on the parchment whereon he wrote no otherwise than as they were in the great book of the magician that lay on the lectern in the room that was sacred to magic. Father Joseph watched the work of the pen that he guided, and all the while saw those syllables growing clearer, until, although he knew not what they were, nor the language in which they were written, he saw unmistakable omens and threats about them, and all those omens were magical, sinister, evil. Ramon Alonzo carried it off lightly, saying he but made idle strokes with the pen, believing he deceived Father Joseph. That hour for which he so often yearned went by, when the shadows of other men were the same as his, and still he worked at the pen. He saw, still close in his corner, the red and level rays shine in and lend a splendour to Father Joseph's knick-knacks. He saw the evening come, and those big Cathayan shapes that he made, black and bold in the gloaming. Then Father Joseph arose to light his tapers, and before he did that Ramon Alonzo thanked him and hastily bade him farewell, and was soon away on his circuitous journey that should lead him wide in the dark round Aragona.

So Ramon Alonzo came next night to the house in the wood. But Father Joseph saddled his mule in the morning and rode away by the very earliest light, and came in the afternoon to the hilly house of a priest he knew who had much knowledge of magic; and with him he brought that parchment on which all day Ramon Alonzo had practised those curious signs. This priest went sometimes down to the church in Aragona, but dwelt mostly alone in his house, where he worked on a scheme for the mitigation of sin, or read books exposing magic. Up the rocky track to that house on his struggling mule Father Joseph arrived; and when the gaiety of their greetings was over he showed his friend the marks that were on the parchment.

"I fear, Aloysius," he said, "we have naught good here."

Brother Aloysius took it. "Naught good," he said. "Naught good at all."

Then he put it down and put on great spectacles and looked at the parchment again and consulted a book, repeating now and then, "There is no good here," and shaking his head often.

And suddenly he became sure and spoke with a clear certainty.

"Indeed," he said, "it is a most heathen spell."

CHAPTER XX

The Magician Imitates
a Way of the Gods

And that day went by with its splendours and was added to past days; and night came up and covered the skies of Spain, and the magician sat all alone in his house in the wood. He was not wholly hostile to man; but, sitting there leaning forward upon a table whereon one taper flared, he was brooding on problems so far from our work-a-day cares, so far beyond even that starry paling which bounds our imaginations, that men and women were not to him that matter of first importance they are to us, but only something to be noted and studied as we might study whatever rumours may come of life upon planets of suns that are other than ours. His care for humanity was solely this, that amongst its children, whether in Spain or elsewhere, were those that were worthy to receive and cherish, and carry to those that would bring it to the far dimness of time, the mighty learning that he himself had had from the most illustrious of all the line of professors that had held the Chair of Magic at Saragossa. For the rest, his care was more

150

with the dominion that he held over captive shadows, and their far wanderings, the messages that they carried and the inspirations they brought, than with that narrow scope, and the brief stay, with which we are familiar. Could we know the supplications that his shadows sometimes took for him to great spirits that chanced on a journey near to Earth's orbit, could we know the songs and the splendours with which they often replied, it might be that our hearts would thrill to his strange traffic till we might forget to blame his aloofness from man. Only in rarest moments, perhaps as an organist sleeps, and his hand falls on to the keys playing one bar straight from dreams; or just at the apex of fever in tropical forests when strange birds are mating; or, eastwards from here, where a player upon a reed in barbarous mountains hits ancestrally on a note that his tribe have known from the days of Pan; or when some flash from the sunset shows a world-wide band of colour that is not one of the colours that man has named; only at rarest moments comes any guess to us of those songs and splendours that the lonely man drew from the spaces that lie bleak and bare about the turn of the comet. And only that day he had learned a curious story, a legend of the interstellar darkness, from a spirit that was going upon a journey, and had passed through the solar planets wrapped in thunder, and had been that morning at his nearest to Earth.

Ramon Alonzo had been absent now for six days; and, having no pupil to whom to transmit the mysteries that he himself had had from so glorious a source, the Master was solely occupied in his loneliness with legend and lore that are not of Earth or our peoples. And as he brooded on matters that are of moment outside our care and beyond the path of Neptune, the step of Ramon Alonzo was heard in the hush of the wood.

The young man entered vexed at that notable failure of the potion he had compounded, and angry for Mirandola, his father and mother, and the whole household of his home. He had pictured the consternation of that house, of which Peter had told him tremblingly not only all, but more; and he laid the blame on the author of the spells, which had seemed too easy for mistakes to be possible, rather than on his own forgetfulness. He entered believing that he owed nothing to the magician, and determined to learn no more of the making of gold so that he should still owe him nothing, and to get his own shadow back as his lawful due, and to rescue the charwoman's as an act of Christian chivalry. The two men met, one brooding upon a wrong, the other upon affairs beyond the orbit of Neptune, so that they each spoke little. And presently Ramon Alonzo, drawing forth a parchment, said: "Master, this script which was brought to Spain by a wandering man of Cathay, perchance hath matter of moment, and may even be worthy of your skill in strange tongues."

And with that he handed the parchment to the magician. The master took it and held it low near the candle. "Ting," he said. "Ting." Then was silent and shook his head.

So the first syllable was "Ting." All the rest were nonsense that Ramon Alonzo had written in levity. More than that one syllable he durst not write, lest the Master should know that he was seeking his spell. There remained two more; and these he would get in the same manner hereafter, when the Master's suspicions should have had time to sleep. For this he bided his time. But he thought within a week to have the key of the shadow-box.

"I know not what language it be," said the Master.

"No?" said Ramon Alonzo.

"None of Earth," said the Master.

And the young man took back the parchment, apologizing for troubling the Master's learning. All had been as he had planned; and he went then to the dingy nook below the wooden stairs to share his high hopes with the charwoman. And there he found her among her brooms and pails, about to lie down for the night on her heap of straw. Her eyes flashed a welcome to him. And at once he said: "I have the first syllable of the spell."

Then thought overcast her face, and a little slowly her old mind turned to the future and tried to find all it would mean if he came by all three syllables. And while youth, under those old stairs, was swiftly building hopes on the roof of hopes, age was finding objections.

"How will you find the others?" she asked.

"The same way," he said, and told her how he had carried out his plan.

"He will suspect," she said.

"He does not yet," said he.

And she shook her head as she thought of old wiles of the Master.

"Has he taken back the false shadow he made?" she asked.

"I have not yet asked him," the young man said, "but he will."

"If he does not," she said, "the false one will show whenever your own true shadow dwindles at noon."

But these objections he had not come to hear in the triumphant moments that followed on his success. He had thought that his own high hopes would have driven away her melancholy, but now it was saddening him.

"You shall have your own shadow back," he said, "and shall wear it in Aragona."

That was his final attempt to cheer the old woman. Then he left while he still could hope.

He went to his spidery room in the lonely tower and

there lay down to sleep, but plans came to that mouldering bed instead of dreams, and far on into the night he plotted the rescue of shadows. How many a man through hours of silent darkness has laid his lonely plans for things more insubstantial.

Plans of caution and plans of impatience came to Ramon Alonzo that night; and by the early hours he blended them, and decided to wait three days before asking the Master to read another script; and he satisfied his impatience, so far as it could be satisfied, by planning to go the next day into the wood to bring back another parchment, with a tale, when the time came, of a meeting with one from Cathay. And a certain radiance in the youthful mind decked the plan with glittering prospects of success. Then Ramon Alonzo slept.

Descending a little late on the next morning the young man found the food awaiting him that the magician never failed to supply. He ate, then went to the room that was sacred to magic. And there was the Master seated before his lectern considering things beyond the concern of man.

"Would you learn more of the making of gold?" he said.

"No," said Ramon Alonzo.

A thin streak of joy passed through the Master's mind. For it was the established duty of all the masters, more especially of those that were as glorious as he, however far they might fare down the ages, surviving the human span, to secure a pupil to whom when he might be worthy the ancient secrets should be revealed at last: so should the wisdom that had been brought so far, by caravans that had all crumbled away and were long since dust blowing over desolate lands, pass on to centuries that would surely need it. And he had thought that Ramon Alonzo might after years of toil, and loneliness, and study, and abnegation, be fit one day far hence for the dreadful initiation. But if he persisted with his uncouth interest in so trivial a matter as gold, then he was not the man. Therefore the Master's mind was briefly lit by a joy when he heard his pupil renouncing this light pursuit; and then his thoughts were afar again with those things that lie beyond the concern of man. From these he was brought back by the young man speaking again.

"Master," said Ramon Alonzo, "I would fain go to the wood, and walk there awhile before I study again."

"As you will," said the Master, and returned to the contemplation of the curious way of a star, which had not as yet been seen by any mortal watcher.

Again those contemplations were interrupted. "Master," said Ramon Alonzo, "I thank you for that shadow that you designed for me; and having no longer any need of it, I pray you to take it back."

However old he was, however far were his thoughts beyond the orbit of Earth, he was not to be wholly duped by that young mind. Doubtless he knew not Ramon Alonzo's plan; yet the stir of a fetter upon a floor of stone may betray the hope of a slave to escape his prison, and Ramon Alonzo's wish to be rid of that shadow showed that something was afoot which if left unchecked might rob the magical Art of a chosen pupil. Therefore, calling back his thoughts from beyond the path of the comet, across all the regions known to the human imagination, he replied to Ramon Alonzo, saying: "We that follow the Art, and that imitate so far as we are able the examples of the gods, do not take back our gifts."

No protestations moved him; and Ramon Alonzo, seeing at last that by every word he said he was disclosing more and more clearly the existence of a plan, turned away silent at last and went into the wood.

CHAPTER XXI

White Magic Comes to the Wood

Through the wood to which Ramon Alonzo had gone with his plans he walked disconsolate. What would he do when all his plans had succeeded and he had got back his shadow, if this sinister thing of gloom was to show at his heels whenever his human shadow should shrink in the noonday sun? And his plans had seemed so sure.

Yet he was pledged to the knightly quest of the charwoman's shadow, whatever embarrassments might befall his own, and from this the laws of chivalry did not allow him to swerve. And the more that she was an ancient and withered crone, the more he knew that he must be true to his pledge, for she had no other knight; no sword would stir for her into the light but his. But he walked disconsolate because of his own redundance of shadows, which he foresaw to the end of his days.

It seems but a little thing to have two shadows, too slight a cloud to darken the gaiety of any mood of youth; how often on glittering evenings has a man or a maiden danced, happy below the splendour of arrayed chandeliers, and followed by scores of shadows? But Ramon Alonzo had learned, as those only learn who have ever lost their shadow, that side by side with great things and with trivial, there are deviations that are outside human pity; and this, the most trivial of them all, any unusual shape of a shadow, was no more tolerated than horns and tail. So absurd a prejudice cannot be credited unless it has been experienced.

He came in his melancholy walk to the mossy roots of an oak; and there he sat him down, and leaning back against the bole of the tree took out from a wallet the parchment and pen and ink he had brought and began to write supposed script of heathen lands, and amongst it the second syllable of the spell, which should shape for him two-thirds of the key of the shadow-box.

Hardly had he written that one Cathayan syllable, and added a few fantastic shapes of his own, when he heard a rustling a little way off in the wood. He sat upon the moss and listened: it grew to a pattering, a sound as of small feet scurrying over leaves, pushing through bracken, leaping rocks and dead branches, in a hurry that seemed to have suddenly come to the wood, and was stirring bramble and briar before him and far on his left and right. And it was coming nearer. Then Ramon Alonzo heard shrill little squeaks above the sound of the scurrying; and all at once an imp came bounding by, and two more and then another. Then the snap of a twig and a rustle drew his attention upon his other side, and six more were running past him; and soon he saw a line of imps fleeing desperately through the wood, not troubling to keep out of sight of him on the far side of trees going by, some passing barely out of reach of his hand. He saw their small round bodies bobbing by, then heard them brush through the bracken into the distance, and not for a moment did one of them cease to scurry. They were jabbering to each other as they went, evidently in great perturbation. And then a gnome came by, carrying a bundle, an old fellow three times as large as an imp and wearing clothes of a sort, especially a hat. And he was clearly just as frightened as the imps, though he could not go so fast. Ramon Alonzo saw that there must be some great trouble that was vexing magical things; and, since gnomes speak the language of men, and will answer if spoken to gently, he raised his hat, and asked of the gnome his name. The gnome did not stop his hasty shuffle a moment as he answered "Alaraba," and grabbed the rim of his hat but forgot to doff it.

"What is the trouble, Alaraba?" said Ramon Alonzo.

"White magic. Run!" said the gnome, and shuffled on eagerly. More than this he did not say, nor thought more necessary, for he had uttered the one thing that magical folk dread most.

A few more things ran by that haunt woods that are subject to magic, one or two elves and their like; then a deep hush came on the wood, for everything had fled. Ramon Alonzo wondering, and listening quiet in the hush, heard after a while shod hooves, coming from that direction from which everything had fled. Then he heard branches brushing by, far noisier than the soft scurrying of the flight of the magical things, but leisurely and calmly. This was nothing that fled: this then was the white magic. The hooves drew nearer, and the brushing of large branches. Then a mule's face came through the foliage, and, bending low to avoid the bough of an oak tree, there appeared Father Joseph.

His face was very red and very moist, for riding through a wood is no joyous pastime. He did not look a shape to have driven to terror all magical things that dwelt in the dark of the wood.

"Good morrow," said Father Joseph.

"Good morrow, Father," replied Ramon Alonzo, rising up from his mossy seat and doffing his hat. Then Father Joseph turned awhile to the business of clambering out of the saddle, after which he took his mule by the bridle and walked up to Ramon Alonzo.

"What brings you to the wood?" said Ramon Alonzo uneasily, for every dealing with magic leaves its trace on the conscience.

Father Joseph beamed towards him with his red face. "I came to see you," he said.

Again Ramon Alonzo doffed his hat. "And what brought you to me?" he said.

"Peril of your soul," said Father Joseph jovially.

Ramon Alonzo was silent awhile. "Have I imperilled it?" he asked lamely.

"Have you had no dealings with the Black Art?" smiled Father Joseph.

"None to risk my salvation," said the young man.

"Let us see," said Father Joseph.

Thereupon he made the sign of the Cross before Ramon Alonzo. At which, though Ramon Alonzo did not see it, for his face was towards the sun, the false shadow fell off from his heels. Then Father Joseph took a bottle of holy water, a hollowed rock-crystal that hung on a small silver chain from his belt, and cast the holy water upon the moss round Ramon Alonzo's heels. And the false shadow lying upon the moss got up and ran away. Ramon Alonzo saw it rush over a sunny clearing and lose itself amongst great true shadows of trees.

"Gone!" he exclaimed.

"Yes," said Father Joseph.

Thus passed from the young man's sight, and was lost for ever, a shadow false, growthless, and magical, which none the less was all the shadow he had. A little while ago he had longed for this very thing, and had grown despondent with longing, but a new feeling came to him now as he stood there perfectly shadowless.

"What shall I do?" he said wistfully.

"Get back your own true shadow," said Father Joseph.

"But how if I cannot?" replied Ramon Alonzo.

"At all costs get back your shadow," said the priest.

"Is it so urgent as that?" asked Ramon Alonzo.

Then the benign red face of Father Joseph became graver than he had ever seen it yet, like strange changes that sometimes come suddenly at evening over the sun, and he said in most earnest tones: "On Earth the shadow is led hither and thither, wherever he will, by the man; but hereafter it is far otherwise, and wherever his shadow goes, alas, he must follow; which is but just, since in all their sojourn here never once doth the shadow lead, never once the man follow."

"And what of the shadow that has gone through the wood?" asked Ramon Alonzo, awed by the priest's tones.

"Damned irretrievably," said Father Joseph. "And if a man died with such a thing at his heels, it leads him violently to its own place. Four angels could not drag him from it."

Ramon Alonzo had held his breath, but breathed again when he heard that death with the thing at his heels was needed for its last triumph.

"It is gone from my heels now," he said cheerily.

"Aye, and be thankful," said Father Joseph. "But wait! Where is your true shadow?"

"In a box," the young man admitted.

"Such shadows darken nor grass nor flower in all the lawns of Heaven."

"Cannot they come there?" said Ramon Alonzo.

Said the priest: "They know not salvation."

"And I?" asked Ramon Alonzo.

"I have told you."

"Can a mere shadow take me?"

"They are of more account than man in the Kingdom of Shadows."

"Can one not struggle against them?" said Ramon Alonzo.

"Their power is irresistible," said the priest, "as the power of the body over the shadow is irresistible here."

"Alas," said Ramon Alonzo.

"Can you not recover it?" asked Father Joseph.

"I will try," said Ramon Alonzo.

Father Joseph smiled. He had come for no other purpose than to give this wholesome advice. And now he heavily clambered back to his saddle.

Ramon Alonzo doffed his hat and gravely said farewell, pondering all the while on the key he was making that should open the shadow-box and free his soul from the grip of a doomed shadow. But how if the magician would not read again for him? How if he did not mutter again as he saw the Cathayan syllable? In the anxiety that these queries caused him he hurried back to his mossy seat below the bole of the oak, and hastened to write that sentence in which, like a curious jewel, the crystal of some rare element, he set the second syllable of the spell. And however fantastic he tried to make the letters that he invented, that Cathayan shape still loomed from amongst the rest the most exotic, and even—as he thought—the most dreadful, upon that parchment. With this he hurried back to the house in the wood.

CHAPTER XXII

Ramon Alonzo Crosses a Sword With Magic

Shadowless, Ramon Alonzo went through the wood, as miserable in every glade and every shaft of sunlight as a man that crept through a city after being robbed of his raiment would feel whenever he came to a busy street. Shadowless he entered the house.

Now was a time for caution; his shadow gone, his eternal soul in danger, now was the time to watch the magician warily till an hour might come that should be favourable to a request. But every circumstance that should have urged delay drove the youth onward impetuously. How if he should die that night, and the doomed shadow get a throttle-grip immediately on his soul and drag it down to Hell! He durst not wait. He must win back that shadow.

And even as he thought of the daily pains of Hell, which are far beyond the imagination of such as Ramon Alonzo, but he had been well instructed in these by good men; even as he thought of the round of pains and terrors, he remembered with chivalrous faith the charwoman's shadow.

He hastened along the corridors; the old woman that had been Anemone, at work by her pail, saw him go by and noticed that he was running: he came to the door of the room that was sacred to magic. He entered; there had been no spell on the door of late, so that the pupil might come to the room for work; he came breathless before the magician. That learned man was sitting at his lectern alone with his own thoughts, that were beyond our needs or concern: he raised his head and looked at Ramon Alonzo.

"Master," said Ramon Alonzo, "a script that I had from a man in the wood. Strange words. I pray you read them."

In the look that the Master gave him he saw he had failed.

Nonetheless he spoke again all the more earnestly. "I pray you, Master," he said.

Still that look. And then the magician slowly shook his head; and Ramon Alonzo knew that hope was over.

"Give me my shadow," he blurted out then.

"No," said the magician.

"Why not?" shouted Ramon Alonzo.

"It is my fee."

"I have learned nothing for your fee."

"You have learned from me," said the Master, "the manner of compounding a love-potion."

"I made it," said Ramon Alonzo, "and a man drank it."

"He will love fiercely," the magician said.

"It made him most monstrous sick," said Ramon Alonzo.

"Ah," said the magician.

"Give me back my shadow," Ramon Alonzo repeated.

"I have taught you other learning for my fee, rare learning come from of old."

"You have not taught me the making of gold," said the youth.

163

"I have taught you a rarer wisdom, a more secret thing."

"What?" said Ramon Alonzo.

The magician paused, and in a graver voice he said: "The oneness of matter."

"It is naught to me," said the other.

"It is a most rare learning," the Master answered. "Few know that there is but one element with a hundred manifestations. Few knew it of old. And few have handed this rare knowledge down. It is worth incomparably more than my fee."

"It is naught to me," repeated Ramon Alonzo. "Give back my shadow."

"No," said the magician, "for you cannot give back this rare, this incomparable knowledge. Neither shall I give back my fee."

"The shadow was worthless: it would not grow. And now it has run away."

"Ah," said the magician.

For the last time Ramon Alonzo blurted out his useless request: "Give me back my shadow."

And the magician answered: "I keep my just fee."

And Ramon Alonzo turned his face toward damnation, yet remembered his knightly quest. "Then only give me the charwoman's shadow," he said.

"She has had years for it," said the Master.

"Such years!" exclaimed Ramon Alonzo.

"They were many," replied the magician.

"Give up her shadow," said menacingly Ramon Alonzo.

"No," said the magician.

And on that No the young man's sword was out and its point was before the face of the magician. He did not move his gaze from Ramon Alonzo or from that glittering point, but leaned his right arm out behind him, the hand feeling

164

downwards, and slightly bending his head as his arm went back. So the Master's hand came to the lid of a box on the floor and felt the rim and opened it and went in, and gripped what lay within all in an instant.

Then, flaming before the eyes of Ramon Alonzo, appeared a flash of lightning fixed to a resinous hilt, that dark and rounded lay gripped in the Master's hand. The flash was little longer than Ramon Alonzo's sword, and more jaggedly crooked, and was rather red than yellow, as though it had slowly cooled while it lay in the box.

At once the two men engaged, at first across the lectern, then working wide of it as they fought. Young Ramon Alonzo had a pretty style with the sword, and the skill of his antagonist was nothing magical, for his years had been given to other studies than those of thrusting and parrying; yet his weapon was magical, and thrilled up the steel the moment it touched the rapier, jarring the young man's arm as far as the shoulder, shaking his elbow and nearly wrenching his wrist. And every time that either of them parried the young man felt that jar and shock jolting along his right arm. So great a blow might have cast his sword from his hand had it been delivered by an earthly weapon, but that lightning-flash with which the magician fought had the curious effect of making Ramon Alonzo's fingers grip tighter whenever he felt the shock in his arm. Had it not been for this he was lost. And even though he kept his sword in his hand he had hard work to parry, for the magician thrust rapidly at him. Soon his arm was growing numb, and he attacked vehemently then, so as to end it while he still had strength in his arm; but the magician parried each thrust and, once returning a lunge of Ramon Alonzo's, brought the weapon so near his face that it singed his hair. And after that the magician beat his mortal antagonist backwards, dazzled and numbed but still fighting. It became clear that had that Master given his days to the sword and studied all the mysteries of the rapier he had been a notable hand at it. None of the young man's thrusts went home; and suddenly a thrust of the magician, partially parried, slipped over the earthly hilt and along the mortal arm, searing the flesh and setting fire to cloth, so that Ramon Alonzo fought a few strokes with a flaming sleeve, till he patted it out with his left hand and still fought on. And now he was near the door and the Master pressing him still, a dark lithe shape lit up by the flash of his eyes, in a gloomy room crossed and re-crossed by the glare of the lightning. A sudden rally Ramon Alonzo made from the lintel, but was beaten back, and again his arm was seared, and tumbling more than retreat-ing he reeled back through the door.

"Cross no swords with magic," said the magician warn-ingly, with his strange sword in the doorway; but he came no further, and Ramon Alonzo was left alone with despair, while the Master returned to the gloom of the room that was sacred to magic, and to occupations that are beyond our knowledge.

Ramon Alonzo stayed awhile by the door, which still opened to the gloom of the magical room, his sword in his shaken hand, and not till he saw that his enemy did not deign to follow did he turn slowly away. But as soon as the thrill of the risk of death was gone, new troubles and even terrors overtook him. On Earth he had lost his shadow and lost a fight; hereafter his salvation. He was defenceless in this sinister house, for his sword had failed him, and im-petuously he had cast his careful and patient plans away. He believed that none could advise him; he saw, as men often do in such times of despondency, nothing between him and everlasting damnation. He would not even pray, counting himself already among the damned, unto whom prayer is forbidden. He heard the charwoman late at her work in a corridor, but moved away from her, being in no mood to speak. But she saw him and came after him, and, seeing all at once the need that he had of comfort, she brought it him, though he would have none of it, so that she had to give comfort without his knowledge.

He did not tell her that his false shadow was gone, and would not tell her that the magician had beaten him, nor that the shadow-box was locked for ever, and his soul involved in the doom of his true shadow; but he said, "All is lost." And this he repeated often, whenever he thought she was trying to give him comfort.

"But you have the first syllable of the spell," she said.

Little had this comforted her when first he had told her, but now that he needed comfort she said it as earnestly as though by this one syllable alone the long box could be opened.

"All is lost," he repeated.

"The first syllable is Ting," she said.

"All is lost," said Ramon Alonzo.

"The next might be Tong or Tang," said the old woman. Idle enough such a remark, unlikely to be true, light words on which to build a hope of escape from Hell; Ramon Alonzo did not even answer them; and yet they started a thought in the young man's mind that later led to a plan, out of which he built a hope, as slender as that last bridge that the Moslem crosses, but the hope seemed to lead to salvation.

CHAPTER XXIII

The Plan of Ramon Alonzo

When the charwoman found that the despair of Ramon Alonzo was so vigorous that she could bring him no comfort then, she went back to the dismal haunt of her brooms and pans, while he went lurking down the passages to watch for the egress of the magician, bent only on clutching the shadow-box, without any thought or plan how to rescue the shadows within it. He found his sword was still gripped in his hand and, looking at it, even in that dim light, he saw that its glitter was gone and all the steel gone grey from its meeting with magic. A long while he waited. And, shadowless there amongst so many shadows, he envied once more the common inanimate things that had their simple shadows and excited no man's wonder. The magician lingered in his gloomy room, till Ramon Alonzo wondered what dreadful plan he was working out against him for having drawn sword in the room that was sacred to magic. But already he had forgotten Ramon Alonzo and was brooding on problems beyond the young man's guesses. That he had fought to protect his shadows was no more to him than it is to a master chess-player that he has locked the door of his room, when he goes to study alone the mysteries of the Ruy Lopez. Fight and antagonist were soon forgot, and he was following intricate orbits of unknown moons, a lonely imagination.

From such studies he rose late, and Ramon Alonzo saw his dark shape loom through the doorway when the light of evening was far gone from the corridors. To his joy he saw that the door had been left wide open, and before the magician's steps had died wholly away the young man rushed into the room that was sacred to magic and had his hands on the shadow-box. First he put his sword's point to the crack between box and lid, then he smote the box with the edge of it. But not thus easily are souls won from damnation. The open door would have hinted to any mind that was calmer that there was something about that box that was not to be opened by the first earthly implement. The gap between lid and box was narrower than the gap between one granite slab and the next in the temple beside the Sphinx, narrower than the line between night and day; the delicate point of the rapier looked gross beside it. And as for the material of the box, it was not of wood, which the young man had thought to shatter, but some element that cared for the edge of steel no more than steel itself cares for the edge or point of a thin feather. He picked at the padlock then; and something about the padlock's glittering hardness brought him to calmer ways, and taught him that, though his soul was in peril of loss, yet unreasoning haste would help him no better in this than it would in any trifle of daily things.

He put the shadow-box slowly back in its place and sheathed his sword, from which lustre and temper and ring seemed all to have gone, and walked thoughtfully thence and came to the stairs of stone, and ascended them and saw his spidery bed. There he lay down for such a night as men have who see doom close. Though the doom be only earthly they plan and plan, and mix up their plans with hopes, and then again they mix them with despairs, till all over the web of reason that makes their plans come curious patterns of the despairs and hopes; and least of all the weaver knows which is which. And the stars go slowly gliding by, and the gradual affairs of Earth; and the plans race on and on. And if the doom be earthly, often towards dawn fatigue overtakes their plans and they sleep when the birds sing. But Ramon Alonzo did not dare to rest from his whirl of plans, and did not sleep till he saw clear reason shine faint through his hopes and despairs, and then it was broad morning.

That ray of reason that shone at last on his plans came from that remark of the charwoman that she made in her feeble efforts to bring him comfort: "It might be Tong or Tang." Some time between dawn and midnight these words had come back to him in all their absurdity. Of the myriad sounds that might form a syllable in an utterly unknown tongue, how would it be possible thus lightly to guess the right one? "Tong or Tang": the suggestion was ludicrous. And it could not be Tong or Tang in any case, for the second syllable of the spell was far too unlike the first for the difference to be in no more than the change of a vowel. What might it be? He had much of the night before him, with all its wide spaces for fears and lost hopes to roam in: he had ample leisure in which to wonder what was the second syllable. But not until light began to creep through the wood did he order his wonder and guesses into a plan.

His plan was this: the number of possible syllables was

limited; he knew the first syllable, he would suppose the last to be "ab," and he would say the spell over and over again to the shadow-box varying only the second syllable. When every possible sound had been tried for that he would change the last syllable to "bab," and try again. Then to "bac," then "bad," then "baf," and every time that he changed the last syllable, going through all the sounds that could possibly form the second. He would work through all the hours of day and night in which the magician was away from his room. And one day years hence he would hit on the three syllables and see the shadow-box open before he died. He calculated it might take forty years.

That he would hold on to the end, crouching upon the gloomy floor murmuring three syllables to the padlock, he did not doubt. Sooner or later a man might have stopped, saying, "Is it worth it?" if the box had held the whole wealth of the Indies; but Ramon Alonzo would work for his soul's salvation. And all the while he remembered the knightly quest to which he had pledged his chivalry. Morning shone wide on the wood and he fell asleep.

When Ramon Alonzo woke his plan was as clear in his mind as though he had pondered it further during his sleep. It was then late in the morning. He went to the charwoman, following the sound of her pail, and putting aside the old woman's efforts to comfort him obtained from her carefully the hours at which the magician left his room, the result of all her experience. Often before he had discussed plans and hopes with her, but not now, for he based upon this plan all the hope that he had in time or eternity, and would discuss it with none. Thence he went straight to the room that was sacred to magic, and offered his sword, hilt foremost to the magician. The magician bade him keep it, for, whatever terrors vexed him from beyond the path of the comet, he had no fear of any earthly sword. Neither man desired to continue their quarrel, the youth because he saw that his folly already had brought his soul to the very brink of Hell, and he regretted his haste, the magician because his need of a pupil, upon whom to unburden himself of some of the wisdom he had carried alone down the ages, was a greater need than Ramon Alonzo knew. So that the tensity between them passed; and the magician turned his mind to the obligation, that is laid upon all magicians, of handing on to a pupil the lore that has come to them from the Dread Masters; for so the magicians of old are known by all that follow the Art; thus is there magic even to this day. Ramon Alonzo meanwhile was only planning and waiting to rob the box within which the magician enslaved his shadows. He knew not when the day would come on which he would rob the box: it might be years hence; he might be grey when he did it, but all his fervour and patience were centred on this. His scheme may seem little better than the Black Art; but he had been taught from childhood that such crafty ways were justified in cases that touched the safety of the soul, nor did he hold that the Master had earned his fee. His whole attention lost in the plans he was making, arranging in countless formulæ a legion of possible syllables, he scarcely heard the suave voice of the Master speaking across the gloom to him.

"What learning would you have of me?"

Back came his thoughts from a far imagined year, in which with a sudden spell that was right at last he should free his shadow from that eternal doom that ownerless shadows share with the souls of those who were once their masters; back came his thoughts as alert as though they had wandered never an hour away from that very morning.

"I would learn the making of some more durable thing," said Ramon Alonzo, "than gold."

And the Master smiled thereat, as Ramon Alonzo had hoped.

"We shall therefore study," the Master said, "the making of Persian spells, which, more than any other inscription of magic, charm spirits whose courses are not within this sphere; and thus they shall be remembered after Earth."

He rose and placed upon the lectern a tome in a leather binding as rough and black as a saddle on an old battlefield, written by one of the Magi in his old age before the fall of Sidon.

"If speech would be had by the folk of Earth with those that dwell not here, and spell be sought that shall compel their answer, it is in this book," said the Master.

Then began the teaching of heathen script, with its dots and curious flourishes, the pronouncing of alien vowels, and strange intonations, and all that labour that thoughts must undergo to bring up wisdom out of a former age, which is no lighter than the toil miners who dig up bygone forests from out of the past of the Earth. And all the time that Ramon Alonzo learned, his attention was fixed upon the approach of that hour when the magician would leave his room that was sacred to magic and sail away a dark shape down the corridor, and he should have leisure at last to attend to his soul's salvation. And that hour came so slowly that in one of those lingering moments the fear came to Ramon Alonzo that time was done and eternity was begun and his doom was to learn heathen spells in the gloom for ever and ever, while the blessed sat in the sunlight singing in Spanish. And this fear passed, giving way to one more terrible, that told him far worse awaited him than this, unless he could rescue his shadow from the doom it must share with his soul.

The hour came at last when, with an earnest reminder of the way of a heathen vowel, the magician arose and went bat-like out of the room. For many moments Ramon Alonzo sat motionless, listening to fading echoes from the feet of that master of shadows; then he was down by the shadow-box eagerly uttering a spell. Not a flicker made the padlock. Rapidly he uttered another, and then another, and with a kind of sing-song intoned spell after spell in the gloom and dust of the floor, bending above the shadow-box. The first syllable was always Ting, which he knew to be right; the last was always Ab, which was only an assumption that he meant to vary slowly through weary years; the second syllable he changed every time. The thought of the years that he should spend in that room murmuring spells to the box did not appal him, for he knew that the relation of all time to eternity is as a drop to the sea: he only feared that those years might be too few. Close to him lay the box that held the magician's weapon, the old flash of lightning. It had neither padlock nor keyhole and, when he tried to raise the lid, it seemed to be shut for ever: by what magic it opened he knew not. He rightly reflected that the magician, having gone from the room without it, had other and probably more terrible weapons. He turned again to his monotonous work.

Towards evening the magician came back again; and Ramon Alonzo ceased his lonely mutterings, and soon was learning again old Persian lore, for the plan was growing in the Master's mind to make of him a magician. Had he studied with such a master, patiently following that lore whose splendours have made many forget salvation, he could have had a name that would have resounded through Wizardry, and hereafter have had great honour among the damned. Of this honour the magician had spoken once, when Ramon Alonzo had wonderingly enquired of the present state of that illustrious professor who had held the Chair of Magic at Saragossa. "He walks through Hell," said the magician, "flaming, an object of awe and reverent veneration, while all abase themselves as he goes by, their faces low in the cinders. He is, as many have told me, an apparition of glory, and amongst the first of all the splendours of Hell."

From such a fame Ramon Alonzo now willfully turned away. Such choices have often to be made.

Whenever the Master blamed his inattention he apologized gracefully and pretended diligence, but his heart was far from Persia, and never a spell he learned that would have hailed passing spirits and given him news unbiased by the narrower views of Earth. And thus he lost what he lost, and gained what he gained.

And at last night came and the magician left him; and, rising as though he too would go, he tarried in the room and joyfully looked to have the long night alone with his work. He had no light but the gleam of a sickle moon, for he did not dare to burn the magician's taper, lest its shortening should show how late he had been at work; and the young moon soon sank. He had forgotten food and even water, and sleep seemed unnecessary and impossible to him. He needed no light except to watch the padlock; and for this purpose he laid a finger upon it all night long, to feel if it moved for any spell that he said. Owls going afield for their nocturnal hunt saw Ramon Alonzo bent over the box, and saw him again as they returned in the chill; bands of moths to whose glowing eyes the night is luminous saw his shape in the corner, and with other hours of the night came other moths of wholly different tribes—they saw the same shape there; mice that at first were terrified at the sound of the human voice grew used to its long monotony, and ran all round the motionless crouching figure; stars that he knew not saw him kneeling there.

And then, as a greyness paled the night and made all hopes seem groundless and his long labour absurd, there came a sudden quiver into the padlock just as he uttered a spell; he felt it vibrating his finger-tips. He had said thousands of spells that night, and for none had the padlock moved; and now it had quivered, but it did not open. Hopes had shot through his mind in that moment of quivering, singing to him of salvation, only to fall like dead birds. He said the same spell again: again the padlock quivered. Yet it remained shut. Ramon Alonzo sat back on his heels and wondered. Then he said it again, and over and over; and always the same thing happened. By dim grey light that came in he now saw the padlock, and no movement in it could be perceived by the eye, but always he felt the quiver along his finger-tip whenever he said that spell. Somehow it increased his despair, for he believed that the spell he was using was the correct one and, for some reason he could not guess, would do no more when uttered by him than to make that faint vibration. Again and again he repeated it, and always the same thing happened. The spell was Ting Yung Ab.

He would not leave it to continue his formula, because no other spell he had used had moved the padlock at all; so he went on hopelessly repeating it while the dawn grew wider and chillier, and more and more objects appeared out of the dark with their shadows; and their shapes seemed to bring him back to his shadowless situation, and all these material things seemed to be triumphing over him one by one, like an army of victors marching by one of its prisoners. Amongst these fancies of despair he noticed at last that the quivering of the padlock occurred at one part of the spell he uttered, and not quite at the end of it. It occurred at the word Yung. He said the spell slowly then to make sure of this, for hitherto he had spoken rapidly. And sure enough, just as he said the word Yung, the padlock always quivered, and was quiet again as he said the word Ab.

A hope came to Ramon Alonzo, glorious and sudden as sunrise, but he would not acknowledge it in that chill hour, burdened by his despairs; yet he planned a change in his formula and went to bed and slept. And when he awoke in the broad and brilliant day the hope was still with him, and it had grown since dawn.

CHAPTER XXIV

Ramon Alonzo Dances With His Shadow

Ramon Alonzo descended, ate hungrily, and hastened to the room that was sacred to magic; and there was the Master in his usual place. There was reproach in the Master's eye for the young man's lateness, but words he did not waste, reserving them for that instruction in heathen spells which he immediately commenced. Every day the Master's intention was growing clearer and the young man guessed it now: *his* was to be a name as revered, as dreaded, as his who had held the Chair of Magic at Saragossa; *his* wisdom, *his* loneliness, *his* aloofness, were to be as those of the dweller in the sombre house in the wood; his should be power at which the just should shudder; and mothers that could not call their children from play in the long evenings when they should be in bed would in the last resort shout Ramon Alonzo to them. Against this terrible fame the young man's blood cried out, and the birds aided him, calling out of the wood, and the sunlight seemed on his side and against magic. Yesterday he had dared to make no protest against

178

anything the Master might teach him, for he had seen in years of obsequiousness his only chance of ever recovering his shadow; but a new hope strengthened him now, and he asked a question that was in itself a protest. The Master was teaching him slowly a spell of terrible potency when Ramon Alonzo said: "Master, what chances of salvation hath a man that shall make use of this spell?"

"Salvation! Salvation!" said the Master. "A thing common to countless millions. The ordinary experience, hereafter, of half the human race. Is this to be put against knowledge of the hour of the return of the comet, against speech from these small fields, with spirits that wander from world to world, against strange tongues, runes and enchantments, and knowledge of ancient histories and visions of future wars; is this to be put against a hold upon the course of a star? Rather would I flame beside the Count of the Mountain, who held the Chair of Magic at Saragossa, and burn in that bright splendour that torments but cannot subdue him, than share with the ignorant populace any bliss that is common to vulgar righteousness. Aye, and upon the sulphur that he treads, damned if you will but held in reverence, kings have not hesitated to abase themselves in honour of his fame that resounds beyond time and far beyond earthly boundaries."

Ramon Alonzo did not dare to say more: it was as though a student at work in a dingy classroom had claimed that some boyish game for which his own heart was longing was of more importance than the honoured learning that was being taught from the desk. The magician was growing angry; Ramon Alonzo bent his head to learn those Persian spells, but his mind was far from them with his hope and his formula. He learned in silence, while the magician bent to the work of making him his pupil and rendering him worthy of the terrible wisdom that had been brought down through the ages by the labour of the Dread Masters. And at last the black shape of the Master went out of the gloomy room and Ramon Alonzo was all alone with his hope.

His hope was that the first two syllables were right, that the quiver in the padlock was its preparation to open, as the spell thrilled through the brass, till the final syllable "ab" disappointed its expectation. He had therefore to try only once the thousands of possible sounds that might make the last syllable, instead of multiplying them by thousands more and working on till old age. The magician would be gone for some hours, returning again in the afternoon for another weary lesson. Spells guarded everything round Ramon Alonzo in the room that was sacred to magic while the magician was gone; spells, had he known it, could have brought to life one of the crocodiles when he drew his sword against magic, and it would have eaten him had the master not needed a pupil. But Ramon Alonzo cared only for one spell. He was down at once by the shadow-box, and this time all the spells that he tried began with "Ting Yung," while he changed every time the last syllable. Once more, whenever he touched the padlock he felt it quiver as he uttered the second syllable, while it calmed again as it heard the end of the spell. He became more and more certain that he held two-thirds of the secret, and that hours would free his shadow instead of years. Then, giving her shadow back to the poor old charwoman, he would flee from the sinister house, and work in some simpler way for Mirandola's dowry, amongst unlearned folk, and have no more to do with such as should scorn salvation. The work of those hours surpassed in patience the labour of many a scholar studying mathematics, or chess-player analysing position or opening. Yet, when the Master returned again, he had tried little more than the syllables commencing with "b," and the padlock upon the shadow-box was shut as fast as ever.

More weary hours passed with the heathen arts of Persia, Ramon Alonzo thinking all the while of Heaven, as a boy in school thinks of the green fields. I would not convey the dullness of those hours. They passed with the exact speed with which other hours pass, if measured by those movements of the Earth by which time is recorded; but, if spiritual measurements be used, and the hours be marked by the impatience, longing, and weariness felt by Ramon Alonzo, by that measurement they passed slowly. But the impatiences of man have their endings, as each of Earth's revolutions; and night arrived and the magician left. Whither he went Ramon Alonzo knew not—perhaps to sleep, perhaps, he thought, to commune across the gulfs with the damned. Want of sleep and too much work, far from wearying Ramon Alonzo, had lit a fever in his veins that drove him to fierce activity, and he was down by the shadow-box rapidly uttering spells. Small winds and faint sounds went by, and the moths and the owls and the stars; and the mice went round and round. And midnight came, and that solitary shape crouching above the shadow-box had uttered to the padlock all the syllables that begin with "c" or "d." No inspiration came to lighten that labour, but he clung to his formula which was one long monotony, thousands of phrases that all began with Ting Yung. He did not look at the slow changes of night, he scarcely saw the window; and yet black branches slanted against the stars remained a memory for all his years, and the sight of branches and stars whenever he saw it afterwards would always bring to him the weariest thoughts. His mind was peopled with hopes and disappointments as the wood was peopled with little hunters going abroad through the dark; but despair never came that night, for he was determined not to admit despair till the last of the sounds was tried for the third syllable. The stars paled as with illness; with intensest weariness, as it seemed to Ramon Alonzo, the dawn dragged upwards; the voices of the birds jarred on his hearing, made delicate by fatigue; and still he murmured on. To the syllables he had tried he had added now all beginning with "f" and "g." They had gone slower than those beginning with "d," because "d," as he believed, could not be followed by "l," which halved the number of sounds that he had to try. And now came "h" which, as he hoped, could not be followed either by "l" or "r."

Dawn grew wider. Again he felt a hopelessness at the myriad shapes of matter appearing out of the darkness, all of them possessing what he lacked so conspicuously, each master of a shadow and he alone without one. Now the sun had risen but was hidden yet by the trees. And all of a sudden the hasp of the padlock opened. The spell was Ting Yung Han.

Hastily Ramon Alonzo removed the padlock, and cautiously opened the box. It was full of shadows. He closed the box again, as he saw them flutter, and went to the window to stuff his kerchief into a broken pane so that they should not escape; then he returned to the box. Then he opened the lid of the box a little way and took out a shadow in finger and thumb by the heels, as he had seen the magician hold his. This he laid on the floor and put a small jar upon it, which he took down from a shelf, trusting any piece of matter to hold down so delicate a thing as a shadow. Then he took out another and treated it in the same way. Then a third and a fourth. They were shadows of all kinds of folk, men and women, young and old. The red sun peeped in and saw the shadowless man laying out this queer assembly and holding them one by one with little weights. They did not grow as the red sun looked at them, for they were masterless and lost. They lay there grey on the floor, fluttering limply. And then, and then, Ramon Alonzo found his own shadow. He recognized it immediately. He put it to his heels. The shadow ran to them, and the instant that it had fastened there, never again, as Ramon Alonzo swore, to be removed as any fee or for any bribe whatever, it grew long in the early morning. At that moment they danced together as though they had been equal in the sight of matter, both of them ponderable and tangible things, both of them having thickness. And indeed for some while Ramon Alonzo could not feel any of that superiority that matter feels towards shadows; he only felt that there had been restored to him here the proud place that humanity holds amongst solid things, and hereafter salvation: they danced as equals, not as master and shadow. Round and round the floor went Ramon Alonzo dancing, and round and round the walls the shadow pranked behind him. Past every material shape in that room he went rejoicing, knowing that with whatever dull feeling matter has, these shapes had scorned him as being less than them, remembering that he had marked himself their inferior by envying all that had shadows. The fatigue of the night and his dread had fallen away and he danced in sheer joy, and a wildness and fantasy about his leaping shadow seemed to show that it also had a joy of its own. As he watched its silent leapings following his merry steps, he began to understand how a soul might follow a shadow, as here on the solid Earth a shadow followed heels. He danced till a new fatigue overtaking happy muscles, not the fatigue of dread and monotony, began to weight his steps. Then he and his shadow rested. Again he went to the box, and the very next shadow he drew from it was the lithe shadow of a slender girl, with curls that seemed just now shaken by a sudden turn of the head, which showed in profile with young lips slightly parted. There was a grace about this young shadow as though Spring had come all of a sudden to one that had waited, wondering, at dawn while her elders slept. A maiden in Spring. And, as Ramon Alonzo looked long at that delicate profile, his fancies began to hear bird-song and distant sheep-bells, and all happy sounds of lost seasons that had made that wondering look. Who was she, he wondered, that could be so fair? Where was she? What fields lent such beauty? He was a man now, with a shadow. He could face the world. He need envy nothing among material things. He would search all Spain for the girl with the curly shadow. And his thoughts ran on into golden imagined days.

It was some while before he came back from those thoughts and remembered his quest and the promise he gave to the charwoman. He returned then to the shadow-box; but he would not weight down the shadow that had the waving curls, and it floated lightly about the room, while he took more from the box. The sun was not yet up to the tops of the trees, but was shining between the trunks when Ramon Alonzo took out the last of the shadows. There were shadows of two plump old women, there was the sweet curly shadow; all the rest were shadows of men. No shadow was there that could possibly belong to the charwoman.

Before he imprisoned the shadows again in the box he made sure that he should be able to free them again. So he shut the box and put the padlock on, and said the spell to it; and it opened again. He did this two or three times. Then he picked up the shadows again in his finger and thumb, and put them back one by one. Last of all he went up to that slender curly shadow that was wandering free round the room, and it ran away from him and he ran after; but soon he caught it, for it ran no faster than it had learned to run when it ran at the heels of a young girl straying along the fields in Spring. This also he put back into the box, although he wept to do so. His own shadow only he kept. Then he fastened the padlock and hastened away from the room, for there was much to do. He had first to find the charwoman and to tell her of the failure of his quest, and to offer her the protection of his sword wherever she wished to go, if she desired to flee away from that house: this much he was bound to do when he could no longer hope to find the shadow that he had promised to rescue. Next he must return to the room in which the shadow-box lay, before the Master came, and wait in the gloomiest corner, so that the Master should not see that he had robbed the box of his shadow. And then he must part from the Master upon such terms that he could return to his house one happy day, when he had found the girl that had lost the curly shadow. This shadow he meant to rescue and give to her, and so to restore to her her lawful place among material things, and to marry her and forsake magic for ever. But his sword was still in the service of the charwoman, and already he had planned another quest; and he had not yet escaped from that house. Were the magician to see his shadow before he went, or to go to the shadow-box and find it missing, it was unlikely that any of his impetuous plans or golden hopes of youth would ever come to fulfillment. He would perish upon that red flash of lightning, or under some frightful spell, and the Master would have his fee.

He ran to find the charwoman. Morning grew older with every step that he took, and brought the hour nearer when he must meet the magician; he came all out of breath to the nook where the old woman lived with her pails.

"Anemone," he said, "I have opened the shadow-box." There was a sudden catch in her breath. "It is not there," he said.

"Was it the shadow-box?" she asked.

"Yes," he said. "Look. I have found my shadow. But yours, it was not there."

She looked, and more joy came into her face at the sight of his rescued shadow than he had ever seen there before. He told her how his false shadow was lost and how he had found his true one. He told her of the other shadows that he had found in the box, he described the shadows of the two plump old women that could not have belonged to Anemone, he described the young slender shadow a little shyly, saying little at first; but some kind of power the charwoman seemed to have, though she scarcely spoke, made him tell more and more; and soon his love of the shadow with blown curls and slightly parted lips became transparent.

"But your shadow was not there," he said, "and I can never find it now; but if you will flee at once away from this house you shall have my sword to protect you instead of your shadow, to whatever place that you may wish to go."

She pushed some straw together into a heap.

"Sit down," she said.

CHAPTER XXV

The Release of the Shadow

"Long ago," said the charwoman, "a long long while ago, I dwelt in my father's cottage in Aragona. I had naught to do in all those sunny days but to tend his garden, or sing; unless in winter I sometimes fetched pails of water for my mother from the stream if the well in our garden were frozen. I think the days of those summers were sunnier than those we have now, and the Springs were more sudden and joyous; and I remember a glory about the woods in autumn, aye, and a splendour about those winter evenings, that I have not seen, ah me, this many a year. So, having naught else to do, I grew in beautiful seasons and breathed and saw loveliness, and through no merit of mine, but only through borrowing in all idleness of God's munificence through listless years, I grew beautiful. Yes, young man," for some expression must have changed on the youth's face, "charwomen were beautiful once.

"I had not loved, for of those that came sometimes with guitars at twilight, and played them near our garden, none

187

had a splendour fairer than my day-dreams, and they were of Aragona.

"There came a most strange man at evening, when I was seventeen, all down the slope from the wood, walking alone. I remember his red cloak now, and his curious hat and his venerable air. He came to our village on that summer's day at the time that bats were flying. At the edge of our garden he stopped—I saw through my window—and drew a flute or pipe from under his cloak and blew one note upon it. My father came running out at that strange sound, and saw the man and doffed his hat to him, for he had a wonderful air, and asked him what he needed. And the Master said, aye it was he, the crafty magician said that he wished for a char-woman, some girl that would mind the things in his house in the wood. My father should have said there was no such girl in his house. But he talked; and then my mother came out; and then they talked again. I know not how he satisfied them, but he had a wonderful air. There are just men with far less a presence. They were poor and looked for work for me, and gold to him was ever stuff to be given by handfuls uncounted; yet I know not how he satisfied them.

"My mother called to me and told me I was to go away with the señor to work for him in his great house in the wood, and he would pay me beyond my expectations, and soon I should come back to Aragona, a girl with a fine dowry. Aye, he paid me beyond my expectations; but I never came back, I never came back. I tried to once but they would not let me.

"He would not wait. I must pack my bundle at once. So I did as I was bade, and said farewell to my parents, and went away after the stranger through the evening. I turned my head as I went beyond the garden and saw my mother look-ing doubtfully after me; but she did not call me back. I was all sad walking alone after this strange man in the evening, thinking of Aragona. And then without looking round at me he drew out a reed from his cloak and blew another note upon it; and all the world seemed strange, and the evening seemed haunted and wonderful, and I forgot Aragona. I walked after him thrilled with the wonders that that one note seemed to have called from the furthest boundaries of wizardry. They seemed to be lurking just over the ridges of hills and the other side of wild bushes, things come from elfland and fancy to hear what tune he would play. But he played no more. And so he brought me to his house in the wood.

"Ah, I had eyes then not like these, not like dim pools in rain: they could flash, they were like the colour of lakes with the sunlight on them in summer. I had small white teeth, yes I. And I had little golden curls, I loved my curls; God wot it was not this hair. My figure was slender then, and straight and supple. And my face. Young man, it was not these wrinkled hollows!"

Ramon Alonzo stirred uneasily. Who will believe in a beauty he cannot see? Withered infirmity claims pity, and he had given it her to the full. But beauty demands love. Could he give that to a legend of beauty, to an old woman's tale? He felt that silence were best. He could have pitied her more deeply without this sorry claim. Words could not build again a beauty that was gone. He patted her hand a little clumsily, where it lay all veins and hollows upon the straw. "Yes, yes," he said. "All passes. I make no doubt you were fair."

And she saw that she had explained nothing to him.

"It was *then*," she said, with a sudden flash in those old eyes, "*then* that he took my shadow."

Ramon Alonzo knew from that look and that voice that

he was being told a thing of strange import, before he understood anything else. He gazed at the charwoman and she nodded to him, and still he understood nothing. And all of a sudden he shouted, "The beautiful shadow!" She went on nodding her head.

The morning was growing late. At any moment he might appear whom they dreaded. He leaped up and ran to the room that was sacred to magic. Once more he bent over the shadow-box. Once more the spell. The padlock opened again and he found the charwoman's shadow. The rest he left locked in the box, and carried the lovely young shadow gently to the old charwoman.

For all the haste that was urgent he carried the shadow slowly; for friendship and his knightly quest demanded that he should give it to the old woman; and as soon as this was done his love must be over. For he knew well enough that shadow and substance must be alike, and that an old charwoman could never cast the shadow of a lithe and lovely girl. He looked at that glad profile and those curls as he walked, murmuring farewells to them. For he had loved this shadow from the moment he saw it, as he had loved no mortal girl. It was that earliest love at which elders sometimes laugh, prophesying that it will pass. But now, thought Ramon Alonzo, it must pass for ever, taking a glory out of his life and leaving all grey. He did not reason that he had only loved for an hour; he did not reason that his love was given to a mere shadow; he did not reason at all. But a grief as profound as the argument of the wisest of elders was settling on him, and not an argument could have removed its weight.

A little while ago he had planned a future in which he should wander through Spain, seeking always for the girl that had lost that shadow; and now that the girl was gone the future seemed empty.

He came to the dingy haunt of brooms and pans where

the charwoman sat on straw, and stood still and looked long at the shadow.

How long he stood there he knew not. There are loves that are each one the romance of a lifetime. Such a love must illumine the whole of a man's memories and light up all his years. It goes down time like lightning through the air. The length of it in hours is not to be measured. How long he stood there he knew not.

Then he went to the charwoman. "Your shadow," he said.

If consolation had been possible to him, the joy he had brought to the old woman's face might have indeed consoled him.

"Yes," she said, "that is my shadow."

And she spoke all hushed as people sometimes do watching rare sunsets, or about the graves of youthful heroes too long dead for grief.

And then she would have fondled it and patted its curls, but drew back her hand ere she did so, for it would have clung to her and she did not wish to take it there. So they stood there looking at it a while longer as it lay on the young man's arm; and the moments on which their lives depended went wasting away, for the footsteps of the magician tapped faintly in a far corridor: he was about, and they did not hear him.

"You were most lovely once," said Ramon Alonzo.

"Aye," she said smiling, and gazing still at the shadow.

"Take your shadow," he said curtly, after one sigh.

And at that moment she heard the steps of the magician plainly coming towards them.

"He is coming here," she cried.

Ramon Alonzo listened. It was clearly so. And then he remembered his kerchief that he had left in the pane in the room that was sacred to magic. After that they spoke in whispers.

Nearer and nearer came the steps in the corridor; the

magician was between them and the door to the wood. Ramon Alonzo stepped hastily towards the old woman, the shadow outstretched to her. "No, no," she whispered, "he must not see."

"It is dark in this corner," he said, pointing.

"No, no," she said, "we must flee."

They fled down the corridor away from the door to the wood, and the magician came slowly after them. They tried to guess from his footsteps how much he suspected. They wondered how much their flight had increased his suspicions. They wondered what weapon he carried, whether of Earth or Hereafter, whether a blade to sunder mortal flesh or one deadly to shadows. They feared a wound that might end all earthly hopes, or a stroke that might rip their shadows clean away from salvation, leaving their helpless souls to share the doom of their shadows. The house was full of fears.

They ran on, Ramon Alonzo still holding the curly shadow, and heard the magician plodding after them. Did he suspect or know? Had he had time at that early hour to open his shadow-box and examine all his shadows? If so, he knew. But if at that hour he had just entered his room, seen the kerchief and looked for Ramon Alonzo at once, then he only suspected. Yet his suspicions were often as shrewd as mortal calculations. Thoughts like these went through their minds more swiftly than they ran.

When the magical footsteps were now some way behind them the old woman pulled Ramon Alonzo suddenly sideways, and they huddled or fell past two loose planks in the wall to a cranny behind the wainscot. She had known of this place for years. Rats, damp, and wood-worm, and other servants of time, had gradually made it larger. There was just room for the two to hide there. They lay there waiting while the steps came nearer; and all the while Ramon

Alonzo held the shadow, though it fluttered to come to the charwoman. Somehow she stifled her breathing, though she had been nearly gasping; and the steps drew near and passed. That he was looking for them they could not doubt, but they felt as he passed so near that he had not learned as yet of the opening of his shadow-box. For he was muttering questioningly to himself as he went: "Ramon Alonzo? Ramon Alonzo?"

The charwoman held the young man by the wrist, and listened, as she held him, to the footsteps going away.

"Now," she said suddenly.

They rose in cautious silence, though one of the timbers creaked; they left the mouldering nook and tiptoed away; they heard the magician turn and come back down the corridor; and then they were running for the door to the wood.

The magician had quickened his steps, but they reached the door in time, and were out into the wood before they saw him, though they often looked over their shoulders. They ran through the wood not only to avoid his pursuit, but to be as far away as they could before he used his enchantments, for both of them feared that as soon as he found they were gone he would go to his sinister room and take from a spell-locked box some potent weapon of wizardry and loosen its deadly power towards the wood. And they did well to run, though they did not know, as those know who have studied the science of magic, that the power of any spell or enchantment lessen according to the square of the distance.

And the magician never caught them either with weapon or spell, but they ran on safe through the wood; and at the edge of it in the wholesome sunlight, which, more than anything else yet known to science, arrests the passage of spells, the old woman sank onto the grass exhausted.

CHAPTER XXVI

The Wonderful Casting

They felt that they were safe in that honest sunlight. And Ramon Alonzo, sitting near the old crone while she rested, looked longingly at that young and delicate shadow which he had not thought to see for so long as this. He held it still in his hands, but now the time was come to give it up, for his old companion was shadowless, and to this he had pledged her his word. He must give it up to take a wizened shape, for shadow and substance must be alike in outline, as all the world knows. He must give it up and end his love-story that was not three hours old. He would see that profile change; he would see those curls scatter to thin wisps; he would lead the old woman back to her Aragona, and then go forth alone to join the forlorn companionage, that he felt sure there must somewhere be, of men that had loved a shadow. Meanwhile the old woman rested; she could spare him a little longer that shadow on which all his young dreams were builded, dreams that he knew, as youth so seldom knows, would soon come tottering down.

He turned from dark thoughts of his future to think of hers. What would the old thing do, back in a world again that had gone so far without her? Her parents would be dead, who knew how long? None would know her in Aragona. How would she fare there?

He turned to her to make again that offer that he had made once before. "If ever you weary of Aragona," he said.

"Ah, Aragona," she interrupted. "How could one weary of it?"

"If you wish for a warm house," he said, "for light work, for little comforts, I know my father will give you employment."

Again that strange smile that he had seen amongst her old wrinkles when he had offered this before. He had intended to say much of his home, telling of the comfort of it, its quaint old nooks, its pleasant rooms, the mellow air about it; and how a charwoman might saunter there with none to vex her, dusting old tapestries slowly and resting when she would, doing easy work to keep just ahead of the spider, dusting as quietly and leisurely as he spun, till the rays came in all red through the western windows; sitting and watching then the faces of olden heroes reddening to life in the rays, and all the tapestries wakening in the sun's moment of magic. No, he would not have used that word, for she was weary of magic. He would have spoken of the sun's benediction, which truly those rays would have been, on that old face in the evening in the happy quiet of his home. But his words all halted before that smile, and he said no more at all.

"Then I will take you to Aragona," he said after a while.

"As you will," she said.

He did not understand such listless words about her loved Aragona; he did not understand her smile. But she was more rested now; the end was near; she must have back her shadow. He gazed again at the young curly head, the happy lips and slender shape of that sweet shadow; then, looking up, he saw that the end which was near was now. For a man was coming towards them along a track that wound across the hill outside the wood, driving before him a donkey that bore a green heap of merchandise. If Ramon Alonzo waited any longer to fulfil his knightly word the man would see she was shadowless.

He sighed once.

"I pray you stand up," he said.

He stood up himself.

She arose without a word, and stood as he said, a calm, serene over her agitation, as the calm of lakes that freeze amongst the mountains in the midst of winter's violence. Then he carried the shadow to her and kneeled down on the grass near her heels. He turned his back to her as he laid the shadow down, to look his last on the form that he so much loved before it should be a shadow cast by a substance on which time had wrought its worst. He knew that from these last moments there is nothing to be had but sorrow, and that it were better to have turned away towards the charwoman, looking, as it were, time full in the face. Yet he gazed long at the shadow. And now the shadow was to the charwoman's heels. It slanted a few degrees to its left, to be right with the sun; the lines of its clothing fluttered a little. But his eyes were only on the merry head, to see the last of the curls. Still the curls crinkled there; still the lips parted in wonder. He kneeled gazing there silent and motionless, as a prophet might kneel and listen before a revelation, whose words were dying away. And still the shadow had not taken the shape of the old substance that cast it.

Then he heard a soft laugh behind him; and its tones

were akin, if there be any meaning in tones and any speech in mere merriment, to the tones of streams to which Spring has suddenly come, rushing down Alpine valleys, unknown as yet to the violets, and unbound them from months of ice. And the shadow, the young shadow with wondering lips, responded. It was the shadow of one that laughed under swinging curls.

And as he gazed, as lost mariners gaze at sails, he saw the little curls move backwards and forwards, and the parted lips shut. Still he waited for the change that he dreaded; still no change came. And a wonder came on him greater even than his unhappiness. How could this thing be? How could a withered substance cast such a shadow? Again that low laugh.

He looked round then and saw her, saw the form that cast that shadow, saw the young girl he loved; for the shadow was stronger than the magician's gift. That weary immortality was gone; and the ravages of those years that magic had given had all fallen away; wrinkles and lank hair were gone at the touch of the shadow; for, although weaker than all material things, yet, amongst spiritual things and the things that war against them, the shadow, for the sake of its shape and its visibility, is accounted as substance; and it was stronger than magic. She had had magical years for a shadow; now the shadow was back and the evil bargain over, and the work of all those dark years was brushed away at the sudden touch of reality; for the shadow was real and had its rightful place amongst our daily realities, while magic was but the mustering of the powers that are in illusion.

Ramon Alonzo wondered to see substance taking the shape of a shadow, for he had become so accustomed to the withered shape that magical years had fastened upon the charwoman that he thought it her own true shape. But her true shape was laughing gently at his wonder, with blue eyes, in the sun, while golden curls were bobbing with her laughter. One wistful look she took at her fair young shadow, and her laughter ceased as she looked on it; then those blue eyes turned again to Ramon Alonzo, and Anemone smiled again.

"Well?" she said.

"Did you know?" were his first words to her.

"Yes," she answered.

"How?" said he.

"By the long time I have lived with magic," she answered ruefully.

"Can magic come and go like this?" he asked.

"That is the way of it," she said.

And still he could hardly believe what he saw with his eyes.

"The bargain is over," she said, "and my shadow is back."

"But your shadow is casting a body," he said in amazement, "not your body a shadow."

"It was only a shape of illusion, that body," she said.

"But you? Where were you?" he said.

"It was not my true self," she said slowly.

He asked her more of this wonder, but she answered more slowly still, and with confused words and fatigue of mind. She was forgetting.

The dark house, the magician, the evil bargain, the long long corridors, and the peril of soul, were all slipping away towards oblivion, after those lank wisps of hair and the long deep wrinkles. Her efforts to recall them became harder and harder; and soon the flowers, the gleaming grass-blades, the butterflies, or any youthful whim, turned her so easily away from effort that Ramon Alonzo saw he would learn no more from her about the ways of illusion, and perhaps never quite understand the power that shadows held amongst shapeless invisible forces such as magic. And while her memories of magic waned, his own interest in the things of illusion was waning too, for he had found the one true illusion; and in the light of love all other illusions were fading out of his view—aye, and substantial things, for the man and his donkey passed by them, and the high load of green merchandise, and neither Anemone nor Ramon Alonzo saw anyone go by, or any donkey or merchandise, and though they answered the greeting that the man gave to them, they did not know they had answered. But in a haze that was made of golden sunlight and many imagined things, and that moved with them and shut them from what we call the world, they wandered together slowly away from the wood.

CHAPTER XXVII

They Dread that a Witch Has Ridden from the Country Beyond Moon's Rising

As Ramon Alonzo and Anemone wandered away from the wood her memories of pails and old age and the magical house dwindled faster, and she seemed even younger than her face amongst its little curls, and that was the face of a girl of seventeen. Often she glanced at her shadow to see if it was there, prompted by some dark memory like the fears that frighten children, but when she saw it going lightly with her light steps over the grass and small leaves she laughed to see it and forgot the memory. At such moments Ramon Alonzo tried to comfort her for those dark ages that she had known and all those wasted years, telling her that the future and years of his love should repay her; but more and more as they wandered away from the wood he noticed that talk of the past would puzzle her. She would listen attentively as though trying to remember or trying to understand, and then she would suddenly laugh to see a butterfly scared at her shadow, or to see the glint of a flower change as her shadow went over it. Then she would go grave again when she saw the grave face of Ramon Alonzo offering her sympathy for all she had suffered; and, puckering her forehead, she would half remember and half understand until she saw a lizard run in the leaves, or a young goat leaping, then all the memory she had of those dark years would go again. So he spoke only of the present and his love, and of the future and how his love would endure, and how it would be with her still in old age to shield her latest years from any sorrow. To this she listened, though when they spoke of old age it seemed to both of them like the ending of a story often told, and even pleasant to hear, but not wholly true. This defeat of invincible youth on a distant day was no more to them than is the thought of defeat to the men of a great army just fresh from their first victory.

Far into the future the radiance of that day shone for them, from where they walked on the hill-side hand in hand in the morning, till all the years to be seemed to shimmer and glow in the gold of it, as though shafts of that one day's sunlight could flash across all time. And even backwards its splendour seemed to pierce the mist of the past, casting a glow far off even on years that were gone; but the past, to Anemone, lay in Aragona and not in the dark house. Across a gulf of time that she could not measure, gardens and cottages of Aragona now glowed with a brighter light for her because of the radiance of one wonderful morning. They spoke awhile of those gardens and those cottages, Ramon Alonzo's swift fancies racing back through the years from far dreams of the future to hear of them; for all ways that were ever trod by Anemone were to him enchanted paths, because they had brought her at last to him. She told of her early days, of her childhood that should have been yesterday, but that magic had separated from her by a bleak waste of years; and now her memories flitted across those years not knowing how many they were, as the swallows come back to us over leagues of sea, straight to their own eaves. And as she told of that old home of her memories, a cottage-garden at twilight in Aragona, the sky all haunted by the hint of some colour too marvellous to tarry till we can name it, but caught and held in her memory, the flowers shining softly with a faint glow of their own, the voices of children playing who must all long since be dead, the air trembling towards starlight, bells and their mellow echoes, faint notes of a lonely far music—as she told he lifted his gaze for a moment away from her lips, and saw, though dazzled a little by the shining gold of her curls, saw Aragona.

This was not the Aragona of her memories, in which every flower welcomed him to come and walk in her garden, and every soft song called him to share old joys of her childhood: it was the Aragona in which night and day men watched with swords at their sides for the man with the bad shadow. And Ramon Alonzo saw that he must look into the future, to pick difficult paths, that would not be lit by any light shining from day-dreams. Immediately before him lay Aragona; and what after that? Would his father receive Anemone? He thought of her fair young face, her delicate curls, the rippling light of her eyes, her fairy figure, her merry childish ways rejoicing in girlhood, to which she had returned after such wanderings: day-dreams all; his father would not see her as Ramon Alonzo saw. Then he thought of soberer things more reasonably. His father was going to marry Mirandola, with those lightning eyes under that stormy hair, to the neighbour, Señor Gulvarez. If they asked where Anemone came from, she too was a neighbour. If they asked who she was, who was Gulvarez? And if Anemone were unknown, was that not better than to be known as

Gulvarez was known, a gross mean man that had excellent pigs, but not himself excellent? So Ramon Alonzo argued, and I give the theme of his argument, considering it worthy thus to be handed down the ages, not for any intrinsic brilliance in the logic, but because it was remarkable that out of that glittering day-dream, that was lulling him and Anemone from all the cares of the world, he was able to awake to argue at all.

Then he told Anemone of his father's house, and how they would marry there and be happy for ever after, and of the welcome that his father would give her. And in his vision of their future there, long languid days of summer and beautiful springtimes, and October suns huge, red and mysterious through haze, and gorgeous fires in winter and hunted boars brought home, all blended to build one glory. He told of his mother and Mirandola, and Father Joseph and Peter, and the great dog that he loved, who, as he believed, could have killed a boar alone. A little he told her of hunts that he had had, but told not much of the past, because it seemed to him so bleak when compared to their future. Of the future he told in all its magnificence and so came back to his daydreams. Once she questioned him about his father's welcome, but his faith in Gulvarez had grown since first he had thought of him, and Gulvarez presided now over all that situation: his father, he said, would surely welcome her. Yet her question brought him back again to the things that are outside day-dreams. They had come nearer Aragona now, and its walls shone bright at noon, but with none of the light that shines from happy dreams. Now they must plan. Whither their steps? Aragona first, said Anemone. And then the Tower, said Ramon Alonzo: they could be there that evening. But Anemone besought him for some days at Aragona, now that she had come back to it after all that mist of years, that seemed banked up, impenetrable to her memory, although over them all shone clear the roofs of the old Aragona.

"But in what house?" he asked.

She knew not.

"With whom?"

She cared not.

Aragona, Aragona—the memory of it was in her mind like bells, and she besought some days there.

Then he told her how men waited there for the man with the bad shadow, because of what had happened there on the hill at evening. And he drew his sword as they went towards the village. She laid her hand on the arm that held the sword and made him put it up.

"Not now," she said. "We will go in the evening late, when shadows are long. And they shall see that your shadow can grow and is as good a shadow as any Christian man's. Aye, and better; and better. Look at it now on the flowers. Who has a shadow equal to it? And at evening it shall be beautiful, dark and long; and who'll dare speak of it except in envy?"

And this seemed wise to him, for he could not believe that any prejudice against a man on account of a short shadow could remain when he had a long shadow for everyone to see. So he praised Anemone's plan and said they would wait. But prejudices die slowly, as they were to find out that evening.

And on the bright hill-side they waited, spending the shining hours in happy talk. They had neither food nor water; they had fled too swiftly to have brought provisions away from the house in the wood. But it was the time of year when pomegranates ripen, and a grove of these was near them; and the pomegranates were food and drink to them. Sitting amongst the flowers their talk went on all through the afternoon. There is no memory of what they said. The sound just came to them, from the limits of hearing, of bees in a tall lime; swift insects flashed across the yellow sunlight with sudden streaks of silver; butterflies rested near them, all motionless, showing their splendours; a wind sighed up out of Africa to turn the leaves of a tree; children a long way off called across the bright fields to their comrades; the flowers sparkled, and drank the sunlight in; their talk was part of the joy with which Earth greeted the sun.

But when rays slanted and shadows crept afield, and more and more appeared where there had been only sunlight, till multitudes of them were gathered upon the hill, and they seemed to possess the landscape more than the rocks on trees, and Earth seemed populated chiefly with shadows, and even destined for them; then Ramon Alonzo and Anemone, hand in hand, their two dark shadows stretching long behind them, walked confidently into Aragona.

And those who watched espied them. Then bells were rung and men ran out of houses, and there were shouts and musterings; and the murmur arose of a crowd in its agitation, and above the murmur one phrase loud and often: "For the Faith. For the Faith."

Ramon Alonzo drew near them with Anemone, thinking to satisfy them with the sight of his long shadow, but when they saw it they only cried, "Magic. Magic." For, having come out of their houses to look for a false shadow, they would not recognize a true one though it lay there for all to see.

Again Ramon Alonzo drew his sword. Without a ring it came from the scabbard and was all leaden to look on and tarnished, not like the bright swords flashing here and there in the crowd, for it had been dulled and disenchanted when it had crossed the lightning-stroke in the hand of the Master.

Then Anemone stepped forward before Ramon Alonzo and raised her voice above the sound of the bells and the cry of the crowd for the Faith, till they all stood silent and listened, halted by her bright vehemence.

"No magic," she said, "no magic; but a young man's shadow. Watch, and you shall see it grow, as it hath grown ever since noon. See it now fair and shapely. Can magic do this? Who hath a longer shadow? Who hath a shapelier? See how the daisies rest in it. I know what magic can do, but this never."

And one lifted his voice from the silence that lulled them all, as with one arm high she spoke her speech in their faces; he lifted his voice and said: "What is this stranger?"

Then all who listened to her looked at her strangely and noted that many times she had used the word magic. What was she? Magic too, maybe. And a fear fell on them all.

"Aye," said another, with more in his voice than the first, "what stranger is she?"

They thought that voice, those questions, and all their looks, had quelled her. But she flashed a look at them and spoke again with irresistible voice.

"Stranger?" she said, "stranger? I am of Aragona, I!"

And an elder peered at her awhile and slowly said: "You know not Aragona."

"Aye," she said, "every lane of it."

"Maybe the roadway," the elder said, "and our notable belfry, but the small lanes never."

"Aye, every lane," said Anemone.

"Easily said," cried another.

And one said: "Let her tell us tales of it. Let her tell us of this Aragona that she has known."

And Ramon Alonzo, behind her with his sword yet in his hand, would have stopped them, for he feared that the Aragona she knew would be all faded away, and that, telling of olden things that to her were dearest, she would bring upon her their derision. So he tried to turn them but they did not hear him, and all were crying out: "Tell us what you found when you travelled to Aragona." And they made pretence that Aragona was some far town that they knew not.

Then she raised her hand and hushed them and spoke low, and told of Aragona. She told not of things that change when old men die, or when children grow and leave gardens, but she told of things that abide or alter slowly, even now when time has a harsher way with villages. She told of yew-trees, she told of the older graves, she told of the wandering lanes that had no purpose, with never a reason for one of their curves and no reason for altering them, she told the place of the haystack in many fields, she told old legends concerning the shape of the hills and the lore that guided the sower. She crooned it to them with her love of those fields vibrating through every phrase, fields that had shone for her across the bleakness of unremembered years. She told them their pedigrees, quaint names to them in faded ink on old scrolls in their houses; but she knew with whom their grandfathers went a maying. She told and perforce they listened, held by her love of those fields. And when she ceased crooning the last word to them, that told of some old stone there was on a hill, when the last sound died away like a song that fades softly, a low hum rose in the crowd from wondering voices. She stood there silent while the hum roamed up and down and back again.

Then one spoke clear and said: "She is a witch-woman, for none knows her here, and hath seen our village upon starry nights riding by broom from the Country Beyond Moon's Rising."

"Aye," said the others, speaking deep in awe. "She is from that land."

And they opened their eyes a little wider, looking towards

her in horror; for that land lies not only beyond salvation, but the dooms of the Last Judgment cross not its borders either, so that those who have trafficked in magic and known the Black Art walk abroad there boldly, unpunished—a most dreadful sight. Only they must come to it before ever they die; for then it is too late.

"No," she said, "not from the Country Beyond Moon's Rising."

"Whence then?" said they.

And again she said: "Aragona."

And one asked her, "What house?"

She pointed to it where one window had flashed and blazed at the sunset; but now the shadow of the hill went over it and someone lit a candle then and placed it in the window.

"There," she said. And no more words than this came to her lips.

"It is empty," they shouted.

"And hath been for years," said one.

"The candle," she said.

"An old custom," one answered. "It is clear that you know not Aragona."

"No," she said, "I know not that custom."

"A girl lived there in the old time," one told her, "and left it, and came not back."

"And the candle?" she said.

"The folk that dwelt there put it there all their days, lest she should come back," he said.

"And after?" asked Anemone.

"They left money by testament, as all men know, for a candle to be lit there always at sunset. The money is long since spent, but we keep the custom."

Aye, they waited for her yet. Then she looked long and saw how the thatch had sagged, and doors and windows were gone except that one window, and it was indeed as they said: the house was empty and had long been so.

There was a hush to see what she would do; all the crowd waited; Ramon Alonzo stood there with his sword to defend her: none stirred.

They waited for her yet. And how could she claim to be the one that legend expected? A tale for a winter's night, with none to doubt it of those that warmed at the fire. But in the open air, with the sun still over the sky-line, who would believe her? And how tell of the long black years without speaking of magic?

A long long look she took at that tumbled cottage, then turned away and touched Ramon Alonzo's arm.

"Come," she said.

They went back to the hill and none followed. But they set guards about the boundaries of Aragona lest he or she should return to corrupt them with magic.

For a while he did not speak, seeing her sorrow. But when voices hummed far behind them, their accusations blurred and harmless with distance, and he saw that none pursued, he turned to Anemone. "Where now?" he said.

And Anemone answered, "I know not."

"Then to my home," said he.

And at these words she smiled, for they came to her thoughts like lights to a dark chamber. The past was all gone, but there was still the future. She let him guide her whither he would; and he made a wide circle about Aragona, and then walked towards his home. The sunset faded and a star came out, and peered at them; others stole out and watched them, and still they strode on swiftly through the night.

Anemone spoke little, for she was troubled about the future. What if it should crumble like the past? What if the parents of this splendid young man should refuse to receive one whose natal house was mouldering walls under a sagging roof that was more moss than thatch, upon which oats were growing.

Only once she spoke of this on their walk through the dark. But he, thinking yet of Gulvarez, answered so certainly that his father would receive her that she feared so great assurance to be unreasoning; for she knew nothing of the mean gross man that the Lord of the Tower was to receive as a son-in-law.

The stars that had come out earliest beckoned quietly to others so soon as they saw that pair, and the others came up hastily, and all that peering multitude all night long saw Ramon Alonzo and Anemone walking, till the lustre went out of their watching and they all faded away.

In the paleness of morning the young man saw his home lifting a gable above the dark of the forest. He did not tell Anemone what it was, for there was a certain spot from which he wished her to see it first, because from there he believed that the Tower looked fairest. But he told her that they were very near his home, for he saw that she was weary. Before they came to that spot from which he wished her to see the Tower, they saw a man coming towards them. It was too far to see his face; yet at the first glance Ramon Alonzo thought of Peter, though it was not ever his wont to be up so early and he had no cause to be going by that road. Then he watched awhile to see who it could be. Peter it was. And with a letter for Ramon Alonzo that his father had written overnight.

"I started full early," said Peter.

Ramon Alonzo took the letter, while Peter's eyes drank in the sight of his young master; then he looked at Anemone and saw how it was, and said nothing.

"My lady," said Ramon Alonzo to Peter, looking up from his letter.

And Peter went down on one knee in the road and kissed Anemone's hand. And this first greeting that she had from the Tower, an omen full of good fortune, heartened Anemone for a fleeting instant. Then she turned to Ramon Alonzo, and saw him reading the letter with great astonishment. At first the news, however strange, seemed good: she could not read the parchment, yet this she read clear in the face of Ramon Alonzo. But then the tenour of the letter changed, and she saw him read the end with troubled anxiety.

CHAPTER XXVIII

Gonsalvo Sings What Had Been the Latest Air from Provence

Thus it came about that the Lord of the Tower sent again for Father Joseph, and bade him write him a letter; and the letter was folded and sealed and given to Peter to bear to Ramon Alonzo at the magical house in the wood.

On the day that Father Joseph had left the Tower to go to his own small house the Duke lay in his bed all day very restless. It was the third day of his strange illness. Whenever a step was heard outside his room he watched his door with a fierceness alight in his eyes which only faded from them when he saw Mirandola. He seldom spoke to her, but he could not curse her; he accepted the food that she brought him, and none else ventured near him. And so that day went by and the evening came, and Gulvarez, in the room where the boar-spears hung, took an old guitar of his host's, that years and years ago Gonsalvo had played; and striking up a tune, Gulvarez sang. And the tune was one that so long haunted valleys of Andalusian hills that none knew who first sang it or whence it came. It was a common love-song of the South. The words were vague, and varied in different villages, so that a lover had wide choice how he would sing the song. Gulvarez sang it with a heavy feeling, looking towards Mirandola and singing all the tenderer lines the loudest. When he had finished his hostess thanked him, and Gonsalvo began to tell of old songs that he too had known, but his lady checked him that Mirandola might speak; and they both sat silent, waiting for their daughter to thank Gulvarez.

Then Mirandola said: " 'Tis a pleasant song. I pray the Saints that the Duke hear it not."

She said it with such an awe that alarm touched Gulvarez. "The Duke?" he stuttered.

"Yes, I pray he hear not," she said. "For he hath a most strange fury, and small sounds trouble it much. I fear lest he should rise from his bed and slay you."

And she listened, even as she spoke, to hear if the Duke were stirring. And Gulvarez grew red and said: "Not at all," and "By no means"; and the Lady of the Tower said "Mirandola!" and the Lord of the Tower knew not what to say.

And a silence fell and Gulvarez still glowed red, like a misty autumnal sun in a still evening. And only Mirandola was quite at ease.

At last to break that silence Gonsalvo sang a merry love-song that in his own young days was newly come from Provence. Only those had known it then who kept an ear to what was doing in the wider world beyond the boundaries of Spain, and who watched the times and were quick to note whenever they brought a new thing; and of these Gonsalvo was one; and so he had got that song, no great while after its arrival in Spain (brought over the Pyrenees by a wandering singer, as birds sometimes carry strange seeds), but the song was old among the troubadours. As Gonsalvo sang he thought of the days when it was something to know that song, showing either that the singer had travelled far or was one of those quick minds that caught all things new; the merrier the notes the more he thought of those days. And the more he thought of them the more he regretted that they were all gone over the hills. A melancholy came into Gonsalvo's voice. Each line of the song seemed to roll him further and further away from that young man that had known so long ago the latest air from Provence. Ah well. Such feelings must come sooner or later to all of us. But Gonsalvo was not a meditative man, and to him they came most rarely, troubling him scarcely ever; now they all welled up in him at the sound of that song, and at the thought that for aught Gonsalvo knew it was no longer the latest air. His melancholy deepened. His memory drew those merry lines from the past, with a tone as sad as the groans of an aged man who winds up a pail of bright water out of a well, with pain in all his old joints.

Gulvarez no more than Gonsalvo knew the Provencal tongue, yet the lilt of the tune should have told him that it was a merry song. But he watched his host's face with care and saw there what he heard in his tones; he therefore mopped his eyes with a kerchief, thinking to please Gonsalvo. Then Gonsalvo sought to explain that it was a merry song, and was highly thought of as such in better years if not now; and all amongst his explanations Gulvarez thrust in words, seeking to explain his kerchief. Why was it that during all this time Mirandola seemed to sit there smiling? For her lips never moved. Then the Lady of the Tower, seeing that the silence, that had hung so heavily over them after Mirandola's remark, had not been bettered, though broken, by Gonsalvo's merry song, rose from her seat and beckoned to Mirandola; and, closing the explanations of the men with fair words to Gulvarez, went thence with her daughter. So passed the third day of that illness that so strangely afflicted the Duke.

And the fourth day came; and on this day Father Joseph was seen riding away on his mule. When Father Joseph walked over to the Tower, and for a few days left the little village, the folk sinned there gladly; but when he rode away on a mule they knew not whither, and was not back by evening, a piety came uneasily down on the village, and not only no one sinned but they scarcely sang; for none gave absolution like Father Joseph.

In the Tower it was as yesterday, for an anxious hush still hung over all the house because of the dreadful thing it had done to the Duke. And none dared trouble that hush by suggesting a new thing; and events came slowly. The Duke's strength still gained gradually, and his magical fury gradually faded, if indeed it faded at all. Mirandola still saw a glitter of wrath in his eyes whenever she opened his door, which only faded when he saw it was her, bringing him food or drink. And the wrath with which he watched the door seemed to Mirandola magnificent; for it seemed to her that no more than lightnings or splendid dawns would he turn aside to let mean things have their way, or assist gross things to prosper; and she had seen gross men and watched mean ways, and had had a fear that for aught that she could do she would come amongst grossness and meanness in the end; so what was crude and common would teach the mundane way once more to the rare and fine.

They spoke little; for the Duke's wrath would not easily allow him to speak to any of that house that had so strangely wronged him, although it could not rage at Mirandola.

Downstairs Gulvarez said tender things to her; but, as it was ever his way to say these the loudest, she hushed him

215

with one hand raised and an anxious air, lest the Duke should hear any sound and be moved to yet fiercer humours. And none knew how the Duke fared except Mirandola, and she told all truthfully; yet always with an anxiety in her voice which made all the future uncertain and checked Gulvarez' boldness, as though he had suddenly come to the verge of a country that was full of a damp white mist. Amongst such uncertainties this day passed like the last.

The fifth day of the Duke's strange illness came. A troubled piety reigned in the village, and Father Joseph was still far away, being then with Ramon Alonzo in the magician's wood. In the Tower none knew if the Duke's illness abated, but now he had grown accustomed to Mirandola's entry, and knew her step and her hand upon the door, and no longer watched the door with glittering wrath whenever he saw it move. But none knew if he would yet suffer the approach of any other, and none touched his door that day but Mirandola.

Gulvarez enquired of her how the Duke fared.

"I fear," she said, "he will never forgive our poor house."

"I will speak to him later," said Gulvarez.

"I trust he may forgive you for bringing him here," she said. "If so, he may well forgive us."

It was thus that Mirandola would speak to Gulvarez. Such words did not at first seem wrong, but there was no comfort in them. Rather they stirred anxieties, and, on thinking over them afterwards, it often seemed as though nothing less than a slight to Gulvarez were hid in them. Mirandola's mother spoke to her about this, telling her how she ought to converse with Gulvarez; and Mirandola listened readily. Still it was a hushed house, in which it seemed that nothing dared happen until the Duke was cured. So the fifth day passed. And the next day brought back Father

Joseph, tired on his mule to his little house by the village.
And the folk rejoiced and made merry when they saw him
riding their way in the afternoon, and through the evening
they kept up their rejoicing, and into the starry night with
dancing and song; and of this came things that are not for
this tale.

But over the Tower a hush still brooded heavily. It was
like a prisoner who waits in the dark for his trial. He knows
not how great his crime will prove to have been. Again and
again he guesses its consequences. Meanwhile his judge
eats and sleeps and has not yet heard of him. Something of
this uncertainty hung over all that household until they
knew how gravely the Duke had been wronged and if he
would surely recover. And still none dare approach him
but Mirandola. And on this day the Duke spoke with her,
not merely answering questions that she asked of him concerning the food or drink that he desired, but talking of
small things distant from that house. And she sat so long
while they talked that all the house grew troubled; for only
from Mirandola could they learn how the Duke fared. All
the while that she tarried their alarm was growing, and
when at length she appeared it was anxious questions they
asked of her.

The Duke was no worse, she said.

"And his anger? What of his anger?" one asked of her
tremulously.

"He has his whims," she said; "But he is not angry."

She returned to the room in which her parents sat with
Gulvarez. And there she found a certain restraint as they
spoke with her, for the same strange thing all at once had
surprised all three; and this was that in the sore perplexity
that had come upon them, and of which they had thought
so deeply for six days, the key seemed suddenly in the hands

of Mirandola. She knew how he fared, knew that he would recover; above all she seemed to be able to soothe his wrath. Terrible menaces seemed to be lifting, of which the worst was that the Duke should die; but after that they feared almost as much his recovery, dreading what he might do for the insult that had been offered him. But now it seemed, at least to Gonsalvo, and was indeed obvious to all, that if Mirandola could thus soothe his wrath it might be averted from all of them. Then Gonsalvo and Gulvarez walked in the garden and planned how, when the Duke should be recovered, Mirandola should lead him out to the road with his bowmen, so that he should pass neither his host nor his friend, who would be at that time in the garden; and the Duke should not see Gulvarez till long after, when his wrath was abated, and Gonsalvo never again. From this planning they soon returned well satisfied; Gonsalvo, his mind now eased of a burden that had weighed on it for six days, was telling volubly of old hunts he had known; while Gulvarez meditated gallant phrases, and stepped gaily into the house all ready to utter them to Mirandola. But Mirandola was gone again to sit and talk with the Duke.

CHAPTER XXIX

The Casket of Silver and Oak Is Given to Señor Gulvarez

This was the seventh day of the Duke's illness. Of his wrath none knew, for he had no wrath for Mirandola, and none else durst venture into his presence to see. But his illness was waning fast, and it was clear that all his strength would soon be recovered. Soon he would be up and away. "And then," thought Gonsalvo, "Father Joseph must come, and farewell to my fair fields." So he went that morning to see the three fields that he loved, with the dew still on them, and the shade of the forest lying still over half of them. He had gone wondering if they could be really so fair as they seemed to be in the picture his memory had of them. Alas! They were. It would have cheered him to find that they were but common fields. But no, there was a glamour about them; something dwelling perhaps in the forest seemed to have stolen out and enchanted them; they lay there deep as ever in their old mystery, under a gauzy grey of spiders' webs and dew. And that old feeling lay over them all in the morning, which we feel when we speak of home. They were very ordinary fields, lying under dew in the morning; and very ordinary tears came into Gonsalvo's eyes, for he was a simple man, and the roots of the grasses that grew there seemed tangled up somehow or other all amongst his heart-strings.

Looking there long at his fields he became aware of a man approaching across them and looking carefully at them as he came. It was Gulvarez. He also had come to see if they were really as fair as had been thought.

The sun now came over the tips of the trees, and Gonsalvo stared at it awhile. "Very bright," he said, as Gulvarez came up.

"Aye," said Gulvarez jovially, "a merry day." And then he spake more gravely. "Yonder stile," he said, "will need much repairing."

It was an old stile whose wood was damp and soft, and moss and strange things grew on it. Grand old timbers had made it, and it had been thus through all Gonsalvo's time.

"It was a good stile once," said Gonsalvo.

"Maybe," said Gulvarez.

Gonsalvo sighed.

"They are fair fields, are they not?" Gonsalvo said.

"Aye," said Gulvarez. But he looked all round at them before he answered, which somehow saddened Gonsalvo.

"It is time for breakfast," Gonsalvo said.

"Aye," said Gulvarez, again with that jovial voice, "I have a merry appetite."

So back they went together from those fair fields, and the morning seemed to shine bright for Gulvarez only.

The Lady of the Tower awaited them, but not Mirandola, nor did she appear while they breakfasted. Gulvarez, refreshed by the morning and charmed at the sight of those fields, was full of a joviality that he would have expressed by gallant sayings told to a beautiful girl. But where was Mirandola?

"She is taking her breakfast with the Duke," said Mirandola's mother.

So Gulvarez waited. And the morning went by and still she did not come, and the stress of impatience caused a change in the nature of Gulvarez' joviality, as the nature of fruit changes when it ferments.

She came to them in the early afternoon with little in her face to show whether the Duke fared well or ill, and saying nothing of him until asked by her father.

"He prospers," she said, "and will take the road to-morrow."

"He will go?" said Gonsalvo.

"Yes, to-morrow," said Mirandola.

"Is he wroth with us yet?" said Gonsalvo.

"I know not," she answered.

They would know to-morrow. Gonsalvo thought again of his plan, and went into the garden with Gulvarez to discuss how Mirandola should lead the Duke to the road while he and his lady and Gulvarez were elsewherc. Within the house her mother looked at Mirandola and was about to speak, but in all the moments that she looked at her daughter she saw no sign of the matter upon which she would have spoken, so closed her lips again and did not speak. When Gonsalvo and Gulvarez came back from the garden Mirandola had gone again with more food and drink to the Duke.

And now Gulvarez sat silent, speaking indeed when spoken to, but always returning to brood, as it seemed to Gonsalvo, upon the same theme, whatever that theme might be. He seemed to be thinking some thought, or working upon some problem, that was surprisingly new, and that could only be followed with difficulty, and yet could not be left.

Once he opened his lips to speak, but what he was going to say seemed so strange to him that in the end he said nothing. So he sat there brooding upon his new thought, a man unaccustomed to thinking, and all the more perplexed at having to brood alone, yet the thought was too strange to share it with Gonsalvo; it seemed too near to madness. And, as he brooded there, from amongst the things that he could see in his mind the three fields faded away.

Next morning the Duke rose. The four chiefs of his bowmen, who all that week had moved about the house seldom speaking to any, like stately silent shadows, showed now an alertness such as comes to the swallows when they know that September is here; and all was prepared for departure.

The Duke had breakfasted before he descended. He was all ready for the road. Nothing remained but that Mirandola, meeting him at the foot of the stairs, should lead him by a path through an arm of the forest, the four bowmen following, and out onto the road at a point at which Peter should have his horse for him; when, not seeing his host or Gulvarez where he would be given to expect them, he would ride away, and Mirandola would carry any farewells for him. These were the plans of Gonsalvo, whereby he hoped to escape the wrath of the Duke if that magical anger still smouldered. He had told them to Mirandola overnight, and she had dutifully hearkened and promised to do the bidding of her father. "All will be well," he had said to Gulvarez. But Gulvarez had maintained that silence of his that was troubled by his new broodings.

The step of the Duke was heard on the stair; behind him tramped his four bowmen. Mirandola looked up.

"Your horse is on the road at the end of the path," she said. "I will show you."

"Is it not at the door?" he asked.

"I think my father sent it to the end of the path," she answered. She gave no reason; there was none. It was the weak part of Gonsalvo's scheme. She watched his face a moment with anxiety. But a glad smile came on his face.

"We will go by the path," he said.

Great indeed was the wrong that had been done him in that house, but it pleased the Duke to think, and he invented many reasons to help his contention, that Mirandola could have no part in it. From this he had come to believe that she had no real part in that house, but was something almost elfin that had haunted it out of the forest, or something that had come for a little while to cheer its hateful rooms, as a ray from the sun may briefly enter a dungeon. Indeed it is hard to say what the Duke was thinking, for his brain was all awhirl. Whatever he thought was unjust, for Mirandola was the one light to him in the dark inhospitality of that house. Whereas—but never mind: it all happened so long ago.

So they went by the path. It ran through a part of the garden; then to the wild, then turned from the heather and rocks and ran awhile through the forest and out to the high road. It was the way that Peter and the dairymaids took, for it brought them into the Tower by a small door at the back, but the road went by the front door.

The Duke walked slowly, full of thought and quite silent. He had looked long for this day, when he could go forth again a hale man once more, and be in the sunlight and hear the birds and ride away, and never have any more to do with that house. Yet here were the sunlight and birds, and the house was behind him, and his horse was waiting for him a little way off, and none of the joy he had looked for came near him at all. He was free of that house at last and unhappy to be free. Never had he thought so much or thought less clearly, for all his thoughts were contradicting each other; and Mirandola's eyes made it harder to think than ever. They were happy eyes, caring little, it seemed, for his trouble. And what was his trouble? Something profoundly wrong with the bright morning that could not be easily cured; and the future coming up all dull and listless for years and years and years. Indeed his brain was in a whirl.

"You are glad to be leaving us?" said Mirandola as they crossed the strip of heather.

"Yes," said the Duke, "I am sorry."

It was the Duke that thought over what he had answered more than Mirandola. She said no more, but he pondered on his own words. He had said he was sorry. Yes, that was the truth of it. An accursed house no doubt, and yet it had hold of his heart-strings. Sighing, he walked on slowly and came to the forest, with Mirandola beside him, and the four chiefs of his bowmen a short way behind. And now his thoughts became fewer and simpler.

"Señorita," he said, "are you glad that I am leaving you?"

"Yes," she said, "I am sorry."

She had repeated his own confused words! Which did she mean?

He turned round to his four men, who halted to hear his order.

"Hunt rabbits," he said.

And at once the chiefs of the bowmen disappeared in the forest; and the Duke with Mirandola walked on in silence. And no words came to him to say what was weighing upon his heart to this flashing elfin lady. He that ruled over the deeps of so great a forest had many affairs to weigh and discharged them with many commands, and his words had earned from men a repute for wisdom; but as for the fawns he loved, that slipped noiselessly across clearings, and wide-winged herons that came down at evening along a slant of the air, foxes, eagles, and roe-deer—he knew not their language. And now he felt as he had sometimes felt, watching alone by the clearings, when the things of the wild came gliding by through a hush that seemed all theirs; and he loved their beautiful shapes and their shy wild ways, and his heart went out towards them; but there lay the gulf between him and them across which no words could call. So he felt now as he looked on Mirandola, fearing that words were not shaped for what he would say. He halted and looked long on her, and no words came to his lips. They were near the road at the spot where his horse waited, and he feared that they soon might part, with all unsaid. But those proud eyes of his were saying all he would say; the twinkle of merriment in Mirandola's eyes died down under the gaze of them, and a graver look came to her face, and her merry look did not return till he spoke and she heard common human words again.

"Will you marry me, Mirandola?" he said at last.

It was then that the twinkle dawned again in her eyes.

"I am engaged to Señor Gulvarez," she said.

"Gulvarez!" he said.

"Yes, my father arranged it," said Mirandola.

"Gulvarez shall hang," said the Duke.

"I thought he was your friend," said Mirandola.

"Aye," said the Duke, "truly. But he shall hang."

And one last favour she did for Gulvarez, that had had so few favours of her hitherto; for when she saw that the Duke was truly bent upon hanging him, and was indeed earnest in the matter, she besought him to put it aside, and would not answer the question that he had asked her until he had sworn that Gulvarez should go unhung. Then she consented.

And now from the obscurer part of the garden, where

they had lurked while the Duke went by, Gonsalvo and Gulvarez came forth. Gonsalvo walked with all the lightness of one from whom a burden has slipped, and Gulvarez with downcast head and moody air, and silence grudgingly broken when at all: so they walked in the garden.

"He never saw us," said Gonsalvo cheerily.

"No," said Gulvarez.

Little light shells crunched under their feet along the path while Gonsalvo waited for a further answer.

"He is gone," said Gonsalvo.

This time Gulvarez made no answer at all, and the shells crunched on in silence.

Gonsalvo believed that all things were as bright as his own mood, but when he perceived that this was not so with Gulvarez he spoke to him of the three fair fields, though it cost him a sigh to do it. And even this made no rift in the heavy mood of Gulvarez.

"They are fair, are they not?" asked Gonsalvo.

"Yes, yes," said Gulvarez impatiently, and fell to nursing again that curious silence.

And at this Gonsalvo wondered, until he wondered "Where is Peter?"

Peter was holding the horse of the Duke a little way down the road: why had he not returned? Was the man straying away to wanton in idleness when there was work to be done in the stables? He peered about in vexation, and still no sign of Peter.

The Duke must have reached the road long since, and ridden away: Peter should have returned immediately. No work, no wages, he thought. And in his anger his mind dwelt long on Peter.

And then he thought: "Where ever is Mirandola?"

"It is curious," he said to Gulvarez, "I do not see Mirandola returning."

Almost a look of contempt seemed to colour the gloom of Gulvarez as he turned to the Lord of the Tower.

"No," he said.

"It is curious," said Gonsalvo.

And an uneasiness began to grow in his mind slowly, until it was two silent men that walked in the garden together.

"A little this way," said Gonsalvo, going through a gap in the hedge to a knoll that rose in a field outside the garden, from which one saw more of the road. Gulvarez moodily followed. And there was the Duke's horse, and Peter waiting; not even wondering, as his whole attitude showed, but holding the horse in the road and merely waiting, as flowers and vegetables wait. "Still there," said Gonsalvo. And Gulvarez grunted.

There was nothing to gaze at—a patient man and an almost patient horse; and presently Gonsalvo turned from them, and came with Gulvarez slowly back to the garden. They walked again upon the small seashells.

And then, with the summer burning in their faces, with the splendours of wonderful hopes and imaginations, led by such inspirations as trouble the hills in Spring, came Mirandola and the Duke of Shadow Valley, together back from the forest.

"He returns," said Gonsalvo.

Gulvarez nodded his head.

"But he comes back," Gonsalvo said.

And on walked Mirandola and the Duke of Shadow Valley, as though they had crossed the border of a land full of the morning and were walking further and further into its golden brightness, which lit their faces more and more as they went, while behind them lay colder lands, lonelier and lacking enchantment.

And Gonsalvo said nothing but little words of surprise,

and Gulvarez said nothing at all, for his gloomy mood was set for these very events. But the Lady of the Tower, as she passed by a high window, looking out saw all at once Mirandola's story. Soon these five met by their separate ways, at the door that led to the garden. And the Lady of the Tower looking out on the huge gloom of Gulvarez and the radiance of Mirandola, while her husband repeated phrases and questions all shrill with surprise, recalled a thunderstorm she had seen long since, coming over the sea at sunrise, while small white birds ran crying along the coast.

And then with a gasp Gonsalvo's eyes were opened to the obvious situation, which had long been clear to Gulvarez. They entered the house, Gonsalvo walking behind in silence. My story draws near to its close.

In the room where the boar-spears hung they planned the future—as far as men ever do—for they turned blindly and confidently towards the strange dark ways to speak as though they could see them; and would have spoken, but the Duke talked instead, fervidly, gaily, and lyrically: it was a great while before Gonsalvo had opportunity to touch on the matter that had long lain near his heart, the matter of the casket and Mirandola's dowry.

"As for dowry," said the Duke, "give me . . ." but he spoke incoherently, naming foolish things, a lock of her hair, an eyelash, a common fan.

"Then Your Magnificence," said Gonsalvo, when opportunity came to speak again, "accept at least that casket which, had the fortunes of my house been grander, had long been filled with gold; for it was ever destined for my daughter's dowry, though still by ill fortune empty as you shall see."

And he took its key and opened the casket there, showing it to be empty as he had said, and was about to hold it forth in his two hands to the Duke. But Mirandola said: "Father, it was promised to Señor Gulvarez."

Gonsalvo, as he bowed forward with his casket, stopped with a sudden jerk and looked with amaze at his daughter. But Mirandola's eyes under curved black lashes remained unwavering, and she said no more. And after a while, in silence, and puzzled at his own action, Gonsalvo handed the casket to Gulvarez, who took it without any thanks, midmost in that courteous age, and put it under his arm and walked from the room and went away from the house. And then the Lady of the Tower would have spoken, but the Duke spoke again. It was more like the words of such songs as they sometimes sang in youth, upon moonlight nights, in the Golden Age, to the tune of a mandolin, than any sober prevision of the future. And as he spoke, thoughts so swam through Gonsalvo's mind, so swift and so unrelated, that he longed with a great yearning for Father Joseph, who had such an easeful way with unruly thoughts, and wondered upon what pretext he could summon him, for the need of a priest was not yet. And then he thought of his son, and that business of gold for the dowry, and the propriety of acquainting him with his sister's betrothal. The occasion was well worthy of a letter. And he slipped from the room and sent Peter in haste for the priest.

Plump and mellow and calm, in due course Father Joseph appeared; and his calmness came to Gonsalvo like snow upon torrid sands. And they greeted and spoke awhile, and Father Joseph said soothing things that were easy to understand. And this was the letter that was written: "My dear Son, a thing has befallen so strange that I am readier to marvel at it than to acquaint you with the truth of it or to tell you how it befell, if indeed this could be told, but it is of those things whose ways are inscrutable and that befall as they may and are not to be traced to their origins, or to be studied by any of the arts of philosophy, but are only indeed to be marvelled at. The Duke of Shadow Valley is betrothed to your sister and will marry her. That is as it is. Ask me not how it became so, for I am no philosopher to unravel the causes of events; and methinks that many events are only made for our wonder, and have no cause and no meaning but that we should wonder at them, as indeed I do at this event most heartily. Now this being as I have said, with the aid of Father Joseph, whose pen has been most ready in this matter, there is no need any longer of that business which we have discussed heretofore. Return home therefore with all speed and abide with us. But of all earthly needs place this the foremost: to wed in due course (and may the Saints whose care it is hasten the happy occasion) only the daughter of some illustrious house; for the Duke of Shadow Valley is, as the world knows, the loved companion of the King's self, and they have hunted the magpie together with their falcons, and have strolled abroad when all the city slept, seeking such adventures together as were appropriate to their youth. Bring no shame therefore on so illustrious a head by marriage with any house not well established in honour before the coming of the Moors. Your loving father, Gonsalvo of the Tower and Rocky Forest."

After the dictation of so long a letter and the work of signing it with his own hand, and all his wonderings and perplexities, Gonsalvo sat in his chair so much bewildered that he could not wholly extricate his thoughts, nor could even Father Joseph make their meaning perfectly clear to him. And in this perplexed state there came to him all of a sudden one vivid, lucid thought of his three fair fields. He rose, and though Father Joseph would have assisted him with his counsel, he went forth in silence out of the house alone. And soon he was walking on those remembered grasses, dewy now with the evening.

With folded hands in a chair Father Joseph ordered his thoughts. But to Gonsalvo, pacing his fields again, there came a calm along the slanting rays, and out of the turf he trod, and from the cool of evening and glitter of leaves; it came from that quiet moment in which day ceases to burn, and it welled up out of memories of other evenings that had illumined those fields. Far off he saw the form of Gulvarez riding away, bent on his horse, his two men-at-arms behind him: he turned to call to him some word as he went: he filled his lungs to hail him—but turned instead to some flowers among the grasses that the sun had touched in his fields.

CHAPTER XXX

The End of the Golden Age

When Ramon Alonzo read his father's letter a fear came into his day-dreams, and he stood a long while wondering. Peter stood before him gazing into his face, and Anemone by his side was quietly reading his thoughts; and both saw trouble there, rushing up black and suddenly to darken the coming years. And there he stayed while two phrases went up and down amidst his dismayed thoughts—"the daughter of some illustrious house" and "well established in honour before the coming of the Moors." What should he do? Were those two phrases to wither away his happiness? And, yet what way of escape? Hope herself seemed blind to it.

"What is the matter?" Anemone said, as he stood there still and silent.

"It is from my father," he said.

And she knew then that his father would not receive her, but she said nothing.

"Peter," he said after a little while, "I must go on alone. Guard my lady."

To her he turned to give excuses and reasons for leaving her awhile in the forest; but she left all to him and needed no reasons.

A little way further they went on together, Peter walking behind; and then Anemone and Ramon Alonzo parted as though it had been for years, though they were only a few hundred paces from the Tower, and Ramon Alonzo had sworn to return to her long before evening. Then he left her and went down to the edge of the forest where it touched the rocky land at the end of the garden; and Peter assured Anemone that his young master would soon return, for that he ever kept his word to the last letter of it: but she was full of heaviness from that dark news that had troubled Ramon Alonzo; although she knew not the words of it, yet she felt it as on sultry days in summer we feel the thunder before we have seen a cloud.

When Ramon Alonzo came to the edge of the forest he hid himself carefully by an old oak that he knew; then he looked towards the garden.

And soon he saw walking on those remembered paths his sister with the Duke of Shadow Valley. They were coming towards him and he saw her clearly, a new gaiety in her dress, and a look in her face that was almost strange to him. Then they turned back again. The next time that they approached he watched her face to find a moment when he could show her that he was there without the Duke perceiving him. And for long he only saw that new look increasing the spell of her beauty; and though the Duke looked seldom toward the forest, and had she glanced for a moment he might have signed to her, yet he caught not one of those glances roving from under her lashes, and the pair went back again to a further part of the garden.

The Duke was talking to Mirandola, that handsome

head bending towards her; and suddenly she lifted her head, looking far beyond the garden, and her gaze was out over the forest where Ramon Alonzo hid. And suddenly he waved his kerchief to her by the hollow old bole of that oak by which they had played of old. She saw the sign and at once walked nearer to him, the Duke walking beside her. And when he saw that tall and slender figure in black velvet and sky-blue plume coming towards him with her, he signed to her again and again to come alone; but they still walked on, and left the end of the garden, and crossed the strip of rocky heathery land. They found him standing by the old hollowed oak. He doffed his hat to the Duke, then hastily said what he had tried to sign: "Mirandola, I have a word to say to you apart."

And she said: "My secrets are his."

Then Ramon Alonzo felt that his judgment had not been trusted, and that Mirandola, his sister, should have doubted that he had good grounds for his request troubled the lad to the heart. And when she made no motion to draw apart with him alone he blurted out in his pique every word of his father's letter, though the Duke was standing beside him, petulantly bent on showing how right he had been to ask her to hear him alone. And then he told her mournfully how he was engaged to wed a maiden whom he had rescued from the magician, and who was fairer than the earliest flowers on bright March mornings in Spain.

When the Duke heard this he smiled.

"And she is of no noble house?" he said.

"Aye, there it is," said Ramon Alonzo.

"Where is she?" asked Mirandola in her quiet kind voice, whose very tones seemed to know her brother's heart, as the echoes of chimes know belfries.

"There in the forest," he said.

Mirandola looked at the Duke.

"Let us see her," he said.

So Ramon Alonzo turned and led the way, and the be-trothed pair followed together. He strode on as though all alone in the wood with his sorrows, disappointed at having had no talk with Mirandola alone, for he had had much hope from her wisdom if he could have talked with her thus, as so often he had talked when they were younger, smoothing the difficulties of tinier troubles. So he walked downcast and moody, though once he fancied that he heard behind him the sound of soft laughter.

When Ramon Alonzo came where Anemone waited with Peter he was silent yet, extending an arm towards her where she stood smiling, fair, as indeed he had said, as any flower looking up at the morning through dews of the earliest Spring. The Duke doffed his hat and bowed, and Miran-dola went up and kissed Anemone. "So I must wed illustri-ously," said Ramon Alonzo in bitterness.

During one of those brief moments that Destiny uses often to perfect an event with which she will shape the years, none of them spoke. Then Anemone slowly turned towards Aragona, towards her own people that rejected her.

"Hold," said the Duke. "I will write to the Just Monarch. Bless his heart, he will do this for us."

None knew till the letter was written quite what would be asked, nor what the Just and Glorious Monarch would do; yet suddenly all seemed decided.

Back then they went to the Tower—Mirandola, the Duke, and Ramon Alonzo. But not Anemone, for Ramon Alonzo knew not yet what to say of her to his father, though the Duke had suddenly lit his hopes again and they shone down vistas of years. So with one swift thought, that long pondering would not have bettered, he remembered Father

Joseph, and commanded Peter to lead her to the good man's little house. This Peter did, and there she was lodged awhile and honourably tended; and, had her memory held any more than hints of those dark ages in the sinister house in the wood, Father Joseph would have been, as he nearly was, surprised; and this, so well knew he man and his pitiful story, he had not been since long and long ago when he was first a curate and all the world was new to him. In the Tower, while his parents were greeting Ramon Alonzo and hearing halting fragments of his story whose whole theme he must hide awhile, the Duke of Shadow Valley, with toil and discomfort, yet still with his own hand, inscribed a letter to the Victorious King. Therein he told his comrade in many a merriment the glad news of his happiness, then added a humble request concerning Anemone, and closed with a renewal of the devotion that his house ever felt towards the illustrious line. And now with meagre spoils his bowmen were coming in, for he had bidden them hunt rabbits; and to one of these he gave at once this letter, bidding him haste to its splendid destination. And the bowman hastened as he had been commanded, and travelled for all the remainder of that day and through most of the night, so that he saw the next sunset glint on the spires of that palace that was the glory and joy of the Golden Age. And there the most high king, the Victorious Monarch, sat on a throne of velvet and wood and gold; and lights had been brought but lately, and two men stood by the throne holding strange torches that the King might see to do any new thing; but the King had naught to do but to ponder the old cares over, for he had wide dominion. Then into the hall came the bowman.

When the King read he rejoiced. Then he rose and gave a command, commanding preparations. And these preparations were for his own presence at the wedding of the

Duke and Mirandola. But amongst his rejoicings, and those august preparations, and the grave cares he inherited, he forgot not his friend's petition and the humble affair of Anemone. So again he commanded, bidding his pen be brought. So one bore the pen down the hall on a cushion of scarlet and yellow, which are the colours of Spain. And the Victorious King took up the pen and wrote upon parchment, writing out with his own hand the humble name of Anemone. And in that illustrious hall, the pride of the Golden Age, he wrote an ample pardon for her low birth, and set his name to the pardon that he had written and sealed it all with the glorious seal of Spain. And the pardon was carried then, on the cushion of scarlet and yellow, to that Archbishop that waited upon the King, watching his spiritual needs from moment to moment. And when the pardon was come before the Archbishop, he raised his hands and blessed it.

The bowman bore the pardon back to the Duke, who gave it to Ramon Alonzo. Thenceforth it became treason to speak of the low birth of Anemone, nor may historians allude to it to this day: that pardon had annulled it; she became of illustrious lineage. And in their loyal avoidance of any reference to Anemone's occupation the Spanish people let drop into disuse the very name of charwoman, lest inadvertently they should ever apply it where it was treason to do so. Still they speak there of broom-lady, woman of the pail, crockery-breaker, floor-warden, scrub-mistress, but never of charwoman, unless a light and unreliable spirit blown over the Pyrenees by a south wind out of Spain has grossly misinformed me.

What more remains to be told of the fortunes of Ramon Alonzo and of the allied House of the Duke of Shadow Valley? Of the wedding of Mirandola good old books tell, in words whose very rhythms dance down the ages with a stately merriment and a mirthful march that are well worthy of their most happy theme. To them I leave that chronicling. In London alone the lucky wayfarer going north by the Charing Cross Road, and taking fortunate turnings, will find in the Antiquareum at the end of Old Zembla Street sufficient of these to his purpose. There, if the old curator dreams not too deeply of bygone splendours of the enchanted days, as may happen on long dark Saturdays, he will find the books that he needs. For there sleep in their mellowed leather on those shelves, and laugh in their sleep as they dream of the Golden Age, such books as *Fortunate Revelries*, *The Glorious Waning of the Golden Age*, *The Sunset of Chivalry*, and *Happy Days of the Illustrious*. And all these tell of that wedding, illumining the event with a dignity and a splendour such as our age considers presumptuous for any affair of man. I make no mention of such books as may be stored in Madrid, nor such as pedlars are likely still to be selling in hamlets of unfrequented valleys of Spain. Suffice it that no full tale is told of the Golden Age that does not revel happily over that day. Of the wedding of Ramon Alonzo and Anemone the good and glorious books tell a briefer tale, for no archbishops performed the holy rite, and the King's self had returned to the burden of his dominion. Yet were they well wed; for Father Joseph did this with his own hands, and blessed them out of the store of his kind old years. And she, with the years of magic cast away, aged as we all age, slowly and mortally. And all those golden books agree on one quaint exaggeration, and record, sometimes with curious and solemn oath, that she and Ramon Alonzo lived happily ever after.

And what of the magician: he whose strange threads have run so much through all the web of this story? He sent no spell to follow after Anemone and her lover, as for a while they had feared, but went all alone to his room that was sacred to magic, and took from the dust and darkness of a high shelf a volume in which he had written all he had learned about boar-hunting; and indeed no more was known of that art in any land, for he that had taught him had followed the boar well. In this he read all that day and all the night, assured that therein was the manifest way to happiness that all philosophers sought. But about the third day, when none returned to him, and he was quite alone, and he felt it was vain to look for another now who should be worthy to receive from him the tremendous secrets of old, he rose from his book and said, "The years grow late." He went then to his tower and quaffed one gulp of that fluid that was named elixir vitae, and, carrying the bottle to that passage that for so long Anemone scrubbed, he cast it heavily down upon the stone. And then he took from a box a flute of reed, and cloaked himself and went out of his magical house.

He went a few paces into the wood, then raised the reed to his lips. He blew one bar upon it of curious music, then waited, listening eagerly. And there came to his ears the scurry of little things, nimble, elvish, and sprightly, over dead leaves of the wood. At that he strode away, going swiftly northwards, and there followed him all manner of magical things: fays, imps, and fauns, and all such children of Pan.

In the open lands he raised his pipe again and blew on it two strange notes, which seemed for a while to haunt the air all round him; then they drifted slowly afar. And to that call responded the things of the wold, tiny enchanted folk from many an elf-mound and many a fairy ring; they joined the fantastic group that had come from the deeps of the wood, and followed after the Master. And with him went old shadows, some taken from earthly folk, and some that seemed cast upon other fields than ours by other lights than our

Sun. He led them on through all the beauty of Spain. On the high hills he blew those two notes once more; and all that had their sole dwelling in moonlight and river-mist, or in the deep romance that overflows from old tales, told at evening in glamour of firesides, came out from their lurking-places at the edge of the olden years, and the dimness of distance, and the other side of grey hills, and followed him over the fields and valleys of Spain, till there came in sight one morning the tips of the Pyrenees. Soon he was crossing these with that wild crew behind him, and butterflies that had followed him out of Spain. He blew his strange notes once upon a peak, where his tall cloaked figure looked tiny seen from the fields, and his uncouth following only specks on the snow. Nevertheless Spain heard him; and as those notes, with their lure and persuasiveness, went murmuring among the villages, singing and promising I know not what, and calling away as naught should call from the calm and orderly ways, all the cathedrals rang their bells against him. And the chimes filled all the valleys and lapped over the rims of the hills, till all the air of Spain was mellow and musical with them, and yet the things of romance and mystery went leaping after the Master, and yet more hearts than ever told of it after turned that day towards the peak and the pass of the Pyrenees. Through the pass he went and the children of Pan followed. Then they turned eastwards and away and away. In Provence to-day there are tales that few folk tell, yet still remembered in the hearts of the peasantry; they tell how once the things of the olden time came that way from the mountains. And away they went through Europe, leaving a track of fable and curious folklore that, except where it is lost near cities and highways, can be followed even yet. And after them always went whatever was magical, and all those things that dwelt in the olden time and are only known to us through legend and fable.

On and on the magician strode, undaunted by rain or night or rivers or mountains, going onward guided by dawns, always due eastwards. Weariness came on him and still he strode on, going homeless by quiet hamlets in the night, and waking new desires by the mere soft sound of his footfall and the scurrying of little hooves that always followed his journey. And there came upon him at last those mortal tremors that are about the end of all earthly journeys. He hastened then. And before the human destiny overtook him he saw one morning, clear where the dawn had been, the luminous rock of the bastions and glittering rampart that rose up sheer from the frontier of the Country Beyond Moon's Rising. This he saw though his eyes were dimming now with fatigue and his long sojourn on Earth; yet if he saw dimly he heard with no degree of uncertainty the trumpets that rang out from those battlements to welcome him after his sojourn, and all that followed him gave back the greeting with such cries as once haunted valleys at certain times of the moon. Upon those battlements and by the opening gates were gathered the robed Masters that had trafficked with time and dwelt awhile on Earth, and handed the mysteries on, and had walked round the back of the grave by the way that they knew, and were even beyond damnation. They raised their hands and blessed him.

And now for him, and the creatures that followed after, the gates were wide that led through the earthward rampart of the Country Beyond Moon's Rising. He limped towards it with all his magical following. He went therein, and the Golden Age was over.

THE END